I0742048

Formatting by Pour Over Ink Designs LLC
Cover design by Paula Silva Alonso (@jinku.pumpkin)
Editing by Hannah G. Scheffer-Wentz, English Proper Editing Services

ISBN (Print): 979-8-9928604-1-2
ISBN (Ebook): 979-8-9928604-0-5

Better *than* Bookends

Russet Ridge 1

A. Smith

Dedication

♥ ♥ ♥

To my book besties
Thank you and I love
you!

CONTENT THEMES/WARNINGS

♥ ♥ ♥

Discussion of mental health (Anxiety, ADHD, etc.)
Toxic family
Toxic Ex (Not toward or by MCs)
Body shaming (Not toward or by MCs)
Sex shaming (Not toward or by MCs)
Derogatory remarks against LGBTQ+ (not by MCs)
Outdoor accident Including MCs
Violence (One punch by MMC)

prologue

scout

SLEEPING above where you worked may seem like a great idea, except when you were supposed to start renovations and your contractor just ghosted you. *Jackass.* Taking a sip of coffee, I scrolled through the replies I received about potential leads on a new company to hire. While the bookstore my family owned had been renovated, the apartment had been left in shambles. No one had lived above the store in at least a decade. It was not an unlivable space, but it was dated and needed major updates. The contractor had promised he could do it in half the time and at a lower cost than the other quotes. I didn't realize that meant dipping out with the five hundred dollar deposit I gave and never returning my phone call or emails.

Listening to the rain pelt the windows and roof, I took a moment to appreciate the present. I knew the work would get done, but patience was not my strongest virtue. My watch began to vibrate, letting me know to get downstairs and open up. I tried to stay organized and be on time, but that was not always the case. Reminders and alarms were my best friends that kept me moving in the right direction at the correct time. Pouring what was left in my coffee pot into a travel mug, I made my way to the door, grabbing my keys to lock up before descending the stairs.

Unlike most of the buildings downtown, my stairs were in the building verses out back. This was especially nice on days with nasty weather, like today. Reaching the store, I turned, heading back to the office. As my hand touched the doorknob, a loud bang rang out from the back door.

A startled "SHIT!" left my mouth just as my travel mug slipped from my hand, another banging thud causing me to jump. Retrieving my phone from my pocket, the security camera app alerted there was motion caught on camera. *No shit, Sherlock.* Standing outside my door were two men. I couldn't make out much more than one was larger and broader, while the other man had longer hair, that looked almost black with how wet it was, and a bright smile.

I cleared my throat before hitting the microphone button. "Hello, can I help you?" Both men immediately looked up at the camera. The one with long hair spoke first.

"Hi, neighbor! Some of your packages were dropped off next door. I'm afraid they got a little wet before we got here." Leaning back slightly, he showed the box he had in his arms before shielding it again. "The address is High Point Publishing. Addressed to Scout Frazier."

"Damnit." Swiftly moving to unlock the door, I threw it open only to be met by the two most beautiful men I had ever seen. *Was I drooling?* The second man cleared his throat, snapping me back to reality. "Sorry, come in." I moved, giving the two men space to come through. Moving to the boxes, I used my key to open the first box, praying the books were not ruined. I let out a breath when I saw the books were bagged inside the box, leaving them completely dry. Moving to check the other box, a low voice came from behind me, causing a delicious shiver to race up my spine. "Are they ok?" I turned my eyes, meeting the larger man's gaze.

"Yes, thankfully my friend who shipped them made sure they were ready for any weather." Pulling the books from each box, I pushed the boxes to the side before standing. I would have to send a thank you to

Kane for packing the books up so well. "Thank you for bringing them over. I don't think I have met either of you," I said, wiping my palms together before extending it to the dark haired man.

"Gatlin. Gatlin Ford. I own the outdoor adventure store next door." He shook my hand with a wink before releasing, my palm tingling from where we touched.

"I'm Leland Boone, ma'am. I own the bakery next door." His cheeks were tinted the lightest shade of pink as he shook my hand. His big, warm hand engulfed mine. I never really ventured out of the store once we opened. I tended to stay in that back, working. Lettie, my best friend who also worked at the bookstore, would often buy things from the bakery. I had never gone into either building and had obviously never laid eyes on the two men who owned the places. I was trying to collect my thoughts, but my brain had temporarily gone offline. We stood there for a moment before a low bark came from the back door.

"Shit. Sorry, Mud." Gatlin's voice broke the weird tension, my hand slipping from Leland's. "This is Mud. He is goofy and sweet, but demanding."

"Like father, like son," Leland said, the words no more than a whisper.

"Aw, Boone, you think I'm sweet?" Gatlin turned from the dog back to Leland.

Leland shook his head before a deep chuckle left his lips. "Never said that."

Unsure what to say or do, I looked from one man to the other. *Why are they so beautiful? It doesn't seem fair.* Glancing down at my fingers where I unconsciously fidgeted with them, squeezing them gently together, I cleared my throat to speak. "Well, I guess I will see you guys around, right? Since you sandwich me." As the words left my mouth, I felt my face flame. "No, I mean since I am between you. *Shit*, like *my store. My store* is between your stores." While Leland was pink-cheeked with a soft smile playing across his lips, Gatlin's smile was wide, and his eyes were bright with mischief.

Gatlin broke, his words laced with humor. "I think we might be better than book ends." With a wink, he turned to the door, leaving. My gaze had shifted back to study the floor, trying in vain to hide my face. I sensed Leland's gaze burning into the top of my head.

"See you around, honeysuckle." His voice was deep and rough, but still soft. His simple words washed over me. Before I had the chance to reply, I heard the soft click of the back door.

I am in so much trouble.

chapter 1

. . .

scout

"OH, SCOUT," Lettie sing-songed my name as she perched her elbow on the corner of the desk. I jumped at her sudden appearance. I wished it because I was hard at work entering inventory, but that would be false. "A little jumpy are we, Miss Scout? Would that be because of the daydreaming? Maybe about the hunks who I saw leaving when I pulled in?"

"Remind me again why I hired you?" I looked at her, squinting as if I was trying to come up with a sound reason for employing her. Though we both knew I would be lost without her.

Her smile widened, knowing she had caught me. "Well, you love me a whole lot, but also, you didn't hire me. Your grandfather did. Then there is the whole besties box to check." She laid her chin in her hands, watching me.

This was the game. Lettie wanted gossip and all the juicy details and I wanted to torture her a little, to keep her guessing. When she began to hum that stupid game show tune, I broke. "Yes, *fine*, I was daydreaming about the two hot men. They are fucking gorgeous. I know it, you know it, and every person that goes into their businesses knows it. They seem to be close—"

"Oh, do you mean like close or *close, close*?" Raising an eyebrow to her, I wondered for a moment if that even made sense to her. "You know what I mean. Crossing of swords, and all."

"*Lord love a duck*. Lettie, I don't know. I met them and they are obviously very attractive, if you like their type of goodlookingness." Which was exactly my type, and Lettie and I both knew it. Did I want to know? Hell yes. All those hands and mouths all over. Damn it. No. Nope, bad Scout.

"If you like their type of *goodlookingness*? You mean the ridiculous hot kind? You know you want to know." She snickered then fanned her face. "Can you imagine those two going at it? I mean hot damn, th—"

"Good morning, Ms. Harper. How are you?" I shot a pointed glare at my soon to be ex-best friend before I turned my focus on Ms. Harper.

"Haven't I told you no need for that Ms. Harper stuff? You can call me Nan like everybody else. Did I hear you talking about the bakery?" I loved this woman and wanted to be her when I grew up. She came to the store for the book club that had started meeting here. They were a bunch of grannies who sat around, reading the smuttiest books they could find. Most were old school romance books, which I found amazing and hilarious.

I gave her a gentle smile. "Yes, ma'am. I met the owner this morning and the outdoor store owner. They were kind enough to bring my packages that were delivered to the wrong address to me."

"I'm glad they helped you out, Scout. If they hadn't and I found out, they would be in a world of trouble." She winked at Lettie. "That's my teddy bear and his best friend, Gatlin."

Oh. Oh, shit. How much had she heard of our talk?

Seeing my face caused Lettie to try and hide her laughter with a cough. "I had no idea, Ms. Ha—" Her stern look made me pause. "Nan."

"That's ok, honey. You should get to know them. They are good boys. Been best friends since elementary school. Though, I think they could be more." She paused before looking me over. "With the right person."

Was she really suggesting...? Surely, she didn't mean like in a *relationship* type of more. What would that even be like? *Hot as fuck.*

Before my mind could run down that rabbit hole, Ms. Harper—I mean, Nan—interrupted, "Well, I'll let you two get back to what you were doing. I just wanted to make sure they didn't give you any trouble." She laughed before waving her goodbyes and leaving the store, heading in the direction of the bakery.

Both of them together. My mind played all kinds of dirty situations like a movie. New fantasy unlocked. Damn, now I was getting worked up. This would not do. I needed to put them out of my head and focus.

Before Lettie could start the interrogation, the bell over the door chimed. *Saved by the bell.* I moved back to the books, determined to get them in the system and move on. I would have plenty of time to think about the hunks later. *In the privacy of my bed.*

leland

Nan walked into the bakery just after eleven. "Well hello, handsome. I just heard some very interesting things about you." She smiled at me, walking over to the counter. "Seems you and bee made a very good impression on that cutie who owns the bookstore." I perked up at the mention of Scout. I had hoped for the last few months that she would happen to walk into the bakery or we would meet in passing, but nothing.

I walked around to hug my grandmother, bending low in order to accomplish it. She stretched up, kissing my cheek and then giving it a little pat. "I heard you two boys were mighty helpful with some packages." She smiled sweetly, but I knew better. The 5 foot nothing woman was a force of nature. She had always been sharp and had a knack for mischief.

Just thinking about Scout had my cheeks pinking. She was gorgeous; petite, but still had a figure. I had only seen her a few times, but every time I did, I was struck with how attracted I was to her. "We just returned some of her packages, Nan. It wasn't anything crazy." Had we both basically fell in love with her at first sight? Maybe. But I did not intend to share that. Or how many fantasies I had about her and someone else who I *definitely* wouldn't think about.

"You and Gatlin should try and court her. Then you and bee can get your heads out of your asses and be honest with each other." Under her breath, I thought she said something to the effect of, "I'm tired of losing money to your sister."

I was stuck on the first part of her sentence when the *you and bee* part hit me. "Nan, I told you Gat isn't into guys. We are just friends. That's it. Period. The end. Also, both of us dating one woman? You have been reading too many romance novels." I took in a breath before I finished. "Wait, what do you mean you are tired of losing money to Oakland? Are you two still making bets on me and Gat?"

With no shame, she held her chin up and looked me directly in the eyes. "Well, dear, some of us are not completely blind and dense like you both seem to be." She patted my arm, muttering *bless your hearts* under her breath. "I think the three of you would make a lovely throuple. The only question is, would be MMF or MFM?"

Throuple? MMF or MFM? What the fuck was happening?

Death. That was the only thing that would save me from this. My death would be the more convenient option, although Nan would come back and haunt me. No God or whatever higher being would do this to me. Right? "Nan, please never say that again." My face and neck were now on fire. I had thought about Gatlin that way before. I tried not to, but I had harbored a secret crush on him for years. I never told him, because it's not his fault that his queer friend is stupid and enjoys heartbreak. None of that is on Gatlin. The images and scenes my brain created with Scout and Gatlin were enough to have me jerking off in my room at night.

Nan's laughter pulled me back to reality. "Well, you should do it with them. It's good for the soul to get some lovin', teddy bear." She took the bag I had in my hand, her usual order plus some extra goodies. "Anyways, I'm meeting yours and bee's mothers, so I'm going to get out of your hair. Love you, honey. Tell Gatlin hello and give him a kiss from me."

"I will do no such thing, but I love you, Nan." I gave her a quick hug before she left. I didn't know what all of that was about, but I sure as shit hope she won't say anything to our mothers. The last thing I needed was my mother on me, which would then prompt my sister to get on my case. They had tried for years to convince me that Gatlin and I had something more than friendship, but I would never let myself hope. Gatlin had always been very physically affectionate, from hugs to smacking my ass. We had seen each other in various states of undress to full blown naked. There had always been a running joke that we were an old married couple. Like an old married couple, for every major life event, he has been there. Even if he was into guys or sharing, I would never risk it. *Never say never, teddy bear.* The words filtered through my mind, sounding a lot like Nan.

I walked to the kitchen to grab the lunch I had made for Gatlin and myself before heading over to his store. Maybe I would bump into the sexy bookstore owner. I wondered if she had lunch yet. It would be weird to just bring her something, right? We didn't know each other, but I loved to cook and bake for people. Especially people I liked. *Like bee, and now Scout.*

Damnit. Nan, get out of my head.

gatlin

The bells over the door jingled. "Welcome to Adrenaline Outdoors. Look around and let me know if you need anything." I looked around the pile of clothes that were currently littered around me to see who had come in. Leland walked around the shelves I was behind, almost tripping over a stack of shirts. "Careful. I can't have you getting hurt on my watch. Nan would kill me." His face turned a slight shade of pink.

What's that about?

He cleared his throat before he spoke. "Speaking of Nan, she says hello. She probably would have come by, but she was meeting our mothers." He said the words without actually looking at me.

I stood up, dusting the back of my pants off. "Mom mentioned something about them going shopping, I think." I looked over the side of his face, because he was still not looking at me. "Um, teddy bear, you ok?" I asked, reaching out to touch his shoulder. I grounded myself with touch; it helped me focus on the conversation or person. I also loved to cuddle, which for some people was a turn off. I had done it in my sleep my whole life. Leland had never commented on the fact that anytime we have shared a bed, I snuggled up to him. I was not awake when it happened, but I had woken up with his big body curled around mine. I secretly loved it, and if his morning wood, or should I say *log*, was poking in my back, that would be a topic that was in the *not talked about* file.

"I'm good. You ready to eat?" He held up the bag, giving it a little shake.

"Sure."

I opened the roll up door on the back of the building to let some fresh air in while we ate. Mud was lounging in his bed when we moved the table over before setting the food out. "Thanks, Leland, for bringing lunch over."

"Of course. If I didn't, you wouldn't eat," he said as he pulled out my sandwich, then his.

I scoffed, causing him to glance up at me. "Excuse you, I would eat. I just wouldn't eat well or probably enough."

"Gat, you have literally gone entire days only eating a couple of crackers and some coffee," he deadpanned.

"See? I eat, just not well." I gave him my most innocent smile. "So what trouble was Nan causing? I assume she was at the granny romance book club this morning."

He fidgeted with the bag before crumpling it up and setting it on the table. "The usual, I guess. Trying to get me dating."

Dating? Is Leland dating people?

The bit of sandwich in my mouth went from delicious to tasting like saw dust. It wasn't that I didn't want Leland to date, but the last few people he had been with were assholes. That's what was wrong with me. I just worried about my friend, that's all. "Dating, huh?" I felt like I had to force the words out.

"Yeah, she was saying all kinds of crazy shit. You know Nan, if she wants to say something, she is going to say it." He huffed a laugh. He wasn't wrong about her, though.

I took a sip of sweet tea, trying to wash down the sandwich. "Who is she thinking you should pursue?"

He looked out over the parking lot toward the bookstore. The back door opened and Scout walked out, climbing into her car. Noticing us sitting there, she gave a little wave before pulling out. "No one. What's the plan for this weekend?" Just like that, the conversation was over.

Leland Boone, everyone. The king of diverting conversions. I'll let him have it this time.

chapter 2

. . .

gatlin

IN THE WEEK since Leland's little dating revelation, everything had been weird. The whole atmosphere in the house felt off. What I worried would happen if I said anything was currently unfolding. We had barely hung out or really talked. I wanted to blame being busy, but that was only half true. I was scared. I could admit it. At least to myself. I had avoided diving into the feelings surrounding him with other people. I had also ingested so heartburn medicine that I could have been a paid sponsor. It was selfish of me to want to keep him for myself. He deserved happiness and love more than anyone I knew. As the days wore on, I spent more time at the store, outside, or at the gym. I didn't blame Leland; I wasn't angry at him, but more at myself. I needed to get my head out of my ass and get over myself. The thoughts that crossed the maybe not straight line had come over the years. Leland Boone was the star of the show in every single one. There would be moments where we would be doing something so domestic and simple, I would look at him and want nothing more than to lean into him. To finally know if his lips were as soft as they always looked. While some of my Leland visions were pure, innocent, and PG, others would make a porn star blush. It was always him, though. No other guys did this to me. The fear that always pulled me back was him feeling like an experiment for me, like a test of my sexuality. What I have come to realize was I was just a Leland sexual.

And a Scout sexual.

Damn you, brain.

It never seemed to matter. When I would finally muster up the courage to say something, he would be dating someone or show interest in someone. My feelings would never change. I would watch and support him from the sidelines and pray that I could shove down the pangs of loving I felt. Then there was the jealousy of someone else having his attention. *I sounded like a toddler, not a grown man.*

The worst times were when someone would mistreat him. The worst was a chick from a few years ago. *Fucking Lana. Lana Thompson.* She made comments about literally everything Leland did.

"Why would you want to open a bakery?"

"What about doing something that will actually make money?"

The cherry on the shit show was the day she commented on the granny bodice rippers he liked to read. Those were apparently not very *manly.* Leland was a romantic, but also loved some smut novels. The old school spicy books were something he and Nan had read for years. Nan had a stint in the hospital when we were eighteen or nineteen. He spent every day with her he could. Her one request: smutty granny romance novels. Leland had so many amazing qualities. He was fiercely protective of the people he loves, but not himself. Lana would always pass her comments off as a joke or that she was just asking, not criticizing. The last comment was made in front of Oakland and Nan. When her condescending ass left, Oakland broke down and told him that if he didn't cut the bitch loose, she was going to need bail money and a hot lawyer. From someone else, this would have been a funny joke. But Leland's twin sister? It would be a terrifying threat that would come true. She finished her rant with a final blow, telling him to dump her and find somebody who's actually human, not a troll, or she would stop talking to him. She refused to sit back and watch someone treat him like he was less. Nan took that moment to chime in with a comment about how Scout would be a wonderful option.

Scout Frazier.

Now *that* was an idea I could get on board with. Or maybe even get in on. This was not the first time I had thoughts about the two of them together. We had chatted in passing, slowly getting to know her better. She was funny and sassy, but also sweet and smart. Scout Fraizer was also drop dead gorgeous. Those pesky thoughts of Leland, the sweet and spicy, now had a co-star. There had been nights I had woken up rock hard with my dick in hand to the thought of me with each of them and them together. The ones that sent me over the edge were the dreams that included all of us together. Not just in bed, but life. *Damnit.*

You and your best friend since childhood while Scout watched and pleasured herself, my traitorous, inner voice helpfully supplied, making my cock twitch in my shorts. Not the fucking time, dude. I scolded myself as I took a sip of my coffee. The hot drink scalded my tongue, making me forget the train of thought for now. The backdoor of the house opening was the final kick back to reality. "You ready to get started?" Leland came out to the back yard where I was standing. With it being the weekend, we had made a plan, pre-selfish asshole Gatlin phase, to work on some projects around the house. There had been a building at the back of the property we had been updating. Today, we were tackling the roof. Doing some home projects, like the bestest of friends and roommates. Definitely not anything else. *Super convincing.*

"Yeah, I'm good to go."

I could feel his eyes on me, doing his best to read me. He knew me too well, but this was something that had to stay buried. He could search all he wanted, but I was like Fort Knox. *Impenetrable.*

Maybe.

"SON OF A BITCH, it has gotten hot today." I wiped the sweat from my eyes with the hem of my shirt. We had been working on the roof for close to four hours. When we started, it had been slow going. There had been issues with some of the roof beams and existing plywood. We had planned to replace some of them, not every piece. Instead of getting the majority of the work done earlier in the day, we were hitting the heat of the day with the added extra work.

"Temps I think are going to be high this whole weekend. I just didn't think it would be this bad. I did catch Scout outside the other day and mentioned the cookout to her. She seemed excited to come. I invited her friend who works at the bookstore, too, if that is ok. I meant to let you know, but we kept missing each other this week." He grabbed his drink, turning the bottle to finish the remaining water. I watched the droplets of water run from the corner of his mouth and down his neck, disappearing into the neck of his shirt. *Oh, to be that water.*

I grabbed my hammer to finish the last few nails in the plywood. Leland moved down the roof toward where the shingles were. I hit the first nail in and reached for one of the ones I held between my lips when something caught attention. I froze with the hammer in mid-air, my lips parting to let the nails fall to the roof. I looked over just in time to witness Leland pull his shirt over his head. *Dear Lord in heaven, did it just get hotter? Was I having a heat stroke?* His big, beefy upper body was now on full display. His broad chest was covered in red hair and freckles. The strong muscles of his arm flexed when he wiped the sweat from his face with his shirt. Completely unaware of my drooling, Leland grabbed some shingles and began to work. For the size he is, the man is beautiful.

My body lost all motor function in that moment and the hammer fell. "Oh fucking fuck." The tool landed hard on my finger. It began to throb, immediately swelling and bruising. Jerking my hand up, I caught it on a sharp piece of the plywood, slicing my hand open. *Wow. Smooth, Gat. So fucking smooth.* Leland stood, moving quickly but carefully to me.

"Did you get your finger?" His eyes strayed to my hand. "Oh shit, bee, there is blood. Here, wrap it in my shirt and I can help you get down."

I took the shirt, sending a word of thanks that it wasn't my dominant hand. Once it was wrapped, I stood and made my way over to the ladder. Leland went down first before turning to spot me as I made my slow decent. When we reached the ground, the world went from vertical, to horizontal, and then black.

I came to on the couch. *Wait, couch?*

My head fell to the side, my gaze meeting Leland's worried eyes. He was sitting on the coffee table, studying every inch of my face. "You scared the shit out of me." His anger and fear bubbled just under the surface. "You could have fallen off the roof, Gatlin. You could have seriously been hurt." He looked down at his hands where he was white knuckling a dish towel.

"Calm down, *Dad*. I'm fine." I tried to make my tone light and brush off the feelings his fiery gaze was stirring. "Just a little scratch. I'll wash it and be good to go."

Leland stood so fast it made me dizzy. "The fuck you will. You are going to let me clean the cut and bandage it, and then you are going to stay in the house. If you aren't going to take care of yourself properly, I fully intend to do it. Now, do you want to walk to the bathroom or am I carrying you?"

"Sorry, *sir*. I'll be a good boy." My words dripped with sarcasm. Leland's whole body went rigid. The muscle in his jaw ticced with how hard he clenched his teeth. Even with knowing I was pushing, I couldn't stop. I was a glutton for punishment, so I decided to poke the bear a little more. "Oopsies, must have made Papa bear mad." I got to my feet and thanked God when I didn't fall over. I threw one last remark before I headed to the bathroom. "Me calling you Papa bear doesn't make you my dad or Daddy, Leland. So chill." By this point, I was being a brat. I knew it and he knew it, but dammit I had done this to myself because I was ogling him. I felt guilty and he was being too nice.

When I went to pass, his arm shot out, stopping me. He turned me so we were face to face. The look in his eyes was something that I couldn't make sense of or maybe I wasn't *ready* to dissect it. It was a look that dripped gasoline on the sparks of my hope. *Longing need.* "We both know you like to be good for me. Now, go to the bathroom and sit your ass down on the toilet while I get the first aid kit." His arm moved from my path. My body was in motion before my brain caught up that I was doing as commanded. There have been times, especially since living together, where things have strayed from platonic to whatever this was. When he said things or acted all domineering, it did something to me. *Made you a needy slut.* Shut up, brain.

I made it to the bathroom and did as instructed. I flipped the lid down, letting it slam because I could, and sat down. I looked down to my shirt and shorts where spots of blood were dotted across them. I needed to shower, probably before my hand was cleaned and bandaged.

Leland appeared in the door with the kit before I could make my escape for extra clothes after my shower. He took a knee in front of me, placing the first aid kit on the floor. Wordlessly, he extended his hand out to take my injured one. I immediately relaxed at the feeling of his warm skin on mine. "Good boy." Oh, *fuck me.* Why did that send a jolt of lust straight to my balls?

Shut it down. Think of something else.

I started naming any random facts I could think of. For once, though, my two heads were on the same page. Leland, being basically at crotch level, also added fuel to the fire. *Come on, Gatlin.* Nothing. Fucking crickets. My brain had gone AWOL and was not wanting to listen. Instead, it started pushing every dirty thought to the forefront. I let out a little groan of annoyance at myself. When Leland froze, his eyes flicked to mine, a deep furrow between his brow. "Sorry, bee." I didn't correct that he didn't do anything. I felt like shit letting him believe he caused me discomfort, but I still said nothing. He refocused on the cut and soon finished. He looked at me again, his eyes still searching. It's like something in his soul was telling him I was hiding something. This is why I have never hid things from him. The man knows me better than I know myself. I am about to tell him that I need to shower and get cleaned up, but he speaks first. "Go ahead and shower then I'll wrap it up after." He stood and then stepped away. "Can you manage on your own? I don't want you to pass out again." His face was pulled into a serious expression, eyes still scanning in concern.

"Yeah, I'm good." I didn't move from where I sat. I needed him to leave before I stood up and exposed my raging hard-on that was tenting my pants. *What was I, a fucking hormonal teenager?*

With one last glance, he nodded before turning to the door. "Just yell if you need me. I'll be getting the meat ready for the cookout."

"Okay." I hurried to shut the door once he was gone and stripped. I snatched a towel and threw it over the door. I turned the shower on without giving it time to warm and stepped in. The cold water did nothing to cool the heat coursing through me. By the time the water had warmed, I had grabbed my conditioner and squeezed some into my hand. With my hand now around my cock, I began to stroke slowly. The glide of my rough palm over the smooth skin pulled me closer to the edge. It wasn't enough, though. I let my lids fall closed as the generic images played through my mind. The tight grip of a woman's pussy around me. The warm, wet slide as I thrusted in and out. The image changed to a more familiar body, the face becoming clearer. Scout's beautiful face covered in a thin sheen of sweat. Her tits bouncing as I drove into her body, where it laid on a bed. My climax was there, but just out of reach. I needed more. I craved more. My brain changed the scene again. I pumped into my fist faster as the picture cleared. *Holy fucking shit.*

My stroke stuttered at what my imagination had produced. I focused back on my dick, redoubling my efforts to come. I could see it so clearly and would have sworn on a stack of Bibles it was real. Scout still laid below me, my dick pumping into her. The change came from behind me. Leland was leaning in behind me, his weight resting on my back. His massive cock was pumping into me, fucking me into Scout.

I leaned against the wall, fucking my fist faster. I snatched the towel, not wanting to bite the fist of my injured hand. In my hast, it knocked something over. I didn't give shit. The whole bathroom could have been on fire for all I cared. "Ngh," I groaned into the towel as spurts of cum hit the wall. A moan left my throat louder than intended as the last spurts of my release came. I let the towel fall from my mouth while I pulled in deep breaths, trying to slow my raging heart rate. It spiked again at a soft knock on the closed door.

"You ok?" Leland called from the other side of the closed door. "I was coming to check on you when I heard something fall."

I tried to sound as calm and relaxed as possible. "Be out in just a minute. I just knocked some bottles over." I rinsed my hand before hastily washing my hair and body. Once I was clean, I grabbed another towel to replace the now soaking wet one. With the towel wrapped around my waist, I walked to the sink. When my eyes caught my reflection, the questions that I had tried to push away all tumbled in.

What was going on with me?

What did this mean?

I wanted two people. Both male and female.

I had never wanted a man. This wasn't just any man, this was Leland.

And Scout, I didn't even really know her.

But what if...?

Shit.

IN THE WEEKS following the cookout, this unsteady feeling wouldn't leave. There was a distance between Leland and I that had never existed. I had still been spending time away from the house, not avoiding him, but avoiding my feelings and reactions. Normally, I would talk to tell him what was going on in my head. He would sit me down, talk it through, and help me find a solution. It's what we did. Now, I was floundering in my own head.

Over the years of being friends with Leland, I heard the things that people would say about him. The remarks that older people made. We, unfortunately, live in a world where some people think it was, in fact, their business that you loved. Most people left Leland be. He was a big dude who intimidated people. He also had Nan and Oakland. People may not have always feared Leland, but they damn well feared those two. In every situation, though, I always had his back and always would. We backed each other up and supported each other.

The bell over the door pulled me from my thoughts. I glanced up to see one of my cousins walking in. Orrin had been the only other person I was close to growing up. He had always been like my brother. That all changed when Leland came out. The minute his parents found out, they called my parents. Of course, Mom and Dad knew. Mr. and Mrs. Boone were two of their best friends. They loved Leland like he was their son. The shit hit the fan because apparently my aunt and uncle were not supportive or welcoming. My mom, never being one to back down from a fight, told her brother where to take his backward opinions. That was the last time they spoke to each other. When my grandparents found out about Leland coming out, they seemed ok with everything, not really caring one way or the other. But then the comments started when I would be over there. They seemed harmless on the surface, but escalated. I had loved my grandparents and respected them until then. I knew admitting anything would only break my mom's relationship with her family even more. After all that, I cut contact with them and only stayed in contact with Orrin. My grandparents and his parents moved a few years ago. Orrin bought his parents' house and became like my brother again. Unfortunately, his parents still visited. On those occasions, we all did our best to avoid them.

"You seem lost in thought." He squinted like he could pull my thoughts out of me with just his eyes. "Care to share?"

I didn't respond, knowing if I let one thing out, that the dam would burst. It already had too many cracks.

He turned fully toward the counter, truly searching my face. He remained quiet, just watching me. It would just be my shitty luck that one of the very few people who can make me crack like an egg walked in right now. "Are you just going to stand there staring at me?"

Nothing.

"Orrin, blink twice if the aliens are trying to take over your brain, but you're still there." Again, nothing. Not even a smirk. The seconds ticked by, feeling like hours. I held out for as long as I could before I broke. "Okay, fine. My brain is all jumbled up. I have been having some feelings and thoughts about..." I paused for a moment. *Did I really want to tell everything?*

"Leland," he supplied, like it was obvious.

"Yes, abou—wait, what the hell, dude?" I looked at him wide eyed.

Orrin rolled his eyes before looking back to me. "You want to know what to do? Whether you are as straight as you always believed. Right?" His gaze was piercing as he continued to watch me. "Also, the two of you are the only ones that have been missing the very large flashing signs." He held his hands up and made a flashing motion. "Two dumbass that are meant to be, but can't get their heads out of their asses."

Everyone knew.

No way.

Maybe?

I couldn't tell him that was only part of it, Lord only knew what he would think. I paused, trying to put my thoughts into words. It wasn't just questioning why my body was reacting to Leland, but also Scout. My eyes were laser focused on the countertop, not wanting to look up.

Orrin's finger tapped the wood top to get my attention. "What else? I know there is more. Don't make me wait you out. You know I will win." He started to hum a gameshow tune just to drive his point home.

Damn if he isn't right. "It's not just Leland. It's Scout, the woman that owns the bookstore next door." I looked back down at my hands. "I have never wanted people like I do them. I have known Leland most of my life, but Scout is new. What if I mess up and I'm not actually attracted to men, or well, a *specific* man and woman, and someone gets hurt? I don't know that I want to risk everything based my dick chubbing up."

There was a long pause before he spoke. "No one is forcing you to do anything. You can take time to figure out what you are feeling and organize your thoughts. There are no rules to figuring out your sexuality. Hell, we are the same age and I couldn't give you a straight answer." He laughed, realizing his joke. "Get it, straight answer?"

This is who was giving me advice. The king of Dad jokes.

"Have you ever talked about all the shit *the ones who shall not be named* said?" I shook my head in reply. I had never brought up the comments that had been made at anyone, but to Orrin. A lot was directed at Leland, but it shifted to me as time went on. "Ok, so here's the plan: you are going to get in and talk with someone. You shouldn't have to hold in the shit those assholes said to you and about someone you love." He waited for me to look at him before he continued. "You might feel better talking things through with an unbiased stranger. I do."

"You go to therapy?" I asked, almost in disbelief. I wouldn't have expected it from Orrin. He had always been so put together. He was the one who had been wise beyond his years. It wasn't that I didn't think he had his own issues, but he just always seemed to know how to handle situations.

His lip tipped up in a smirk before he replied. "You aren't the only one who has been putting the pieces of who they are together. Well, I guess I have been working on putting the pieces back together. The damage asshole parents can do is mind blowing."

"Damn, Orrin. I never realized they treated you in any way but good. I feel like such an asshat for being so wrapped up on my own mess. You can always talk to me, you know? Maybe me or my parents could have—"

Orrin shook his head when I was about to continue, my words clogged my throat. "You aren't an asshat. I became very good at hiding things. Plus, you already had a target on your back. There wasn't anything anyone could have done. They weren't physically abusive or even neglectful to me; they were just assholes." He picked at his finger. "I have worked through all that. They don't hold power over me now like they did growing up." We were both quiet for a beat before he spoke again. "Seriously, though, what do you have to lose by talking to somebody?"

"Nothing."

Orrin's head moved in a subtle nod. "Exactly, you have nothing to lose and everything to gain."

Nothing to lose and everything to gain.

I gave his arm a gentle push. "When did you become all grown up and wise?"

He clutched his chest, his expression mock offense. "Excuse you. I have always been wise. You just don't listen to my advice."

Ouch.

WITHIN A MONTH, I had a therapist. And I would never admit it to Orrin, but he had been right. I needed to talk. Unfortunately, I wasn't fast enough, because both Leland and Scout started seeing people during that time. That was the day I gained a new mantra.

It's not for them, this is for you. You are healing you for you.

Rolling my eyes, I locked my phone and put it in my pocket before unlocking the door. *Like he is any better.*

PULLING UP BEHIND OUR BUILDINGS, I let Mud out before getting my stuff from the front seat. The back of the buildings for the most part was uninteresting. A few parking spots and space for deliveries, but the one part that stood out was attached to Scout's building. She had a covered porch added a few months ago, including railing and a gate that kept Mud either in or out of the area. When she mentioned loving the idea of an outdoor space, I will admit I was a bit envious. It was a great place to take a breather from the stores and people. Mud also loved it because he had free rein of the area when he was out there. With some of his favorite toys, a comfy bed to lay on, and food and water, he would never leave if given the choice.

Once he was settled, I walked over to the back of the bakery and buzzed into the back door. As the door opened, the smells of the bakery hit me. The sweet and savory treats battled for dominance. Sitting on a bench, Scout munched on something, probably sugary sweet, and watched Leland place unbaked cookies on sheet pans.

Walking up quietly behind Scout, I leaned in, my voice a whisper. "Where are they, honeysuckle?"

"WHAT TH—" Clutching her chest, she whirled on me. "How are you so sneaky and quiet?"

Smirking at her, I straightened and walked to where Leland had set the small pan of biscuits. "I'm like a ninja," I take a bite before finishing, "you'll never see me coming." Sliding my backpack off, I placed it on the table, unzipping it to remove two pairs of my favorite wool socks.

Turning back to Scout, she extended her hands out, giving me grabby hands for the socks. *So fucking cute.*

I had supported the small business for years and now sold them in the store. Scout now took to stealing my socks every chance she got, even though she had her own that I bought her. I, of course, didn't mind. Her claim was mine were broken in and they felt cozier. She was a dragon when it came to four things: coffee, books, food, and cozy clothing items. Leland had lost at least two, possibly three sweatshirts to her, more than likely some t-shirts, as well. My contribution to Scout's stash was wool socks and flannel shirts. With owning an outdoor store that also led outdoor adventure trips, I had a never ending supply of clothes and gear.

"Thank you! You are forgiven for almost giving me a heart attack." Scout set the socks down before returning to her breakfast.

I stood for a moment, just taking her in. She was stunning. She was always dressed in business casual clothes when at the store. Today, she wore black pants that looked like they were leather, but they weren't because the woman wouldn't harm a fly. The pants were tight, hugging her legs from ankle to her hips. Today, like most days, she wore sneakers. These were white with small black details. For her shirt, or shirts, I should say, it was a simple white collared shirt with a caramel colored sweater over it. Her thick, espresso-colored hair was pulled back into a ponytail. With her hair back, her doll-like features were on display. Even from the side, her silhouette was beautiful. Feeling my eyes on her, she turned, our gazes connecting. The full impact of her big, leafy-green eyes framed by long lashes took me in. Her fair skin turned pink under the small freckles that covered her nose and cheeks before she turned away. Not wanting to make her feel awkward, I shifted my gaze to Leland.

"Will you be able to help with the Nature Nuggets next week?" I asked before taking another bite of my biscuit.

"Yeah, I will just need to let Cleo know so we can plan things out." He pulled a notepad from his pocket, scribbling a note inside. Leland was the most organized person I knew. Unlike myself, who would forget my head if it wasn't attached to my body. It was something we both struggled with when we first became roommates. We would butt heads over the smallest of things in the house. Most of the time, it was me who forgot something, but we had also both lived alone or with our parents. Nan kept saying that it was just the growing pains of our relationship, but we had been friends most of our lives. I moved in after just graduating college. Leland was done with culinary school, working and going to night classes for a business degree. He hadn't planned on doing a traditional degree, but wanted some kind of business knowledge. Leland tended to be over-prepared and the business degree was no different. Nan wanted to move to a retirement community; her plan was always that Leland got her house. She decided one day that it was time to move and that was that. Within a month, she was moved completely out and we moved in. I have never regretted agreeing to the move and probably never will. I can't imagine not having Leland around and sharing a space with him. When it came down to it, Leland had always watched out for me. He had always been someone who took care of the people he loved. Sometimes this came off as being bossy. He was a big softy, but he had a stubborn, domineering streak in him. I was more of a fly by the seat of my pants kind of guy, which did get me into trouble sometimes. We had always been well balanced. Where I lacked he would shine, and vice versa.

I turned my attention back to Leland and Scout, enjoying their ribbing. Scout was giving him grief about his book choices, as usual. "I know you love your granny bodice rippers, but I find it hard to believe that half the stuff in those books could happen." She raised one eyebrow at him, as if challenging him to prove her wrong.

"The only thing I will tell you, honeysuckle, is with the right ones, damn near everything in those books is possible." His gaze flicked to me before locking on Scout. Who had turned as red as a cherry.

"Leland Boone! How dare you say such things in front of a lady." I moved to Scout's side, mock covering her ears. "You know that is for the privacy of your bedroom, young man."

Leland was a reserved person, but when it came to his romance novels, he accepted no criticism. Scout knew this, which is why she always gave him grief. Most of the time she would read the book, as well, and then go into an in depth description of the explicit scene just to rile Leland up.

"Leland, I must say, this is a new side to you." Scout lifted her chin before finishing. "I only have one question." I saw the *oh shit* look that crossed Leland's face. "Is this what you're like in bed? Bossy and all knowing?" She innocently leaned into the table, propping her elbow on the table and resting her chin in her hand.

Checkmate.

chapter 3

· · ·

scout

BESIDE ME GATLIN STILLED, his head shifting back and
forth between me and Leland. "Well, teddy bear?" I knew I had him. We
all three walked the edge of flirting and friends; even when the guys
seemed oblivious to how they sounded. I was seriously asking, but I
would also be terrified to ever make a move in that direction. This was
me goofing off with my friends, or at least that is what I told myself.

"Sweet honeysuckle, only one way to find out." Hot damn. I was
going to need help picking my jaw up from the floor. I could feel
Gatlin's body heat pouring off of him as I sat staring at a now smirking
Leland. I felt Gatlin's warm body press forward into my space.

"I believe that's checkmate, honeysuckle." His words ghosted over
the shell of my ear. An involuntary shiver ran over my body. Why was it
so fucking hot in here now?

"I don't think you could handle me, teddy bear." I looked at him,
batting my lashes.

Gatlin spoke again into my ear, his words barely above a whisper,
but loud enough to reach Leland. "Well, they do say two is better than

one, ya know?" He reaches up to run my ponytail through his hand. "Some might say we would be better than bookends."

"Will you all just fuck and get it over with?" Cleo's voice broke through the kitchen, causing me to jump. When my shoulder connected with some part of Gatlin's face, he let out a yelp of pain. He turned away, swearing under his breath and grabbing his nose. I moved without thinking toward him.

"Oh shit." Leland moved around the table, reaching Gatlin right as I did. "Gat, let me look," he said, his voice coming out soft but commanding. He turned, looking at Leland while still covering his nose.

"Move back, honey, I think it's bleeding." Gatlin motioned for me to step away. Like hell I was.

"I don't care about the blood." Taking the towel that Cleo had brought to where we stood, I brought it up to his face.

"I'm so sorry Gatlin...I didn't mean for you to get hurt. I was just kidding, but I thought you guys heard me come in the back." Cleo began to apologize. "I'm so sorry. I'll grab some ice, that should help. Right?" Before we could answer, she was gone.

I shifted the towel so it was below where he held his hand. "Baby, you have to move your hand," I said, the endearment slipping out.

He grabbed the towel with his free hand and slowly moved the hand covering his nose, replacing it with the towel.

"Um...I think I might need to sit down." Gatlin's words were faint as he looked at the blood that was on his hand.

"Come on, bumblebee." With Gatlin sandwiched between us, we moved to Leland's office.

"Gat, I am so sorry." I could feel tears burning behind my eyes. We reached the couch that was pushed up against the back wall. The office was roomier than what you would expect. Enough room for a couch, Leland's desk and chair, as well as a filing cabinet. The walls had dry erase boards and cork boards along them holding various orders, designs, and photos. Above the desk were shelves mounted to the wall holding various books, binders full of paperwork, and a few pictures of Leland and his family including him and Oakland, and him and Gatlin the day he opened the bakery. In Gatlin's office, there was a mirror image of the picture, only in front of his store on opening day. The most recent addition to his photos was one Oakland took of us on our last camping trip. I am sandwiched between them, with Mud standing at our feet. There are three copies, each placed in our offices.

Leland helped Gatlin get comfortable on the couch, his head tilted back with the towel still covering his nose. Once settled, Leland squatted down in front of him, resting his hands on Gatlin's knees. I stood off to the side, blinking rapidly to keep the tears at bay.

"Honeysuckle, I'm ok. I just got a little dizzy." Gatlin's words came out muffled behind the towel. His eyes were closed, his chest rising and falling as he took slow breaths. "Is your shoulder ok?" The concern for me was the start to my undoing. A sniffle escaped as a tear slid down my cheek. I couldn't make the words leave my throat. I was worried about him and I was embarrassed that I had hurt him. I nodded my head wordlessly, trying to let him know I was fine. When I still said nothing, Gatlin peeked one eye open, looking directly to where I stood before his gaze moved to Leland. "Leland, I'm fine, honeysuckle is not." I wanted a hole to open up and swallow me. As if coming back to reality, Leland turned to look at me, his facing softening when he saw the tears running down my face.

"Baby, come here. He is ok, you are ok. It was an accident." He reached his hand out, waiting for me to move closer to the couch. "Sit down next to Gat." By this point, Gatlin had straightened some, his eyes now open and taking me in. Patting the seat next to him, I moved closer before sitting down.

My fingers tangled together before I began to fidget. Not meeting their stares, I started speaking rapidly. This happened when my anxiety spiked. "I'm sorry, I don't know why I'm crying. It's stupid. I'm not the one that got hurt." Words keep pouring out. "I don't mean to do stupid things or be so jumpy. Then I start crying a-and Leland has to stop focusing on you b-because I—"

"Stop," Gatlin and Leland said at the same time.

Gatlin reached over, giving my knee a gentle squeeze. "I know your brain is telling you a lot right now, but it's none of that true." He paused, waiting for me to look up. He had removed the towel leaving dried blood on his face and neck, the collar of his shirt tinted just slightly. "Nothing that happened was your fault, we aren't mad at you or upset that you were showing emotion." His thumb rubbed back and forth over my thigh as he looked me in the eye.

Another warm palm began to rub my other knee. "You don't apologize for what you can't help," Leland said, both their calm voices soothing my racing thoughts. "If we have to tell you a thousand times a day, we will." My eyes dropped to where their hands rested. I had struggled with eye contact since I was a child. This always became harder when my emotions were high. I could know that I hadn't done anything wrong, but my brain could still convince me that it was my fault. When those neuro-spicy squirrels took the wheel, I would rather keel over than have to see disappointment in someone's eyes. I would be scolded by teachers for not looking them in the eye when they were talking to me. They would assume that if something happened, I was lying because I couldn't maintain eye contact. Older adults would say I was disrespectful for not looking at them when talking. It wasn't that I didn't want to, I physically couldn't make myself sometimes. This wonderful little trait was a battle I fought in every conversation throughout childhood and adolescence and was something I still struggled with as an adult. I instead focused on my fingers rather than looking up.

"This is just a piece of you, honeysuckle. It's not damaged, stupid, broken, or anything else that people or your brain have said. It's just a piece of a beautiful, amazing, wonderful picture." Gatlin reached, taking one of my hands while Leland took the other.

For the millionth time since meeting the two of them, I was thankful to have them as my two best friends. I also gave the cosmos the middle finger because we couldn't be more—not without losing one or both of them. I wouldn't claim to be proficient in relationships. I gather knowledge like any rational adult: through failed attempts at dating, romance novels, and praying to anyone who would listen I would get it right. This was not one of those times. What did I know about having a relationship with not just one man, but two? Nothing.

Fuck. My. Life.

ONCE CLEO RETURNED with the ice, I was significantly calmer and Gatlin's nose had stopped bleeding altogether.

"You are probably going to have a black eye," Leland spoke, pushing up from where he had squatted. "I don't know that I would tell people you were taken out by the shoulder of someone half your size." He smirked before glancing at me with a wink.

"Ya know what, Mr. Boone, I wasn't going to put the blame on anyone, but I do believe it rests solely on your shoulders," Gatlin spoke with a snobbish air to his tone. "If you weren't such a shameless flirt with Miss Frazier, then I dare say this would not have happened," he finished with a huff before looking away.

"As I recall, someone else was also being a shameless flirt. For someone who claims to have never read any of my beloved romance novels, you sure sound a lot like the characters." Leland looked knowingly at him.

With a gasp, Gatlin spoke, "Are you questioning my honor?" He stood, swaying for a moment. "I require a dual, but will have to schedule for a later date, as I am in poor health."

Giggling, I stood by, letting them have their fun. "You guys are so strange," Cleo spoke from the door. "Also, if you are done reenacting a regency romance novel, we have about ten minutes before the morning rush." Pausing, she spoke again. "And again, Gatlin, I am so, so sorry." She turned, walking toward the cake room.

Glancing down at my watch, Cleo was correct. I needed to get over to the store and get ready for the day. "Well, I guess I'm going to head over to the store." I started to leave before remembering something else. "Oh, and they are starting on the next two rooms for the apartment remodel, so it might be a little loud."

"That's awesome, honeysuckle!" Leland's voice carried genuine excitement for me.

"It is, honeysuckle. We know how long this process has been," Gatlin spoke, shifting the ice pack that rested across his nose.

Warmth spread over me hearing them use the nickname they have given me. I have asked why they call me honeysuckle, but never got a direct response. In turn, I have obviously never shared what hearing it does to me.

I let out a breath. "I am definitely ready for it to be done. But I will let you guys get to it. I hope you both have a great day. See you maybe for lunch?" My heart gave a hopeful jump as I waited for an answer.

"Of course!" Gatlin answered. "What does Nan say?"

"Lord willing and the creek don't rise."

Laughing I moved to the door. "Bye, guys."

"Grab your to-go goodies," Leland called. I grabbed my bag, coffee cup, and then the treats Leland packed up for me. I slip out the backdoor, walking toward my building. Mud raised his head when he heard the door close, standing to meet me at the gate. "Good morning, Muddington. How are you, handsome boy?" I spoke to the sweet pup as I move toward the door. "Do you want to come in with me for a bit? I'm sure your dad won't mind." His tongue lazily hung from his mouth, his tail gentle swishing where it laid on the deck. Opening the door, I stepped aside, allowing room for him to move through. "After you, sweet boy." With that invitation, he stood and moved into the back of the store, sniffing around before going to find his bed and laying down. Having the big shaggy dog around always made me feel calmer. He was very much still a puppy, but he was a lazy puppy. Before I could close the door, the construction crew pulled up. Maybe this day will turn out better than I thought.

chapter 4

. . .

leland

EVEN WITHOUT HER HERE, my mind was on Scout. Like most, she tried to hide the parts of herself that made her vulnerable. The first time her mask slipped, as she put it, was only a few months after we first met. The pharmacy that normally filled her medications had been out. Calling her doctor led her down a rabbit hole of trying to get the prescription moved. This led to a few days with no medicine, which Scout handled like a champ. However, when she was ghosted by someone else who was supposed to work on her apartment, it was her final straw. We brought her over to the bakery and just sat with her for a while. We learned that when Scout was overwhelmed and her brain started to run too fast, that the things it told her were usually not kind. That day, we let her just be for a while. The biggest help was Mud; he became her best buddy that day. If Scout was not having a great day, Mud knew and stuck to her like glue.

Mine and Gatlin's phones chimed with a message.

Scout: 7:10 a.m. Mud is in the store with me.

Scout: 7:11 a.m. He said some mean old man left him outside. 🙁

Gatlin: 7:13 a.m. *Shock*

Me: 7:14 a.m. Uncle Leland will take care of him. He has a whole bag of doggie biscuits here.

Gatlin: 7:15 a.m. Which he will get none of if he keeps telling stories.

Scout: 7:18 a.m. Sorry, what was that? I couldn't hear you over him munching on some treats.

Gatlin: 7:20 a.m. When he is spoiled rotten and doesn't listen, it will be you two who will be blamed.

Scout: 7:25 a.m. Aggressive eye roll.

Me: 7:27 a.m. Ok children, time to work. Scout, have a great morning. Message if you need us. 😃

Scout: 7:29 a.m. Ok Daddy. 😋

I felt my face turn red, the blush creeping across my face and down my neck. Clearing my throat, I tried to subtly adjust my dick as it began to chub up. "You can hang out back here for a little while if you want. I need to check in on everything. You know, in the kitchen and up front. Cause the rush and all." *Stop talking.*

My eyes found Gatlin's. He was close to exploding with laughter. "Well, *Daddy*, you might want to handle that before going out front." His eyes glanced down to the bulge in the front of my pants. "Might intimidate the old ladies." I turned, walking out of the office and straight to the bathroom, leaving a cackling Gatlin in the office.

They were going to be the death of me.

I LOVED the morning rush at the bakery. Even though I had employees to cover the front of the shop, I made it a point to engage with my customers. It was a way to connect with the people supporting the shop and me. My employees were amazing at their jobs. Currently, we had four in the back, not including myself and Cleo. Then in the front, I had a rotation of six employees, not including my siblings.

When I opened the bakery, it was just me and the help my family could offer. I was stressed, burning out, and close to throwing in the towel. One family dinner, Oakland and my mother scolded me for not hiring people to help. I didn't say it, but my fear was hiring someone and the business failing. I would feel responsible for that person. Speaking that out into the world made it seem like too much of a possibility. Fortunately, Oakland and I had the twin connection, and she basically knew. We sat down after dinner where she lovingly dumbed down my books and showed me how well the business was doing. I could have done more, but decided to start with three positions. I would have someone to help me in the kitchen, a front person, and then a manger who also did baking and decorating.

Cleo was the first person who came on board. We went to culinary school together and had kept in touch. I asked her if she wanted to become my manager and head baker. She was the easy hire; the other two, not so much. We went through a rotation of hires with none of them working out. When Sebastian interviewed, we clicked and I hired him on the spot for the front. Sebastian was a smaller built guy, fit but lean. He was sarcastic and hilarious, but also sweet. His charm and sense of humor was what made him so good at running the front. The last of our little gang had been Finch. Fin was a guy about my size and was incredibly intimidating. A lot of it came down to him just keeping to himself, but Seb had made it his life goal to get under Finch's skin. He had lovingly given him the nickname of grumps. His exact words were, "Well, he is an old grumpy man, i.e., grumps is the perfect name." Fin was only two years older than me and four years older than Seb. How in

Fin's mind that makes him old, I will never know. Cleo and Scout "ship" them. The first time Scout said "ship" I probably looked like a lost puppy not realizing they meant a relationship. Cleo helpfully chimed in that they think all the tension is sexual and that they should do the dirty and get to dating. A romantic relationship between them could go one of two ways. The first would be they find someone that can buffer them and then all live happily ever after. The second is Fin would kill Seb and get arrested. Then, I would lose two employees and friends. One to the grave and the other to prison.

After handling my situation, washing my hands, and a splash or two of cold water on my face, I head for the front. I spot some of our usuals, greeting them as I make my way down to where Seb is helping our newest hire, Piper, at the register.

"Yeah, that button will take you straight through to the custom part of the menu." He pointed toward the button. "See, now just click on the correct changes or adds."

"It's just these two, right?" Piper asked, her voice coming out a little shaky.

Seb nodded his head before replying to her question. "Yep, that's it. And of course, always double check with the customer that the change is correct. Especially if it is an allergy request, because you will want to click that button. That way, the crew in the back know if it is something they need to change." He patted her shoulder. "You are doing great! Deep breath." Turning to Mr. Simpson, a regular, he throws him a smile. "Mr. Simpson, I leave you in Piper's capable hands. Have a good morning and give that sweet puppy some love from me."

"Thank you, Sebastian. I will give Pearl your love." With a gentle smile, the elderly man waited patiently while Piper finished up.

This was why Seb only stayed a basic front employee for a few months. The minute we hired more people, I asked if he would manage the front. It was the best decision I could have made. He took pride in knowing the customers and taking care of them. With new employees, he gave the same level of care, never talking down to them or making them feel less because they were learning and messed up sometimes.

I checked some of the cabinets, making sure they were fully stocked. When I stood back up, Seb had made his way down the counter toward me. For the morning rush, either myself or Seb were in the front, normally with two other employees. With Piper here this morning, we actually had three front workers and Seb. When we make up the schedule, I am more there for final approval. Seb knew what the crew could work and who preferred what shifts. Usually Cleo and I handled the back crew, trading off who does it.

"Well good morning, sunshine! How is Papa bear this morning?" Seb asked in his most chippest tone, leaning one hip on the counter behind where I'm currently standing. I moved to stand beside him, resting against the counter. Shifting around, he mirrored how I stood, crossing his arms across his chest. "I love morning rush." Seb let out a little laugh looking around the bakery.

"Me too." I also looked around. The place was packed with regulars taking up their usual tables with new faces sprinkled among them. Some were talking quietly, others sipped coffee and munched on breakfast. I turned my head slightly back to Seb. "How is Piper doing?" I asked him, wanting to check in that new hires were working out.

Glancing down to Piper, he turned to me. "She is a sweetheart; learned a lot in a short time. She does get a little nervous when we get busy, but that will get better with time."

"Good, I'm glad she is working out. It will make getting shifts covered a lot easier." I looked around again. "Well, I'll get out of your hair. I know you have this covered," I said, shooting him a quick smile.

Seb let out a little laugh. "Ok, tell grumps when he gets here, I have something for him. Did you know his birthday's this month?" The smile that crossed his face said that Fin was not going to be pleased.

"Seb, don't make the man quit." I let out a dramatic breath. "Also, no, I did not know it was his birthday month." It didn't miss my attention that Seb knew when his birthday was. "That leaves me to question, Sebastian. How did you come upon this information?" Seb didn't reply automatically, but casting a glance his way, I see that his cheeks and ears were blushing.

"Didn't you say you were going to the back to get out of my hair? Now would be a great time." With those parting words, he turned to walk away.

Chuckling, I decided that I will tell Fin. Because I am now very invested in what's going on.

This should make things interesting around here. *Very interesting.*

gatlin

I stayed on Leland's couch for a few minutes after he left. He was the easiest person to work up—always had been. He was also hung. The guy was seriously well endowed. Not that I spent extended periods checking out his junk. *Liar. Nope, don't think about it.* At some point, changing in front of each other went from innocent to dangerous boner territory. Nude Leland was nothing new. He was, however, mouth-wateringly good-looking. Big, broad and beefy. He had always been a big guy. Even in school, he was the tallest kid. While he didn't bring it up often, I knew some of what he experienced before transferring schools and it wasn't the best. When he walked into a room now, most women and some men gave him a good. long look. I was also included in that. This was something my therapist and I had talked through over the last few years. I had come to the realization that the only man I was attracted to Leland. I still hadn't told him anything. It never seemed like the right time, so I put it in the *need to talk to the therapist* box.

"You do know that your store should be opening soon." Fin's low, gruff voice came through the door, causing me to jump.

"Damn, dude! You scared the shit out of me," I said, clutching my chest as my heartbeat wildly.

Chuckling, he kept walking, moving out of the doorway. Scout said I was sneaky, but that man was like a cat. Big dudes like him should not be able to move without making a literal sound. I reached over, grabbing my phone before pushing off the couch. He was correct. I did need to go over to the store. Not only was it shipment day, but I had paperwork to sort through for Nature Nuggets. Even with the trip not happening for a while, I liked to give parents plenty of time to prepare. Most volunteers also liked having the extra time to arrange their schedules and prepare themselves. We would also hold our meetings between now and then, which meant even more prep. It was stressful, but so worth it. I loved getting to share my knowledge and passion for the outdoors with people.

I shot Leland a message, telling him I was headed to the store out the back door. As I passed the back of Scout's building, the crew was starting to take material up the stairs to start work. I was glad she had taken Mud in with her. He wouldn't have done anything or run off, but a big dog and people needing to get anything done usually didn't work well. He also loved Scout as much as he loved Leland. I honestly thought the dog would choose her or Leland over me. *Not that I blamed him.* They were two of my favorite people, too.

Once the store was open, I pulled out the paperwork for the trip and began sorting through everything. The Nature Nuggets was the local nature scout group that helped get kids outside and in nature. I had volunteered with them through high school and when I could while in college. Once I decided to move back home, I started trying to do more. I had knowledge of the area and degrees in wildlife biology and conservation, with minors in business and outdoor recreation. I threw everything into school and came out with the skills to pursue my passion. Opening the store was never my end goal, but it has worked out well. I ran outdoor adventures, helped with the Nature Nuggets, and helped train in the mountains for rescue crews. The Nuggets were my favorite. Those kids soaked up everything and I loved it. Not every kid wanted to be there, but we tried to make it fun while teaching them.

Once the paperwork was sorted, I started the long, labored process of checking my email. I tried to stay on top of it, but when I left the store, I tried to leave work here. I had been scolded by my family, Leland's family, and Scout multiple times about overdoing it. I would commit to everything that was asked. This was me trying to be better.

The bell above the door chimed before a few customers walked in. "Hey, how are you guys doing today?" I asked, smiling as they moved farther into the store.

"We're doing well. You?" the man replied, returning my smile.

I give the only answer that exists in retail. "Doing great this morning. Is there anything I can help you guys find?" This led to the next two and half hours getting the couple prepared for a backpacking trip.

Once everything was rung up and they were heading out the door, it was getting close to time for my delivery. As if on cue, the buzzier for the back door sounded. Time for some heavy lifting.

ONCE THE DELIVERY driver pulled off, I grabbed my phone and turned the music up. It wouldn't stop me from hearing someone come in, but not having something playing would make unpacking boxes suck. I tugged the first box over and was excited to see a new line from one of my favorite companies. To keep stock fresh and interesting, I tried to cycle the items and brands in the store. Even if an item wasn't in stock, if customers had something they liked or something we had carried, I never minded ordering it for them. When the store first opened, I had made it my mission to stock mostly small businesses mixed in bigger names here and there. Some companies were ones that I had supported and products I loved. Others were friends of friends. It was a process, but I was getting to a place where my mission was becoming a reality.

Thankfully, the store was rarely busy in the morning. I would have a few people wander in, but for the most part, it would be me doing stocking and administrative work. Which made the morning crawl by. It also didn't keep my brain from bouncing between all the things I shouldn't think about. Namely, my two best friends. The flirting was something that had slowly begun to happen as we became more comfortable with each other. I had never really thought about my sexuality in depth, until therapy. Even with talking to my therapist, that was not our goal when it came to sessions. Fortunately for me, working through family bullshit has helped me to realize who I am and what I wanted—and casual dating wasn't it. Not that I ever seriously dated people, anyway. I was not a blushing virgin, but most women weren't a fan of how close Leland and I were. They would make comments about the time we spent together or that I should really be looking to have my own place, not living in a bachelor pad. Once those comments started, that would be the final nail in the coffin. After the first few times of this happening, dating became too much work. So I just stopped.

And began to secretly lust over your best friends.

Shut up, brain.

Leland had dated some throughout our adult life, but nothing ever really came from most of them. He always said after they would stop seeing each other that he just didn't get "the feeling." The last guy had ended for that reason. No sparks.

While Scout was relatively private, she had opened up to us after her last break up. The guy was a grade A asshole. Between his know-it-all attitude and thinking he needed to explain everything, his final mistake was commenting on Mud being a "nasty, germ infested mut" that Scout shouldn't have allowed in the store. He was the one who was promptly asked to leave and never come back. I was protective of Mud—but Scout would go feral for that dog.

And now they are single, and so are you. Nothing to lose, remember? The words drifted through my head sounding strangely like Orrin. *Damn him.*

I pulled my phone out to check the time when my stomach growled. I had shared my goodies with the delivery crew. I had known them and their family for a few years, so the biscuits Leland had sent over with me were long gone. Seeing it was getting close to lunch, I moved to the front door and flipped the sign around. I had a group coming in later to plan out an adventure trip, which was where most of my money came from, so closing for lunch wasn't going to break the bank. Plus, I was the boss. I grabbed my keys from under the desk and headed over to the bookstore before Scout and I would head over to the bakery.

chapter 5

· · ·

scout

THE DAY DRUG BY. By lunch, I was so sick of the constant noise from the construction work I feared I may actually go crazy. The constant banging and hum of tools combined with customers coming in and the small book club that met here has overwhelmed me. I felt something warm lean against my leg. When I glanced down, Mud had moved from his bed and came to me, leaning his body on me.

Much like Leland and Gatlin, Mud just knew. I knew people would probably say all dogs can sense things, but Mud was the first dog I had ever experienced it with. I shifted my gaze to him before I reached down, stroking his head. "Mud, you are the sweetest, bestest, most special pupper." Mud turned at the sound of footsteps coming toward us.

"When you live with two awesome people, it's basically impossible not to be the bestest, most special boy," Gatlin said as he came to squat by the dog.

Letting out a little laugh, I said, "I guess his lessons in humility are not coming from you." Gatlin didn't respond, just looked up with a wide smile and winks. Even with the bruising from earlier starting to show, he was still so fucking good looking. Damn him for being gorgeous with a potentially broken nose.

Once Mud had gotten some love from his dad, he moved back to me, bumping my hand before heading for his bed. "Ready for lunch?" Gatlin asked as he stood, wiping his hand on his pants.

"More than ready. Let me tell Lettie and then I'll be good." I moved to where she was putting a display together. "I'm going to get some lunch if you're good," I called out to her. I knew she was totally fine on her own. I had two full-time employees and a handful of part-time workers. Normally, when a full-time worker was here, I didn't stay upfront. However, with all the construction above the back room, I couldn't stand to be in the office.

Her chestnut eyes met mine, made slightly bigger by the glasses she wore. "Having lunch with the hunks?" Her dimples peeked out as she smiled.

"Yes, and you can't say things like that. I don't need to be reminded just how hot they are. I am well aware," I said, keeping my voice low.

Placing one hand on her hip, she gave me her *ok, sassy pants* look. "You know you could do something, like maybe make a move." Her eyes twinkled. "You don't see how they look at you."

I felt my face heat at her words. "We are just friends, ma'am. Now stop making me blush." I moved back to the desk to grab my phone. "Text me if you need me."

I didn't catch what she said under her breath, but when she giggled, I knew I probably didn't need to know. "Ready?" I asked Gatlin once I had what I needed.

Extending his arm, he gestured to me to go ahead of him. "After you, honeysuckle."

The damn nickname again. I wanted to blame Lettie for getting the naughty thoughts run in my head, but that would be a lie. When I was around the guys, I lived in a constant state of annoyed arousal.

Wet panties: 1

Dry panties: 0

ONCE MUD WAS SETTLED back on the covered porch, we crossed the short distance to the back of the bakery. Gatlin pulled the fob from his pocket, using it to unlock the door before holding it open for me. I still have not completely calmed my horny thoughts, so averting my gaze, I give a quick, "Thank you," as I passed.

Walking through the back of the building, I stopped, causing Gat to bump into my back. Leland stood at the sink, his white shirt clinging to his body. The usually opaque material was almost transparent where it hugged the muscles of his back. *Hot damn.*

"You're drooling a little, honeysuckle." Gat's words ghosted over the shell of my ear where he had moved closer to me. I let out a small squeak, causing Leland to turn at the sound. *Holy. Fucking. Fuck.*

The sharp intake of breath by my ear told me I wasn't the only one enjoying the view, and it was a damn good view. Not only was the shirt plastered to his back, but he was dripping water from head to toe. The white material was stretched over his broad chest, molding to the muscles. While Leland was strong as a bear, he was not ripped. I heard him say that he is *fit fat*. The muscle is there, but he has a layer of softness over top. My eye traveled south to where the wet jeans were clinging to his tree trunk thighs. The man had got a set of legs and a clear ass from lifting bakery supplies and working out with Gatlin. I'm sure the material was chilly in the air conditioning. It was doing nothing to shrink the outline of his bulge.

And what a bulge it was.

A clearing throat caused my attention to snap back. I felt Gatlin shift behind me before stepping slightly away from me. "Something is wrong with the sink. I was rinsing pans and the damn thing started spraying water." Leland gestured to his clothes. "I finally got it shut off, but not before it soaked me." He reached to the rack above the sink, pulling a towel down. Oh, to be that towel. I mean, I could help him with that. Get all the places he struggled to reach.

"I know other things that are soaked, too," Gat said under his breath. *Damn him.*

I turned to face him with a glare. "Gatlin, why don't you grab Leland some clothes from the store? I know how *hard* it is for you to see your BFF so uncomfortable." I pointedly looked down as his half hard bulge and paused for a moment, because fuck my life. They were both well endowed.

Gatlin's hands flew to cover his groin. "That—is such a good—" He paused, his eyes flicking to Leland who had moved closer. He visibly swallowed.

"Is a good what?" Leland's voice sounded closer than it should. "What is wrong with you two?"

I spun a bit too fast, losing my balance and almost crashing to the ground. Four hands landed in various places on my body. Leland and I were now almost chest to chest, while Gatlin was pressed close to my back. *Did I die? I fell and hit my head and died.*

"Easy, honeysuckle." Leland's voice came out low and rough. His eyes met mine, checking that I was good before he released my body. Gatlin's hands also fell away. "Sorry if I got you wet. I don't think I did." As if checking, he did a quick once over. "Gat, could I get some pants to wear from the store? I really don't want to have to go back home and this isn't going to dry anytime soon."

I looked over to Gatlin with a shit eating grin on my face. "You know, bumblebee, that is such a *good* idea."

With his hands still covering the front of his pants, his words came a little breathier than normal. "Yeah, definitely. Scout can come and help pick some out. Wouldn't want her to leave her high and dry. Or maybe not so dry." Getting his bearings back a little, he tacked on the last part low enough for just me. The sexy ass wink he gave me tells me that my assumption was correct.

Wet panties: 2
Dry panties: 0

chapter 6

· · ·

leland

I WOULD NEVER CLAIM to know the inner workings of people for the most part. However, the two standing in front of me were a different story. Scout's cheeks were flushed and Gatlin was hiding a very obvious bulge. I was not a fit guy by anyone's standard. I liked to keep healthy, but I owned a bakery and I loved to eat. I'm 6 '9 and on the beefier side, and not everyone's cup of tea. The way my two best friends were looking at me had my brain going into overdrive with what ifs. *Stop thinking with your dick.*

Focusing back on the present, I rubbed the towel over my short hair and down my face. "Do you mind, honeysuckle? There is no telling what Gat will try to do with no one there to stop him. He might try to ravage me." I watched as the blush spread over her cheeks again and down her neck. Gatlin unceremoniously choked on what I assumed was spit.

"Yea-yep, of course, I don't mind at all," Scout spoke before turning and brushing past Gatlin.

"Take a minute if you need to, bumblebee. Wouldn't want to intimidate any potential old ladies passing by." I reached out as I passed him, putting a hand on his shoulder and squeezing.

I USUALLY HATED shopping for clothes. Years of struggling to find things that fit had soured me to the whole idea. Because I was a bigger kid, I couldn't wear the more in style things because they didn't fit. Clothes just never seemed to fit right. As I got older, I found brands that worked and that's what I stuck with. Today's shopping experience was completely different. I had two sets of eyes watching every move. "I hope you two don't expect a fashion show." I tossed a look over my shoulder as I looked at a rack of pants.

Gatlin cleared his throat before he spoke, "Well, I mean, we did bring Scout all the way over. How is she supposed to give her opinion if you don't show off the goods?" He winked at me, regaining his usual confidence after earlier. "Also, you are dripping on my floor. So can you kindly remove your wet clothes?" he asked, throwing a towel at me.

Draping the towel around my shoulders, I glanced at Scout. Her cheeks were flushed, an unchecked heat in her gaze. Her eyes tracked over my still clothed, wet body. The slow perusal caused a shiver to run over me. "He isn't wrong. You are definitely dripping on the floor." Her voice came out raspier than usual. "No sense in trailing water every-where." Normally, I wouldn't say I had an ego or was boastful, but with the way they were both now watching me, I decided maybe a little show was necessary.

I pulled the towel from my neck, reaching over to lay it on a rack. Thankfully, we were at the back of the store with only the back lights on, so no passersby would be able to see in. I towed off my shoes, moving my gaze between Scout and Gatlin. I reached back, grabbing my shirt before pulling it over my head and dropping it to the floor. I felt their eyes on me as I moved. When I went to reach for the button on my jeans, I looked at Gatlin, hoping my face conveyed the silent question. *Is this what you want?*

His eyes dropped to my hands then to Scout. He reached his hand forward, lightly touching her arm. Her eyes, which had been glued to me, snapped to his. "Honeysuckle, are you ok?"

She took a moment before she turned back to me. This was new territory. We had all lightly flirted over the last year, but this was a whole different ball game. This was a line we had not talked about crossing. Hell, Gatlin was supposed to be straight by all accounts. While we had heard all the jokes about us being the old married couple, nothing had ever happened. Same since meeting Scout. We ribbed each other, but nothing physical or otherwise came of it.

"I don't feel like this is a very fair trade off," I said, slowly undoing the button before pulling the zipper down. One of the best parts about having bigger legs and butt is my pants didn't just fall down. They were also wet and sticking to me. The material fell open slightly, revealing my boxer briefs. "I mean here I am, half naked and having to give the two of you a strip show." Shrugging one shoulder, I said, "I think it's only fair that we—"

A loud thud came from somewhere above us, causing me to pause. "What was—" Another thud, louder this time, was followed by the whine of metal. I quickly did my pants up as Scout and Gatlin turned, both running to the back of the shop.

Nothing seemed to be wrong when we got to the parking lot. I looked to where Mud was standing at Scout's back door, whining and pawing at her door. Scout opened the gate and walked up on to the porch, Gatlin and I following behind her. Mud, seeing us, moved back over to his bed, allowing us room at the door. Before she can reach the door, it flew open. Gatlin pulled Scout to his chestas I grabbed them both, pulling all of us back just as the door swung out, narrowly missing us. One of the workers appeared, water pouring down the stairs behind him. *What the hell?*

He stopped when he spotted us. "Miss Scout, we had a problem. Something happened with the main water line. They got it shut off, but it has been leaking behind the wall."

Scout looked at him, frozen in shock, her mouth opened and closed with nothing coming out. Gatlin spoke before I could. "What do you mean, it's been leaking? How long?"

Water still poured out from behind the guy. "The main pipe has been leaking. It has caused damage we didn't know about. I don't know how long. From the amount of water, it's been a while." The guy looked like he did not want to be the one delivering this news.

I motioned to the water around us. "This couldn't have all come from a leak in the wall. Right?"

"No, unfortunately when we shut the water off, we didn't know about the leak, so the pressure built and the pipes burst. It must have had a weak spot. The pipes were old and prob—" The worker looked at Scout's face and stopped talking. The natural flush of her cheeks was gone. All the color had drained, leaving her pale almost sickly looking.

The rush of water had slowed enough that we could walk upstairs and hopefully get answers that didn't make Scout pass out. "Come on, Scout, let's go talk to the lead and see what the damage is." Gatlin placed his hand on her lower back. His other hand tugged one of my belt loops as if to say *you, too*. I had no intention of staying down here.

Scout looked at Gatlin and then me with an almost lifeless gaze. Her moves were almost robotic when she nodded and moved past the worker, walking towards the steps. I gave the man an apologetic smile as we passed, knowing that it wasn't his fault, and headed up. When we got to the top of the stairs, the hope of the damage not being bad evaporated. It was bad. *Really bad.*

Scout stiffened as she took in the state of her apartment. While I looked at the apartment, my attention was lasered in on my sweet honeysuckle. An elbow nudge pulled my gaze to Gatlin. His eyes were wide when they met mine. His expression screamed at me, *what the fuck do we do?*

I gave him a subtle shake of my head, trying to silently communicate that I had no idea. The only thing we could do truly is support Scout. Out of the frying pan into a massive tub of water, in this case.

scout

The day was not turning out better than I thought. In fact, I wanted to rewind back to flirting and strip shows in the store. I looked around my kitchen, at the amount of water that was puddled on the floor and most of the surfaces. I didn't notice it at first, but as I scanned around the room, my eyes snapped to the massive hole in the wall. I must have been in shock to have not immediately seen it. It looked like someone had taken a sledgehammer to it. There were soggy pieces of sheetrock all over the place. I couldn't tell if the water busted through the wall or the crew made the hole. Whatever the case, I felt like I was about to pass out. The only thing keeping me upright was knowing the guys were here. While I considered myself a strong, independent woman, I was feeling very much like a child about to have a meltdown. I wanted to ask how much worse it could get, but the shitstorm those words might bring had me biting my tongue. *Shit. Shit. Shit.*

When hands landed on my shoulder, I blindly turned into Gatlin's chest. With my face buried in his chest, the spicy, wooded scent of him calmed me a fraction. Before my brain could register that something was missing, I felt Leland move in close beside Gatlin and myself. He began to rub soothing circles on my back. Even without his shirt, his citrus, bergamot smell was strong and mixed with Gat's perfectly. I let it envelop me while I tried to match my breathing to theirs. I could feel my pounding heart finally start to settle. Once it seemed like I was able to speak without passing out, I lifted my head up. "This is really bad." My words came out as a whisper, blinking back the tears that threatened to fall. I was not going to break down in front of them for the second time today.

Strong independent women need to be held, too.

"We will get it sorted, honeysuckle," Leland spoke, his words reassuring me.

Gatlin brushed my cheek, wiping a stray tear away. "It will be ok. Come on, let's see what is going on."

I nodded, reluctantly pulling myself away from their hands. I turned, walking toward the couch where I knew one of Leland's sweatshirts was draped over the arm. The guys had followed me into the living room area and stood, waiting for me. I returned to stand in front of them, extending the hand that held the shirt. Leland took the offered sweatshirt, pulling it over his head. Part of me was happy he was covered so no one else could enjoy looking at him, while the other part of me was disappointed to be losing the view. I was possessive of the guys. Sue me. They were freaking hot. Even in my shocked and frazzled state, I could appreciate their sexiness; especially when they were being so sweet.

Gatlin, being his usual self, spoke, "Now that we have covered our sweet teddy bear and restored his dignity, we can get to the bottom of this." This pulled a small giggle from me and an eye roll from Leland.

"Brat," Leland said low and quiet. Gatlin could definitely be a brat and he knew it. They had been friends for so long that they were well aware where every one of the other's buttons laid, and exactly how to push them. They toed the line of friendly banter and flirting, which neither seemed to realize or purposefully didn't notice.

I led the way toward the small hall that led to the guest bedrooms and bath. My panic climbed as I took in the amount of water standing in the hall. I knew the crew was starting on the guest bedroom and spare bathroom today. With the building being three stories and the bottom part being the store, I had two floors for a living space. The main floor was where we were, including the kitchen, living room, laundry, two bedrooms, and one and a half baths. The top floor was my sanctuary. Once everything was said and done, I would have a beautiful bedroom, master ensuite, and library.

Peeking into the spare bedrooms, I didn't see the crew in either room. My heart rate began to climb again. This construction project had been like wading in quicksand. Everything that could go sideways, did. I had hired this crew around six months ago and was pleased with the work they had been doing. Hearing movement and voices above set me in motion. I quickly made my way to the stairs, taking them two at a time with the boys right on my heels. When we reached the landing, my worst nightmare played out.

There was a barricade of towels at the door to the library, the only saving grace being my books were not in there yet. Most were still either with my parents or in storage. The bedroom was not barricaded. I realized as I moved into the room why this was. The water had started there.

Other than my bed and a few essentials, the room was bare at the moment.

I stood, looking at the damage to the drywall and floors. The lead contractor and owner approached me. "Scout, I am so sorry. We had no idea that there had been a leak." He rubbed his hand over his face before he looked around. "When we shut the water off to start downstairs, it must have put too much pressure on the pipes. With this being an older building, a lot of the plumbing has not been updated." He paused, taking a breath before he continued. "There were two places where the pipes busted. The first one was in the kitchen, the second was in here."

My eyes bounced between him and the room. I knew I needed to ask questions, but I couldn't think of a single thing to say.

"Hi, I don't think we have met. I'm Gatlin Ford and this is Leland Boone. We own the businesses on either side of Scout." Gatlin held his hand out, shaking the guy's hand before Leland did the same.

"I'm Amos Harding, it's nice to meet you both. I just wish it was under different circumstances." He slid his hands into his front pockets. "I know this seems like a major setback, and in some ways, it has set the timeline back, but it's better to have happened now and not when we had finished everything. At least this way, everything gets fixed. Good news is with the store already being remodeled, everything was upgraded. Plus, the second floor acted almost like a catch all for the water. If it had been that floor that flooded, there is no telling what it could have done to the store."

I realized he was trying to make me feel better, and while appreciated, it was doing the opposite. Feeling my breathing pick up, I tried to focus and breathe slowly through the panic. Causally, Leland slid his hand into mine with Gatlin's coming to rest at the small of my back. "So timeline wise, what are we looking at?" My voice came out calmer than I anticipated.

Amos glanced at the room, as if inventorying the damages. "I would say a month, possibly two for the two floors that were effected. That would give us time to check the remaining plumbing, replace everything, and repair the damages to what has already been remodeled. Honestly, checking more than just the plumbing would be my suggestion." He looked from me, to the boys, and back. "I know the parts we have remodeled, the wiring and all has been updated, but the parts we were going to skip for now has me concerned." He winced, not wanting to tell me all this.

I silently nodded. *It could have been worse. Your books could have been ruined.* The silver lining to this whole mess. I appreciated his honesty about the situation. The building was old; it should have been updated long before now. But that was neither here nor there.

"How much more is going to be tacked on the bill?" Leland asked, the words coming out more as a growl, which was not normal for our teddy bear.

Amos shook his head before looking back at me. "I don't feel right charging the full labor and material cost. I—"

I interrupted him before he could finish. "No, that's not right. You and your crew deserve to be paid for the work you do." I put on my best boss bitch face. No one should do work for free. These guys had done an amazing job and I wouldn't feel right if they worked and received nothing. This left us frozen in a stalemate.

Rubbing the back of his neck, he took a moment before taking a different path. "How about just materials? I will still pay my crew to work, but you will not pay our labor cost." He glanced from Leland to Gatlin and then to me again. "Does that seem fair?"

"It's not your fault the pipes were old and had weak spots. You had no way of knowing," Gatlin spoke with certainty in his tone.

"I may not be responsible, but this is my business, and in this situation, I wouldn't feel right to charge full price. I know you have not had the best luck with other companies, but I promise you I will make this right, Scout." Looking directly at me, I felt the conviction in his words. I appreciated the fact that he spoke directly to me, which made me like him even more. Even with the guys here, he didn't dismiss me or talk down to me. It was a sad fact, but one I had to deal with as a woman and business owner.

I knew nothing about construction or the cost, but if the boys felt like this man was trying to cheat me, they would have already ripped into him. "That seems fair to me. I'm guessing that you will need me to not stay here for a while?" I guess it was back to the parents' house for a few weeks. I love my parents and brother, but staying with them for an undisclosed amount of time would be...interesting. Four grown adults under one roof can be a bit cramped.

Amos took a moment before he spoke. "It would make it easier. I sometimes like to work a little later than the guys, just to knock out small projects. Of course, it's completely up to you."

The knot in my stomach tightened. My throat clogged with emotion as I tried to hold in my frustrated tears. My therapist always used a spoon and fork analogy. I knew I lived life with fewer spoons and someday I could handle more fork sticks. Today, I was running dangerously low on spoons to finish the day and this was my last fork. *Come on, Scout.*

Clenching and releasing my fist, I was finally able to speak. "Ok. Yeah, I can manage that for sure." I tried to inject some cheer to my words. "I will just need to grab a few things and then I should be good." I didn't want Amos to feel bad about any of this. I moved past him before the tears could fall and went to my bathroom. *Breathe.*

Once in the bathroom, I took a moment to collect my thoughts. I pulled the small travel toiletry bag from under the sink. I really only needed to pack my makeup and skin care products. I kept extras of anything else I would need in the bag already. With my anxiety and ADHD, pre-trip or travel shopping was a nightmare I actively avoided. I zipped the bag, glancing around to make sure I hadn't forgotten anything.

Back in the bedroom, Amos was no longer there. It was just Leland and Gatlin, talking quietly as I approached them. "I just need to go downstairs to grab clothes from the spare bedroom."

I moved to go past them when Leland placed a hand on my arm. "Love, where are you going to stay?" I could still feel the warmth of his palm on my arm.

"I was going to shoot my mom and dad a message. I'm sure they won't mind if I stay with them." I reached into my pocket for my phone. *No time like the present.*

As I went to unlock my phone, Gatlin placed his hand over mine, causing me to look up at him. "You can totally say no if you want, but you can stay with us. We have the extra room. Plus, isn't the guest bedroom at your parents' going to be occupied for a bit?" It didn't register what he was talking about. I'm sure my face was giving confused puppy as I stood there, staring at the two of them. "Flint."

Fuck.

I had completely forgotten. My brother, Atticus, was about to be home for the summer from college. Normally, this wouldn't be an issue, but this year, his roommate was coming home with him. Flint didn't have the best home life, which meant he became our family. He had spent more breaks and holidays with us than the blood family he had. This year, he was staying the summer instead of working or taking summer classes like he usually did.

Shit.

chapter 7

. . .

gatlin

I TOUCHED Scout's arm again, bringing her attention back to me. "Seriously, if you want. You know it's completely fine if you do or don't want to." I didn't want her to feel pressured.

"How about we go down and grab your clothes first, then you can think about it?" Leland spoke low, injecting his usual calm into the situation.

Scout nodded without speaking before she turned to go downstairs. While she grabbed her clothes, I pulled Leland to the living room. I spoke low so Scout would hopefully not overhear. "She can't stay at her parents'. She also looks like she is about to hit the floor," I said, glancing toward the room where Scout currently was.

Leland nodded, agreeing with at least part of my statement. "She is holding it together, but we can't make her stay with us. We offered and if she wants to, then great. But if not, it's ok. She has had a shit day." His hands landed on my shoulders, immediately grounding me.

"I know. I know." And I did. I would never push her, but the thought of her being under the same roof as us had me almost buzzing. The situation that caused her to be displaced sucked major donkey balls, but damn if it didn't light a spark in me. Before I could say anything more, Scout appeared in the doorway, rolling a large suitcase.

She crossed the room to us, coming to a stop in front of us. "Ok, if you guys are sure you don't mind me staying. I know it not the first time I have stayed, but this is a bit different." While she had calmed some, she was still visibly worn out from the events, the shock of everything starting to fade.

Leland spoke, taking the words right out of my mouth. "Of course we don't mind you staying." He looked down at his watch before back up to Scout. "Cleo has the bakery covered and I know Lettie is at the store." He looked at me. "Are you done for the day, Gat?"

"As a matter of fact, I am done for the day." I gave Scout a soft smile. "Let's head to the house where you can get settled and we can do take out and a movie."

"That would honestly be amazing." Scout let out a relieved sigh. "I'll tell Lettie and then I can meet you at the house." She looked a little lighter having a place to stay and a relaxing plan for the evening.

"Sounds good, honeysuckle." I tapped Leland's arm and whispered in mock relief, "Oh good, we have time to rush home and get things cleaned up. We can't have a proper lady over without making sure all the scandalous things are hidden." Leland's cheeks went from his usual color to bright red.

"Really, Gat?" He shook his head at me before turning to Scout. "Take your time heading over, honeysuckle. You will have your pick of rooms. I think there is about to be a vacancy in another room, as well," he said, throwing a pointed look at me.

"On that note. I'm going to grab Mud and my stuff. Ok, love you guys, bye!" I turned without another look and headed to the store. This was going to be fun. Really fun.

I PULLED up to the house. Instead of parking in my normal place, I left the closer spots open for Leland and Scout. Leland and I had our usual spots we pulled into, but I was glad to give it up if it meant Scout would be more comfortable.

Once Mud was inside, I went back out to grab everything I left in the car. Trying to get the massive dog in and all my stuff was a recipe for disaster. He was well-behaved, but was still a puppy. Just as I shut the driver side door, Leland pulled in. He had sent me a message before he left to tell me he was packing up a box or two of treats for us and some drinks from the store.

He pulled up, taking the spot my truck usually occupied, before he climbed out. Our driveway had an area wider off to one side, which was where I had pulled in. With how much space there was, you could easily fit three vehicles and still have room. Once he was out of his SUV, he reached up, setting his coffee cup on the roof before moving to the rear driver's door. My mind went blank when he bent over into the back seat.

My eyes were glued to his firm ass and thick thighs. Scenes ran through my mind from earlier in the bakery and my store. The way that wet shirt clung to his body, showing the sheer size of him, was hard to miss. Leland was built like a solid tank. When Nan nicknamed him bear, it was an accurate name. He was big, strong, and if he let it, his beard and hair would be out of control. I had looked at other guys and appreciated them, but Leland felt different. There was always something more. After close to two years of therapy, things were clearer for me than they had been. I had realized, or rather my therapist made an observation, that the *something more* was the emotional connection I had to him. With all that being said, the way he filled out his clothes had my mouth watering. He was big enough to manhandle a full-grown man. *I wonder if...Wait. What the fuck am I doing?*

Dammit, Gatlin! Stop ogling your best friend.

As if feeling my eyes on him, Leland stood, holding the bakery box. "Um, Gat...You okay?" He raised one eyebrow at me before scanning my face for any signs if something was wrong. Thank the heavens I had not moved around my truck. Otherwise, he would have seen just how not ok I currently was. Totally fine, just felt like I could pound a hole through the side of my truck door with my rock hard dick. *Toootaallly fine.*

Focus, man. Focus.

I forced my eyes to his. "I'm very ok. Like, you can't get more ok than me right now. Just fine as frog hair." *Smooth, dumbass. STOP TALKING. Bite your damn tongue off.*

"Riiight." He rolled his eyes before turning back and shutting the door to the SUV. Leland held the box close as he reached up to grab the coffee cup off the roof. He was still wearing the sweatshirt from Scout's apartment, only at some point, he pushed the sleeves up, exposing his beefy forearms. The bottom hem creeped up, showing a sliver of skin. Like the rest of him, I could see the freckles that covered him from head to toe. *Well, at least the parts that saw the sun.*

The clearing of Leland's throat jerked me out of the trance I was in. "Seriously, Gat, what's wrong?" He set the box on the edge of my truck. "Is it about Scout staying here?" He reached up, running his free hand over his hair. "Or is it about earlier in the store? Listen, I get it, heat of the moment and all." Leland paused, looking toward the road. He was physically here, but his mind was somewhere else. "I mean, Scout would get anybody going." I could see the blush forming on his cheeks. "I know we have never talked about it, but you know if you wanted to—" His words were cut off by the pizza guy pulling up. *Damn it! If we ever wanted to, what?*

I was frozen to the spot. My brain was running a thousand miles a minute. There were so many ways he could end that sentence. The little sparks of hope that had bloomed in my chest were growing. I was done living in *what ifs*. I was not one to sit back and wait, but deep in my soul, I knew this was a situation that required more patience than I normally had. If I pushed, I could very well lose both of them. Everything in me right now was screaming for him to finish that sentence. It was a bone-deep need to know where his brain was going. Without looking at me, Leland moved the bakery box to the bed of the truck. "I got it." That was it. The end of the conversation. We went into the house, Leland moving like he was all but running from the boogieman. Instead of following him like I wanted to do, I decided I would wait. I would wait a lifetime for them. Now was not the time to demand answers to questions I still wasn't completely certain of myself. Like a broken record, my brain went to the usual questions.

What did I want?
Could we do this?
Did they even want more?

leland

I left Gatlin in the living room, moving toward the back of the house. Once in my room, I pushed the door closed, leaning my back against the door. Fuck, I needed to get my shit together. Where the hell was I going with that sentence? If you wanted to go after Scout? If you wanted to explore things? If you wanted to be more with me? Maybe me and Scout? *Shut it down, Boone.*

I would not get my hopes up. The innocent flirting was one thing, but I wouldn't risk losing the two people who meant the world to me. Everything earlier was just Gatlin being himself. Playing along and pushing my buttons. *Right?* Yeah, that was it. He was just messing with me and Scout. He was turned on by Scout. I would have to take the wet dreams and fantasies to the grave. Gatlin had never even remotely shown interest in a man. I hoped he would feel like he could talk to me, but I would never push him. I knew he didn't sleep around, but he was a shameless flirt. With most people, it was a part of his charm. It came more from him just liking to make people smile or laugh.

My phone pinged with a notification from the doorbell camera. I pulled the phone out and opened the app. Gatlin was walking out to meet Scout as she pulled into the driveway. I drew in a deep breath, held it for a moment, and then released it. This will all be fine. I mean, we are all friends and adults. This doesn't have to be a thing. It's not a thing. There is nothing to even worry about. Everything will be fine.

Famous last words.

WHEN THE PIZZA WAS GONE, we moved to the couch, the box of treats I had brought home set on the ottoman. I sat in my usual spot of the sectional, sinking down into the cushions. Scout sat in the middle, tucking her legs under her body before she covered herself with the blanket that was also over the back of the couch. Gatlin took up the other end, stretching his legs toward the ottoman. I pushed the remote to Scout. "You pick, honeysuckle."

Scout took the controller, flipping through the shows and movies. She looked a little calmer than she had been. The day had been shit. She had been trying so hard to hold it together in front of Amos. After everything was said and done, I was thankful she was staying here. She would have made do at her parents' house, and they would have been thrilled to have her, but you can only be so comfortable sleeping on a couch or air mattress for so long. Plus, with Flint being there, it would have made things a bit more cramped. There was no reason when we had space.

I studied her profile in the faint light coming from the TV. She was gorgeous, truly. Her features were petite, almost doll-like. She had leaf-green eyes that were slightly larger and rounder than most people's. It fit with her small nose that was dotted with freckles. I would like to say that I had not had fantasies about what she looked like in bed, but I would be lying. Her perfect plump lips were full, with her bottom lip being just a bit bigger. She had a tiny scar on her chin where she had fallen as a kid and had to get stitches. Her hair was pulled into a messy bun on top of her head. The makeup she had worn for the day was now gone, leaving her bare face on display. Everything about her was beautiful inside and out.

My eyes caught on Gatlin's face just past Scout. I had watched him my entire life. We had been there to witness every physical change the other had gone through. This meant I had studied every inch of his face. The straight line of his nose. The way it wrinkled when something made him truly laugh. The straight line of his jaw that was covered in a well-maintained beard. His olive skin tanned from being outside all the time. His hair was loose and wavy as he left it to air dry from his shower. He had started to grow his hair out when we were around fifteen and had not cut it above his shoulders since, keeping it right at his shoulder blades. In the light, it had small highlights from the sun, which enhanced the slight curl.

I had avoided dating people who looked even remotely like either one of them, even though everything about them called to me. I had ended a few relationships when I realized that I was comparing the person to Scout and Gatlin. The minute my brain would go there, I knew it was time. I always thought if they were the right person, there would be no comparison. I was still waiting for that to happen. I refocused back on Gatlin's profile. Fucking hell, he was just as beautiful as Scout.

As if he felt my gaze on him, Gatlin turned, his stare locked on me. With a slight tilt of his head, he was silently asking me what I was doing. Giving my head a slight shake, I turned my attention to the screen where Scout had chosen a historical romance show. I could feel his eyes borrowing into the side of my face. I forced my eyes to remain on the show. What if he was looking at me like I had him? Did he like what he saw? Or was he admiring how beautiful the woman between us was? *No. Stop. Don't go down that road.*

I needed to get my head out of fantasyland. The questions of *what if* could be no good for me or anyone else. There were only two options: bury the thoughts down for later or talk about them. I was not ready to talk, so setting them aside for now was my best choice. Now to get my head and dick on the same page. The latter was trying to chub up, which was not ideal. I sat up and reached for the box of treats, hoping to use them as a cover. "Anybody want any treats?" I asked as I opened the lid, giving them what I hoped was a convincing, nonchalant smile.

Scout turned toward me, moving the blanket off her before she shifted closer on the cushion. Her knees pressed lightly into the side of my leg when she leaned over, peeking at the goodies. "Is that the new blueberry tea cookie with lemon glaze?" Her eyes bounced up to mine as her tongue darted out to wet her bottom lip. My eyes flicked to her now wet lip. I quickly looked back up. Fuck, she probably saw that.

The darkness of the room hopefully hid my flaming cheeks. "It is," I forced the words out. If she didn't move back soon, my dick was going to bust through the bottom of the box—and that was not a treat I had offered on the menu. Not tonight at least. *Dammit brain.*

She reached in, pulling out a salted caramel chocolate chip cookie first and blindly passed it to Gatlin. While he rarely ate sweets, he couldn't resist a salty-sweet combination. When she pulled out another item, I was surprised when she raised up and leaned across my lap to place a snickerdoodle on the side table. Her baggy shirt grazed my hand as she moved. I wondered if she was wearing a bra? *Fuuuck a duck.* With one final grab in the box, we all had our cookie of choice. I stared at Scout in awe of the way she seemed to automatically care for us like we did for her. By this point, I had a full boner. I was rock hard and had a box of bakery items on my lap. My eyes connected with Gatlin's again. He looked from me to the box, as if he was daring me to move it. What was his problem tonight? *No, fucker, I will not be moving the box without something to cover up with.*

The asshole smirked. *Smirked* at me. Knowing full well the rock and hard place I was currently in, pun completely intended. "Does anybody need a refill?" I asked quietly. My face was burning hot, I needed to calm down. That would only be accomplished not here. I stood, still covering my groin with the box. Scout shook her head before she turned, giving me a soft smile. Gatlin's eyes were filled with mischief as he replied, "No, but the cookies are staying in here, right?" *Asshole.*

"No, I'm taking them with me. Be good and I might bring them back." His eyes widened and Scout giggled. Two could play this game.

chapter 8

. . .

scout

A FEW DAYS after I had come to stay with the guys, I was wound tighter than an eight day clock. Leland and Gat had been front and center for my evening activities for the last year or more. There were many nights that I found release thinking about them, being with them not just for sex, but more. The first dream had been so real I thought it was happening. Unfortunately, my alarm made sure to let me know I was in fact dreaming. Most of the dreams I was sandwiched between them, our hands and mouths all over each other. Since coming to stay with them, though, private time had taken a pause. Masturbating while thinking about them when I was in my own bed was different from them being under the same roof. This was made harder by the fact one or both of them was always home with me. *Were they having the same issues?* We could collectively assist each other. My thoughts were cut short when my phone pinged as I pulled up to the house.

Today was the day I went in early to the bookstore to do payroll and then would head out early. This meant I had driven instead of riding with the guys. I grabbed my phone, pulling up my messages to see a notification for our group chat.

Papa bear: 2:54 p.m. Hey, honeysuckle, it's Gat. My phone is charging. We wanted to remind you that you will have the house to yourself since we will be at Nature Nuggets. Also, it is going to be chaos because Frankie is sick and can't help. Pray for us. Not 100% sure what time we will be done. Probably like 5:30 or 6:00. Papa bear said to send a message when you get home.

Me: 2:56 p.m. Let Papa bear know I made it safe and sound. Now to find something to occupy my time until the men folk return.

Me: 2:56 p.m. Also tell Frankie I hope they get to feeling better!

Papa bear: 2:58 p.m. I just snorted water out my nose. "The men folk". We all know what you will be doing.

Doubt it.

Me: 3:00 p.m. Oh you both think you know me so well.

Papa bear 3:02 p.m. We say it's between reading or you will sneakily watch the rest of the Everest documentary without us, and then pretend you didn't. Just like the one about the guy that free climbed the mountain, Miss "No I would never finish that without you guys."

Me: 3:03 p.m. *Gasp* I represent that comment. It was really good. You guys should watch it. 😂

Me: 3:03 p.m. Any who, off to do busy independent woman things. Be careful, both of you!

Papa bear: 3:05 p.m. Will do, boss.

They did know me, however tonight, I had different plans for the evening. I dropped my stuff in my room before changing into my workout clothes. I tried to run or walk during the week and then would usually do a bit of yoga or go to the gym with the guys. I was strong, but definitely not built like some model. I had the butt and the hips that most of the women in my family had. I was not skin and bones, but was built very much like a pear. There was nothing wrong with being lean and small, but I wasn't and that was ok. I had curves and my stomach was a little softer. I had learned at a very young age that if I was healthy and doing the best I could for my body, that was enough for me.

I changed and grabbed my yoga mat before heading out the back door to the covered porch. Once the mat was situated, I chose a session to go through. I felt my body relax as I moved through the positions. By the end, I had begun to sweat and my muscle had a pleasant burn. I sat and meditated for a moment, cooling down and allowing my mind to calm. My thoughts wandered, but eventually made their way to the usual place. I really needed some relief if I was going to survive being here with Gatlin and Leland. I could see them in my head like they were standing in front of me. Both naked, hard, and wanting to get down and dirty. It would be so good. There had never been any legitimate moves made. I didn't know if they truly wanted me or if it was harmless flirting. The things I want to do with them...When my meditation ended, I let out a final breath and stood. I rolled my mat back up and tucked it under my arm. Grabbing my phone and water bottle, I headed in to take a quick shower. There were pressing matters that needed my attention.

The clock on the stove caught my eye: 4:32 p.m. *Shit, how long of a session did I do?* Checking the video, I realized that I had chosen a longer session, but had also zoned out too long while cooling down. I stripped out of my clothes as I went through the house. Nobody was here to see, at the moment, and the risk of being caught excited to me.

I scrubbed quickly and wrapped one of the fluffy towels around my chest before heading for my room. At the door to Gatlin's room, I paused and then looked to Leland's room. I went to Gat's first, grabbing one of his shirts. Bringing it close, I inhaled deeply. Their smells were like a drug to me. They calmed me and worked me up at the same time. I took the towel off my hair before pulling the shirt over my head. Once the shirt was on, I took the towel from around me, carrying it with me to put up. The shirt rubbed against my bare skin, rubbing over my sensitive nipples. It was like having Gatlin wrapped around me. The next stop was Leland's room. I rummaged for a moment before pulling out a sweatshirt. Pulling it over the shirt, I was hit with a heady mix of their scents. I could feel myself growing wetter by the second. Would some people find my behavior weird? Probably. But in my current, very horny state, I could not find a single fuck to give. Horny Scout was a needy bitch, and what she needed most was to smell the two men she was lusting after as she climaxed. *I need to get to my room.*

From my nightstand I pulled my trusty vibrator from the drawer. I got comfortable on the pillows and started the toy up. The mental images of us together started to flood in. The first was me on my knees with both Gatlin and Leland's hard cocks in my hand. I moved the vibrator down, gliding it down my stomach. I paused before I reached my pussy. I was soaked. At this rate, the sheets would need to be changed. I wanted to take as much time as I could before orgasming. I teased my outer lips, the vibrations ghosting over my skin. Reaching up with my free hand, I grazed my fingers over my nipple through the fabric of the shirt and sweatshirt. The material would have normally caused the sensation to be dulled. Instead, the material moved over my sensitive skin, just enough friction to drive my need higher. The touch sent a wave of pleasure through me.

I carried on, teasing and edging myself for some time before moving the vibrator to lightly circle my clit. At the first contact, my back arched off the bed, chasing more. Behind my eyelids, the new picture had me on top of Leland. He was thrusting deep into my pussy while Gatlin fucked my ass. I had never trusted anyone with anal, but my guys were different. *Wait, my guys? They aren't my guys.*

Not now. Don't think about it now.

It was too late, my mind had latched on to the idea. I focused back on the task at hand, pinching my nipple hard as I continued to move the toy. The thought of them claiming me caused my muscles to clench. I wanted that so much. I could almost feel them thrusting into me. Their bodies were sandwiching me as they drove us higher and higher. I was right on the edge of losing it when the final mental image had me crying out their names. Gatlin was fucking me from behind while Leland fucked him.

"Oh fuck, yes, bear, fuck him into me." My words came out louder than expected, echoing off the wall. "Fuck. Fuck—" I shook with my orgasm, their names coming out a muddle mess. I laid there for a moment, my chest rapidly rising and falling. Beads of sweat had formed in my hairline. I knew it had been a little while, but damn. That was one of the best orgasms I had in I couldn't even say how long. I would credit that to my little dry spell, but it came down to the porn worthy movie that my mind gave me. I heard the distinct clicking of Mud's nails as he walked through the house. *Oh shit.*

I snatched my phone up: 5:47 p.m. Shit, I had gotten lost in the fantasies. How the hell did I lose time so fast? Jumping from the bed, I turned the toy off before throwing it in the draw. I grabbed underwear and darted to the bathroom as a knock came at my open door. "Just a second," I called from the bathroom. My stupid horny self had not even bothered shutting the door. It was wide open for all to enter.

Leland spoke from the hall without entering the room, his voice distant. They had both been so respectful of giving me privacy when I was in my room. It shouldn't come as a shock they would be this way. "Just wanted to let you know we were home, honeysuckle. We were also trying to decide what to eat for dinner. Anything you are craving?"

You and Gatlin.

No. Down girl! We almost got caught, I scolded myself and my lady parts. She was needy and wanted two men in particular. "Um, no not really. I'm good with whatever."

Gatlin called from down the hall, "Breakfast for dinner."

I walked out of the bathroom to Leland who was leaning on the doorframe like a damn book boyfriend. His eyes widened slightly when he saw me. "I wanted to be comfortable after my shower," I replied innocently as his eyes started at my feet and worked their way up my bare legs. His sweatshirt and Gatlin's shirt were both oversized on me, but it was obvious I was not wearing shorts under them.

He pulled his bottom lip between his teeth, continuing his perusal.

When his gaze finally reached my face, the barely concealed lust was definitely a boost to my ego. Gatlin appeared at the door. "Holy shit, honeysuckle." His face mirrored Leland's. When Gatlin spoke, it broke the intense gaze Leland had me pinned under. I began to fidget, nerves creeping in at the fact I was standing here in their shirts after just having a mind-blowing orgasm thinking about them. I literally could not say what I had been thinking. Well, I mean I knew what *parts of me* had been thinking. One way ticket to a solo orgasm, all aboard. Now though, I was considering just locking myself in the bathroom until I either passed from starvation or was able to dig a tunnel out prison break style. *Dramatic much?*

"Sorry I didn't realize what time it was," I started word vomiting. "I just had gotten out of the shower and I had laid down on the bed—" I was cut off by a buzzing pulse coming from behind me. I looked around, seeing my phone still dark. Realization slammed into me. I had not turned the damn vibrator off, just changed the setting.

"Honeysuckle, I think your phone is ringing." Leland's deep voice caused my head to whip back to them. I was completely frozen in place. My eyes darted between them and the nightstand.

I would have giggled at Gatlin's face had it not been for the mortification current running rampant. His head was tilted slightly to one side, almost like a confused puppy. "That doesn't sound like a phone. It sounds like a vi—" Leland turned to look at him, waiting for him to finish.

I started talking before he could complete his sentence. "Better get that it, could be the store or who knows what else. I'll be out in just a minute." I turned toward my "urgent" phone call and waited until I heard their footsteps heading back down the hall.

Good job, lady parts. Your greedy ass almost got us caught.

And that would have been a bad thing? my inner, horny self whispered.

I shut the stupid toy off and moved it to another drawer. *Well, time to face the music. Or find a shovel and start digging…*

chapter 9

. . .

scout

IT DIDN'T SEEM right to have to drive to work. The ride to the shop the day after the great vibrator malfunction, the conversation was very one sided with Gatlin doing most of the talking. I had lived above the store for some time now. Even before the renovations started, I had moved the essentials in and stayed there. While I loved being close to work, I was realizing how nice it was to have some distance between me and the store.

The first few days of staying with the guys was an adjustment. They had lived together for a long time, and had routines and certain ways of doing things. It was easy for the three of us to be roommates. To some, it would shock them how well we fit, but this is how it had been with them from the first time we hung out.

We went through the first two weeks with no issues. *Other than almost getting caught masturbating.* I have not made that mistake again. Leland had to get up and go to the bakery most days before the sun was up. I noticed one night that Gatlin sets up the coffee for him the night before, and then Leland will reset it for Gatlin and me to have coffee when we get up. Gatlin had said once that he couldn't imagine getting up that early and not having coffee. The way they seemed to always take care of each other, and now me, was different, but welcome. I had friends. Lettie was one of my closest friends, but I struggled with making connections like that. The thought of letting people behind my carefully constructed mask and walls was a battle. When I met Gat and Leland, I kept them at an arm's length. They had always been friendly when we would see each other, but never pushy. One day, I noticed Gatlin leaning on the wall behind his store. When I got out of the car, he glanced up from his phone to give me a little wave. I returned the gesture before climbing out of my car. When Leland came from the bakery carrying food, I offered the cover porch and they offered me lunch. After that day, we regularly met for lunch, which turned into breakfast and then hanging out away from work. They became my two best friends. Recently, it has started to get harder keeping them in the best friend category. Especially being under the same roof.

Like right now, I was waiting on Leland to finish up so we could ride to the house together. This morning, Gatlin had driven us here after having a cup of coffee, waiting for me when I came into the kitchen. I had only been half awake when I entered, but had the most amazing morning view when Gatlin came through with only pants on and no shirt. I would absolutely never grow tired of half-naked Gat.

"Sorry, I have to grab a Nature Nugget shirt from the laundry. Muddington decided that I needed aggressive love while holding coffee. We both ended up covered in it." As if on cue, Mud pawed at the back door.

With Gatlin's back to me, I shamelessly checked him out, taking in all the lean muscles of his back down to his firm ass. His jeans were doing wonderful things for his lower half. I bet he smelt amazing. Weird to think, but with his damp hair down, I knew he had showered either pre or post coffee accident. His body wash mixed with his cologne made the most heady scent. I took a slow inhale when catching his scent. Thankfully, it seemed like I was only taking in the coffee aromas. They thought I just took their stuff because it was comfortable. While this was true, it was more because of the comfort even the scent of them brought me.

A low whine pulled my attention. I walked over and let Mud in, just as Gatlin returned now fully clothed. *Damn.*

"Ready to head out?"

I checked to make sure I had everything before I replied, "Yep, let's get this day started." With that, we headed out the door. Time to be an adult and not just a lusty horn dog.

This lasted until the end of the day. The store had been busy, which I loved, but I had also spent most of my time moving books and displays. We had gotten in some amazing indie books that I really thought were going to do well. I loved a lot of things about running my own business, but finding new authors to put in the store as by far the most rewarding. Our store was small in comparison to the big box stores, but I got to help people discover new authors or series they may have never tried. It made all the late days and early mornings worth it.

Now, though, I sat on the back porch of my store, watching Leland unload a supply truck. It was supposed to arrive earlier, but had been delayed. I was not upset in the slightest, this meant I got my second show of the day. Where Gatlin was tall and lean muscled, Leland was big and brawny. I am pretty sure I could hear the seams in his shirt sleeves screaming. I clenched my legs together as he effortlessly moved heavy bags and containers around. *Oh, to be a bag of flour.*

I could admit that I was physically attracted to both of them, but there was so much more than that. I can understand why Nan joked that they were an old married couple. Now the old married couple included me. The most asked question, of course, is which of them I was dating. Some have joked that they must both be with me. Of course, the answer was always a no, even if I wanted to say yes, all three of us were together. By three, I meant *all* three. I had seen the looks they give each other. I would never try to push in on what they have or could have, but I had seen the looks they throw my way, too. Lettie tells me in detail how they looked at me every chance she got.

I was lost in thought when Leland cleared his throat, snapping me back to the present. "I'm good to go if you are. I wanted to stop by the store to grab stuff for the weekend, if that's good with you?"

I tried and failed to speak due to the drooling I had been doing.

After I cleared my throat, my mouth and brain are finally on the same page and I try again. "Yeah, we can definitely do that."

AFTER EVERYTHING WAS in the house and unloaded, I took my stuff to my room. I had my routines, and even though I was not at home, I tried to stick to them. I had been diagnosed with ADHD/ADD as an adult, which came as a surprise to no one. I took medicine now and it had helped, but routines, alarms, and lists are what I live by. I unpacked my bag, plugging in my tablet before setting my current read on top.

Lettie had forced me to start one of her favorite series. I was enjoying it, however I had chosen to skip one of the books that was particularly sad. Now, she was threatening to do a death bed reading when we became two old bats. I mean, honestly, I have seen what happens in the book, *thank you, social media*. It's too sad.

No thank you, ma'am.

When I sat down at the desk, I meant to only do a few social media posts. However, I doom scrolled for what I thought was only a few minutes, but turned out to be close to an hour. A soft knock made me turn to the door. Leland leaned against the door, looking like a wet dream.

"Anything you might want for dinner?"

We traded days for who cooked, but usually we would all end up in the kitchen, helping and joking. "We could do burgers. You know Gat is normally starving when he gets done with the kids. Plus, you have tomorrow off, so it will give you something for lunch." I continued to move around my room. I had worn overalls today with a tank top and one of my beloved cardigans over the top. I took the low bun out, letting my hair loose. Lettie gave me daily lectures about how it being up gave me headaches. This led to saggy, sad buns. Leland stood silently in the doorway as I grabbed a hanger. "I can make up some fries. I saw a new seasoning mix that I think we have all the ingredients for. It looked really good."

Once my cardigan was off and on its hanger, I turned to Leland, wondering why he had not replied. He had moved to lean just inside the door, his eyes raking over me. The outfit left everything but my shoulders and arms to the imagination. *Scandalous shoulders.* Leland, however, was looking at me like I was wearing the most revealing lingerie he'd ever seen. His stare caused goosebumps to cover my body. I stood a little taller under his gaze. When his eyes caught mine, I could see a heat behind them.

He moved further into the room, stopping directly in front of me. Even as he towered over me, my eyes never strayed from his.

leland

I was a simple man. There really wasn't much that I wanted. I didn't want or need all the money in the world or fame, but fuck I wanted, *needed* this woman. I wanted her more than my next breath. I wanted to taste her and savior every noise I knew she would make. I had an all-consuming need to claim her. It wasn't just her, though. My body was screaming to grab her, tie her down, and pleasure her until Gatlin came home and then start again with him, right here with us. *Dammit.*

The way she moved through the house like it was hers. She used the word "we" like a partner did with their significant other. The house had always had a feeling of home for me. This had been where we had family dinners and get-togethers growing up. When I bought it from Nan, I was terrified that I would lose that feeling. When Gat moved in, I felt that familiar comfort again. I thought it was perfect. It was after the first week Scout had been here that I felt a shift. It was like the house settled with us all here. She had stayed here a few times over the last year, but this was different. There were little Scout touches throughout the house and in our daily routines. Things that made it a true home for me and Gat.

She would leave little messages around the house. Some were reminders for herself, others were for us, and then there were just sweet notes. Ranging from how proud she was of us, or that she hoped we had a great day, or a corny joke to make us laugh. There were other things like thinking that I was off the next day and would need lunch. Knowing Gat loved hamburgers and how hungry he would be. *Gatlin. Shit, what was I doing?*

I couldn't make a move on Scout; not without talking to him and her. I felt like shit for not thinking about the man who had been my best friend since we were children. I had seen the way he looked at Scout. The way they looked at each other, honestly. But I also saw how they had both looked at me a few weeks back. I knew what I needed to do, but I could not force myself back.

The squeaky floorboard at the threshold of Scout's door behind us was like a bomb going off. I froze, every muscle locking up as I looked down at Scout, her eyes wide.

"I will say, guys, I'm not normally a sit back and watch kind of guy." Gatlin's voice came closer than I expected. He moved to stand directly behind me, his body heat radiating off him. "Is that what you want, teddy bear?" He reached one hand up to press between my shoulder blades. "What about you, honeysuckle? Should I watch or join?"

A blush crawled its way over Scout's cheeks, matching the one I knew was on my face. I couldn't say that I was upset by what was happening. I had wanted Gatlin for most of our life. I never did anything because for all I knew, he was straight. With Scout, the feelings had come on fast and strong. I never wanted to risk my friendship with them. They were too important to me. *What the fuck was Gatlin up to?*

That seemed to be the million-dollar question I was constantly asking. *What was he doing? What did he want? What did they want? Would it be me?*

The heat of his hand was burning into my skin. He moved where he now stood to the side, his chest almost touching Scout's shoulder, his hand dropping from my back. I immediately missed the touch. I tried with everything in me to hold back the almost whimper that escaped my lips. My lids had fallen closed at the contact. I squeezed them tight in an effort not to move or make a sound. Whatever was going on, I selfishly didn't want it to end. "I know you, too, have felt the tension. I'm not the only one." His voice was smooth and calm, the exact opposite of what I was feeling. I was almost lightheaded due to my blood rushing south.

I opened my eyes and shifted my gaze from Scout to Gatlin before I wet my lips to speak. "What are you doing, bee?" My voice was low, almost a whispered plea. A plea for what I couldn't say. His eyes dropped to my mouth, then darted to our girl. Because that's what Scout was, *our girl.*

I felt a smaller hand reach out and lace their fingers with mine. I looked to where Scout held my hand and then watched as she reached for Gatlin's. Having her hand in mine was one thing, seeing her reach for him as well was like a match on dry leaves. The contrast of his golden-tanned skin made her beautiful, fair skin look like the porcelain dolls Nan collected.

Every possibility played through my head. Gatlin and I laying Scout out on the bed and worshiping her. Scout and I would do the same for him. If he let me. Gatlin might not have been thinking of there being a me and him in this little equation. My dick was not giving up on that possibility. I couldn't just think with my dick right now, though. This could be a massive mistake. We could lose everything. I could lose the two most important people to me. I had to be the rational one. I had to keep us from making a mistake.

I pulled in a breath to say as much when I was yanked down to Scout's level. Her hand slipped from mine, and I assumed Gatlin's, as they both wound around my neck, pulling me closer. Her mouth crashed down on mine. A low groan left me at the feel of her plush lips. When her tongue teased the seam of my lips, I was a goner. I opened to her, but quickly took over the kiss.

I grabbed the back of her legs under her luscious ass, lifting her easily. She knew what to do and wrapped her legs around my waist. She let one hand move from my neck to blindly reach for Gatlin. He was right there, waiting for her. I glanced down to see the noticeable bulge in his pants that matched my own.

Once he was close, she broke our kiss to grab Gat. I held on to her as he placed one hand on the back of her neck, running his fingers through her hair to move her where he wanted. They battled for control, giving and taking from each other. Gat's moan reached my ears as Scout began to move her hips, searching for friction.

They broke apart, both breathing heavily. My grip tightened on Scout as her gaze bounced from Gatlin to me. *Shit.*

I couldn't let this break us. I couldn't lose them. Scout would move back home when the renovations were done, then it would be me and Gatlin again in the house. Unless they got together. My chest tightened at the thought. Even with Scout's legs still around my waist, the thoughts tried to worm in.

They will want each other. Not you.

They might let you join, but you can't have them both.

She might want you and him, but he just wants her.

Fuck, I needed to get out of here. But my body was still locked up, holding Scout, feeling the warmth of her and Gatlin bleeding into my skin. Dammit, I didn't want to stop to walk away, but I was so scared that I was going to be the broken one at the end of this. I would be a puzzle full missing pieces because Scout and Gatlin owned them already.

What idiot falls for his straight best friend and their girl best friend?

Me. I am that idiot.

chapter 10

· · ·

gatlin

I HAD no clue what we were doing, but damn if it didn't feel right. When I had walked into the quiet house, I looked out back, not seeing anyone. I went to search the house. I had been with the Nature Nuggets, but had gotten done a little earlier than expected. I loved the kids, but they were in rare form today. The end of school was fast approaching, then we had the annual camping trip we did each summer. It was a week-long trip of camping, hiking, fishing, and learning about nature. I had gotten a massive donation from one of the outdoor apparel companies that I had supported for years. I was excited to tell Leland and Scout, because this meant more kids would get to come on the trip.

I didn't expect, however, to walk in to my two best friends having a heated staring contest. I can admit that I was a little thrown off at first. We flirted, but this was different. I couldn't lie and say I wasn't a little jealous by how close they were. The problem was I couldn't figure out who I was jealous of. I had been running in overdrive trying to figure out what was going on in my brain when it came to, well, me. *Self-centered much?*

I had only dated women throughout my life, but I had only thought about one man. The one standing in front of me. Of course, I didn't think there was anything wrong with it. I had looked at guys over the years, especially since I had been trying to figure out what I liked or I guess *who* I liked. I had gone to a couple of clubs with Leland and had been hit on by men and women alike. They were never what I was looking for. Really, most people weren't. I would flirt and occasionally have a hook up, but for the most part, I had stayed single, never growing real feelings for anyone. Well, anyone but the two people in front of me.

"Damn, honeysuckle. That was one hell of a kiss." I leaned in, trailing my lips over her neck before scraping my teeth lightly over the delicate skin. The whimper she released didn't cover the sharp breath Leland took in.

Her legs were still wrapped around Leland's waist. I could feel the subtle shift as she tried to gain friction against him. I pulled my mouth from Scout's neck to look at my best friend. The man who had been my rock since childhood. The person who had been with me in every step of my life. I felt more than I saw when Scout slid from his waist. Her feet came to rest on the floor again. She took the slightest step back, enough to make room while still touching us.

Leland's eyes dropped from mine to the floor. He stood quiet for a moment before his gaze met mine again. "What are we doing here, Ford?" Oh, he meant business. He rarely ever called me by my last name. I would have made a joke, but the emotion behind his eyes gave me pause. I could see the questions in his eyes. So much more was running through his head than just that one question. It was an important question, but one I had no answers to yet.

What were we doing?

"I think we should maybe go to the kitchen and start dinner, and then we can talk." Scout's sweet voice broke the staring contest Leland and I were currently locked in.

I took one more moment to look at Leland and then Scout. Leland spoke before I could. "I think that is a good idea, honeysuckle." With that, he turned and left the room. Scout gently brushed her fingers down my arm and gave my hand a little squeeze. I hope I didn't just fuck everything up.

BY THE TIME I got to the kitchen, Leland was getting the grill going on the back porch while Scout cut up potatoes for fries. "What are we having tonight?" I asked before sitting at one of the bar stools that were set to one side of the island.

Scout paused in her prep to give me a soft smile. "Well, we know how hungry you are after running around with the kids, so we thought burgers and fries." *This woman.* "Plus, Leland won't be at the bakery tomorrow, so he will have lunch without having to worry," she finished before going back to prepping fries.

"Do you need any help?"

With the last few potatoes cut, she set them aside before grabbing the seasoning mix. She gave me a pointed look, taking her lower lip between her teeth. "I think someone else needs you instead." She glanced out to Leland before turning back to me. "It's ok not to label yourself, you know that, right? You can just be Gatlin, Gat, bumblebee, and bee. There doesn't have to be anything past that. If you are happy with yourself, then that's all that matters." She reached across the counter, giving my hand a squeeze before starting back with the food prep.

Damn. That was something I didn't know I needed to hear.

What happens when you fall in love with your best friends? *Wait. Friends. Plural.*

Shit it hit me like a truck. I was falling in love with my best friends. With the teddy bear of a man who has had my back my whole life, and the sweet, caring woman who just happened to own the bookstore next door.

I rounded the island, giving Scout a peck on the cheek. She leaned into my touch and let out a soft laugh. I grabbed two beers from the fridge and walked to the back door. Pushing through the screen door, I walked over to where the grill was set up. I didn't know what kind of headspace Leland was in. This didn't happen with us. Our friendship from the very start had always been on solid ground. I knew that whatever was going on with all of us needed to be talked out. Right now, this was between me and him. Scout had made her wants clear with that kiss. I set one beer on the table next to the grill. Leland blindly grabbed the beer before taking a long pull.

The area with the grill was basically set up to be an outdoor kitchen. It would be anyone who enjoys grilling and entertaining's wet dream. I don't think we used the kitchen inside for a year when it was finished. We would go weeks without cooking inside, opting instead to grill out. Leland and I both enjoyed grilling, so it was a well-used area. I turned, leaning back against the counter that was set to each side of the grill.

Scout had been right—his mind was going at full speed. This was an odd change to see. Leland was normally the sure one in situations. He was the constant, the one who thought through things, but made decisions with confidence. I hated seeing the worry that was etched on his face. Even from his profile, I could tell that his brow was furrowed, and his face was guarded.

"Thanks, Gat." His reply came without his eyes leaving the burgers. Anyone who didn't know Leland Boone would think he was just focusing as to not burn the burgers. Not me. I knew this man better than I knew myself. He had thrown up a wall around himself and now I had to try and break through or climb over. I had never been on this side of the wall, though. I guess he forgot that I am one hell of a climber.

"You ok, bear?" I looked at his profile while he did his best to not look at me.

"Yeah, I'm good. Trying not to burn the burgers. Can't tarnish my reputation for being an amazing grill master and burn the food." He forced a smile as he glanced at me before returning to the grill. His whole body was strung tight, giving away that the humor he was trying to lace into the conversation was not genuine. "How were the kids? Getting excited about the camp out?"

Now we were deflecting the conversation. I would let him have this for now, but I would find out what was rolling around in his head. A few pokes and he would crack. *Hopefully.*

"They were good. They are definitely excited about starting to plan the camping trip. Their teachers are going to struggle to keep them focused for the last weeks of school." I took a sip of my beer before waiting for him to say something else. When he didn't, I continued, "They are excited that you get to come."

"I bring them sugary, baked items. Of course they would be happy for me to be there." He gave a small, self-deprecating laugh. *What the hell?*

He knew that was not the reason the kids loved having him come. He had the best stories, the best fishing tips, and yes, the best treats. He also loved helping with events. When I took over the Nuggets group, he had jumped at the chance to get involved. The first time he came to a meeting, he had been nervous that his size would scare the kids off. He tried to act like people judging him for his size was all in the past and didn't affect him, but I knew that wasn't the case. He also worried about his sexuality, not that he went around screaming it from the rooftops, but we lived in a smallish town. Instead of parents and kids having an issue, we had parents grateful that the Nuggets had become more accepting. We had kids from all walks of life. He and one of our moms had made a massive difference for the quieter kids. So this shit he was trying to push about only being there because of the sugary treats was bullshit.

"Come on, you know they want you around—" I was cut off by the lid closing.

He paused without meeting my gaze. "Hey, so all that in the bedroom, I get it if you are looking to have something with just Scout. I mean, three ways are fun, but nobody wants the bi guy getting too handsy. Right?" He huffed a low laugh that almost sounded like a sigh before he clenched his jaw. I was pretty sure if he kept it up, he was going to crack his teeth. "I wouldn't want to make things weird for you or Scout. She is an amazing woman who cares a lot about you, and I don't need to boost your ego. You already know you are awesome. Just wanted to let you know. Not that you need my permission. Just wanted to say I guess that I get it and it's cool." His head gave a slight shake like he was trying to clear something out. Then he turned to head back into the house, leaving me standing there, looking at his back. *The fuck?*

Did he just fucking imply that Scout and I should have anything without him? That she cared for only me? What kind of gentleman shit was this? I went from dumbfounded and confused to seeing red. My heart began to pound, the blood rushing in my ears. What. The. Actual. Fuck.

I was about to try and beat some sense into the big bear of a man and probably lose. Option two was kissing him until his brain hopefully melted and he didn't remember his name. I'm sure Scout would be on board to help with option two. *Maybe?*

I realized I had made a huge mistake. I should have grown a pair of balls and told Leland what I had been feeling for years. At the same time, he was not going to say shit like that about himself. Not to me or anyone. I turned my beer up, downing what was left before slamming the bottle down and storming inside. My head was a little fuzzy. Whether it was from chugging the beer or my blood pressure being sky high, I didn't know.

I ripped the screen door open, my eyes focused on the big man leaning on the counter. Scout had pulled the burger toppings from the fridge and was now slicing a tomato. "Ready to—" Her sentence died when she caught the look on my face. "Gat?" She laid the knife down, her tone causing Leland to look over at me.

When our eyes met, my semi-calm demeanor evaporated like rainwater on a hot sidewalk. "What the fuck was that about? Huh?" My voice came low and sounded even more angry than intended. "What kind of bullshit was that, Leland? How the fuck would you being around, or God forbid, with us, make it weird?" At some point, I had crossed the kitchen and was now standing inches from Leland.

Scout stared at both of us with a look of confusion and a sliver of hurt crossing her face. "Um, what is going on? What happened?"

I turned to her, trying to calm my racing heart. "Leland, being the patron saint of granny bodice ripping romances, has given us his bless-ing. He is a real gentleman, ya know? I think dickhead is a better term, but what do I know? Go ahead, tell Scout what you told me." I turned back to glare at the side of his face. "Tell her all that bullshit you just spouted. I swear, Leland, I have never been so mad at you in my whole life." He was always pale, but he looked even paler now. Like someone had kicked his puppy or he was about to pass out. I almost felt bad. *Almost.*

"Nothing?" I made an *out with it* motion. "You were fine saying it to me. It was ok to hurt me. Honestly, kind of glad you won't say it. I guess I can be the bad guy this time. Well, honeysuckle, here is the gist of it. Apparently, no one wants the bi guy around to get too handsy and makes things weird, whatever the fuck that means," I finished. My body was vibrating. I was so angry with him and myself. I could feel tears starting to form. The silence in the kitchen was so heavy. Tension clouded the room, making it hard to take in full breaths.

"Why would you say that, Leland?" Scout looked at Leland, her eyes soft. She wasn't angry with him. Her tone was laced more with sadness and disappointment. His eyes were down casted, inspecting the counter-top, as if it held all the answers.

He let out an almost pained breath. He was curved so far in on himself, like he was guarding against a physical blow. "I don't want to mess something up and you two would be good together. It would make sense, I have been here before. Plus, we could all still be friends. I —" He was caught off guard when I shoved him, causing us to fall to the side, landing on the floor. He maneuvered where I was on top, absorbing the impact for both of us. His arms banded around me to keep me safe. *Still taking care of me.*

Leland was bigger than me in height and weight, but I was so pissed off at him. There had been very few times that we had fought, most had been when we were kids. This time, though, I was drawing a hard line and he could either get with the program willingly or I would drag his ass over. I raised myself up, bracketing his head between my hands before looking at him. "Listen here, asshole, I don't know what kind of shit is rolling around in your head, but I can promise I can be louder. Whatever that was outside, shut it out. Whoever made you feel that way, I'm not them, and Scout sure as hell isn't, either." My breathing was coming out in ragged breaths. I felt his hands on my thighs like he was getting ready to throw me off or needing the touch to ground himself. He was shit out of luck if he was going to try and get rid of me.

His eyes were closed tight, his face pulled like he was in pain. "You don't get it, Gat. It's ok, though—" I grabbed the sides of his face and crashed my mouth down on his. If he wouldn't listen to words, then I would shut him up with my mouth. Option two it was. His hands tightened where they held my legs.

The kiss went from a firm press of our mouths to a softer touch before Leland turned, slanting his lips to deepen it. His tongue skated across my lips, asking for permission. When I let him in, any control I thought I had was gone. He rolled us, placing his larger body over mine, the weight of his hips pressed down on mine. He slotted his leg between mine, pressing against my hardening cock. A whimpered moan escaped my lips at the contact. It felt like the final puzzle piece had found its place.

Our tongues danced before Leland pulled mine into his mouth, sucking on it like you would a dick. His hand had tangled in my hair, keeping me firmly in place. My hips moved, rubbing my now hard cock against his leg and then his bulge. The low groan that he made in the back of his throat would have made me come in my pants, but a noise pulled me back to reality. *Scout.*

Leland lifted slightly, breaking the kiss, allowing us both to take in a full breath of air. The grip he had on my hair loosened before he removed his hand, resting it beside my head. His pupils were blown wide, causing the ice blue of his irises to be a thin ring around the outside. I reached my hand up to Scout. The floor wasn't the most comfortable place, but that's where we were. She came willingly, sitting next to where I still laid on my back. I laced our fingers together, bringing them to my mouth and pressing my lips to the back of her hand. It was an awkward position, but I was afraid if we moved too much or too fast, Leland would bolt like a scared animal.

Turning my attention back to Leland, I looked at him. Really looked. "Never, and I do mean *never* doubt what you mean to us. I don't know what this is yet, but you are not some bi guy who is not welcome. There has never been a me without you. Period. The end. You hear me, bear?" His eyes shifted from mine, his face turning away from me and Scout.

Scout reached with her free hand to turn him to her, before leaning in to press a soft kiss to his lips. "You two are the most important people to me. I know I may not say it a lot, but you both mean so much to me. Like Gat, I'm not sure what this is between us, but I would like to try and find out." She looked down at me before going back to Leland.

"Both of you. I would never be ok with one without the other. It's both of you or nothing. I can't imagine it not being both of you."

Leland lifted himself up before moving off me to sit back on his heels. I thought he was going to reject the idea. My gut clenched in anticipation. If he thought that I would just go quietly and not try to convince him, he had another thing coming. This was different for us, for Scout, hell, in the town we lived in. It wasn't small, but it also wasn't huge. People had their ideas about things and how they should be. But honestly, I could care less. As long as I had them, I would deal with the rest.

I sat up and moved just as Scout did. We both crowded close to Leland, his arms wrapping around both of us, his face buried in between us. He took a moment, taking a calming breath. Leland had never been a big talker, always being the more strong, silent type, letting his action speak for him. His words came muffled, "I'm sorry, I got so far in my head. I want to try this and see where it goes." He leaned back to look at us. "I'm so sorry." He took a shaky breath before, taking another when he spoke. His voice was sure and more normal. "I think we should finish dinner and eat. Then we need to talk."

I looked at Scout, a small smile lifting the corner of my mouth. "There's our teddy bear."

chapter 11

. . .

scout

WE DECIDED to eat on the back porch, letting Mud out to run around in the backyard. I had always loved this house. From the first time I ever came over, it called to me. The house was a mix of a craftsman cottage and cabin. The outside was dark green, almost black, with a front porch running the length of the front. Most of the house had not been changed from Nan moving out. The biggest changes were to the back. There was a covered area that connected to the outdoor kitchen. The plan was to screen it in, but according to the guys, "they had big plans." This was terrifying as much as exciting.

We ate in a comfortable silence. We all knew we needed to talk about things, but we could enjoy the moment. The burgers, of course, were amazing, and both Gatlin and I told Leland. All of us ended up cleaning our plates before Gatlin grabbed them, stacking them and taking them inside. A moment later, he returned with the fixings to make s'mores.

"Marry me? Both of you." Leland snorted while Gatlin raised one eyebrow at me before letting out a laugh. "I'm serious. You made me amazing burgers and now I get s'mores. How could this get better? I'm not needy, I only require my books, food, and coffee."

"Oh, honeysuckle, I can think of so many things that could make it better. We will have to see about the needy part." Leland's deep, husky voice was laced with the sexual tension that hung around the three of us. A lightning bolt of want went straight to my center. My body reacted to his words, just as he intended. Whatever fear or doubt he had was at least quiet, for now.

Gatlin carried his supplies over to one of the fire pit chairs. With the guys still wanting to make changes to the backyard, the ring of landscaping stone served as the makeshift fire ring. He went about building a fire and had it going in no time; one of the perks of Gatlin being well versed in outdoor activities and survival. With the fire going strong, he checked the sand buckets and moved the hose where it would be in easy reach. He turned back to us, giving a wide grin before he motioned us over.

I walked close to Gatlin, bumping his hip lightly as I passed. "Always glad to have our very own boy scout." I let out a squeak when his arms came around my waist. Pulling me to his chest, he leaned in to nuzzle my hair. Even with the warmth of the fire, I shivered, every nerve lighting up where we touched. He turned us to face where Leland stood, his eyes locked on us like a predator watching its prey. Gatlin began to move us closer, the warmth of the fire now at our backs.

I was sandwiched between them, their body heat seeping into me. A light breeze blew, causing goosebumps to cover my skin. I looked up, meeting Leland's gaze. The fire flicked across his features, catching on the hints of blond in his hair and beard. I have never claimed to be a smooth talker; most would say the opposite was true. What I did enjoy was poking my bear and bee. "Well, this was not the s'mores I had planned. Though, we are missing a layer." I paused for dramatic affect. "I saw my brother and Flint the other day. Flint did seem kind of sad I wasn't staying at the house. I could shoot him a text. He can be our missing layer. Honestly, I'm sure he wouldn't mind. Here I'l—"

Leland's right hand that had been resting on Gatlin's arm was now tangled in my hair, holding me in place while Gatlin's had slipped over my mouth. With the height difference between us, this left my head tilted back, resting on Gat's chest. The look on Leland's face was feral and I could only imagine Gat wore a similar expression. *So we are a little possessive. Interesting.*

What was the pantie count now?

Wet panties: 3

Dry panties: 0

gatlin

Honestly, I'm sure he wouldn't mind.

I, for one, did not give a flying fuck about what Flint would or wouldn't mind. I was not a possessive asshole—most of the time. Scout's eyes were filled with laughter as I felt her tongue press against my palm. I looked down at her, unable to see her entire face, but I felt how she shifted her weight. I trailed my fingers down before letting my palm rest against her throat. Not applying pressure, but just holding it there. I could see, even in the low light, that her pupils were blown wide with lust. Our little honeysuckle liked it when we got all possessive. I lifted my gaze to meet Leland's, speaking over Scout. "Did you hear that, teddy bear?" Scout had always kept us on our toes and she loved to rile both of us up. This time would end differently than the others.

In a sudden movement, Leland crushed his mouth to hers. She let out a gasp from the force of the kiss, followed by a moan. He deepened the kiss before pulling away just as quickly. I watched, my cock pushing against my zipper. Leland released Scout only for his hand to wrap around the back of my neck, pulling me closer to him over Scout's head. My hand fell from her neck, coming to rest on her waist. The feeling of his scruff against my bread was a completely new sensation. How had I ended up with two people who could kiss this fucking good? He pulled back, looking me in the eyes, emotions playing across his face.

Leland looked back down to Scout. "Fuck the usual standard of s'mores layers. I got the only two I need or want."

I leaned down to where Scout's neck was exposed, scraping my teeth lightly over the delicate sin before soothing it with my mouth. I straightened back up. "S'mores are sweet, but I can think of other desserts I would prefer. There are so many options and combinations with this dessert choice. Unfortunately, that will have to wait. If I remember correctly, we are supposed to be talking about some things."

I reluctantly pulled away to put some space between us. "Come on, let's enjoy the fire and eat some sweets. It's too nice out here to waste it." I slipped my hand into one of Scout's, Leland had moved to her other side, putting his arm around her shoulders.

The fire had died down by the time we made it over. I gave Scout's hand a squeeze before I let go. "I need to add a few logs before we start cooking." She sat down in one of the chairs, leaning her head back to look at the clear sky.

Like Leland and I, Scout enjoys the outdoors, especially when the sky is clear. Even though we have spent countless hours in our backyard talking under the stars, this time feels different. There was a hum of energy running just under my skin that said this was more. I thought that Leland and Scout felt it, too. I ran through scenarios in my head of what this could be between us. Mine and Leland's parents had known each other for decades at this point. The first time they met Scout's family, they acted like long lost friends. Within one meeting, all of our mothers had planned coffee dates, shopping trips, and other adventures. The dads had bonded, making plans of their own. Then you had Nan.

She was the only grandparent living or living with the same state. Scout had her grandmother left, but she had moved the year after they lost her grandfather after helping Scout settle into the bookstore. I had my dad's dad who was currently in some other country doing who knows what. He and my grandmother had been young when they had my dad, so he was still very active. My mom's parents were still living, but that relationship went up in flames years ago. That left Nan being the go-to grandma, and she loved it. She was a typical granny who knew everything about everything and everyone. Only difference between her and most others was that she was right almost all the time. She was going to have a field day with this little development.

I finished loading the wagon we kept near the wood pile up and returned to the fire. I noticed immediately that only Scout was outside.

Her head was still back, her eyes closed. She was gorgeous. I spoke softly, not wanting to startle her, "Sweetheart, where's Leland?" I wasn't panicking, but he had gotten spooked earlier. If I had to hunt him down and drag him out here, I would.

"I can hear your brain running. He went in to get a couple of blankets and one of his hoodies for me." A soft smile played on her lips. "And I told him to grab one for you, too." She cracked an eye to look at me. I wasn't normally someone who blushed, but I felt my cheeks and ears start to warm. It was like I was a teenager again, talking to my crush about my other crush. It was a small thing, just a sweatshirt, but warmth spread in my chest at the thought of being wrapped in Leland's smell.

"One blanket and sweatshirt for you, darling, and I heard a certain bee might also want one." Leland handed Scout hers and then held the other one to me. I looked from his outstretched hand to his face. He joked, but he looked a little bashful about the offering. I took the blanket first, laying it in the chair beside me, then reached for the sweatshirt. When I pulled it over my head, I caught the familiar smell of Leland, but also something else. Once I pulled it down, I realized the other scent: *Scout*. She must have worn this one after Leland. The sweet man in front of me looked away. "I thought you would like it if there was a little of both of us."

My heart. It just melted. I'm sure that will kill you, but honestly, what a way to go. I was a puddle of lovey goo.

Not wanting to make a big deal about it, I walked closer until I could grab the flannel he had on. *Wait.* That's *mine.* A company had sent samples and most were too big for me, but I kept them and would use them to layer up. This one fit Leland like it was made for him. "Thank you for the sweatshirt." I gave him a quick peck before I stepped around him. "Also, I like that shirt on you, teddy bear."

Scout sat in her chair, looking like she was watching a romcom. She had a giddy smile on her face and looked like she was about to burst. "That was so sweet. I don't know how you haven't been a thing before." She paused as Leland sat down and I started passing s'more fixings around. As soon as we all had what we needed, Scout's dam burst. "Ok, you don't have to tell me, but have you two really never done or had anything intimate with each other?"

"No, we haven't had any kind of intimate relationship. We were just friends. I honestly thought Gat was straight," Leland answered before he looked at me. "I know the last few years have been crazy. You supported me so much when I came out. I should have made more time for you as my best friend. Not saying that you had to tell me or you owe me something. Shit, I'm messing this up. You can always talk to me. Ya know, if you need to." His brow was furrowed in frustration at himself before he looked down at the chocolate bar wrapper he was fidgeting with.

"Leland, no, don't do that. It has been a crazy few years. You can't be mad at yourself for not knowing." I waited until he was looking at me. "As amazing of a human being as you are, Leland, you can't read minds or see the future. You would have needed both and a lot of patience to find out anything. You had no way of knowing, I didn't really know. I honestly still don't." I reached my hand out for him and felt his big, warm palm wrap around mine. "I know what I feel and what I want, but I don't know that it has a label yet."

Scout stood and turned to the chair she had been sitting in, picking it up and moving it back. She grabbed the blanket off the chair and spread it out on the ground. When she was done, she walked back, coming to stand in front of us. "I know this is a serious conversation, but I can't keep sitting in the chairs so far apart. It may seem silly, but I feel like we need to be physically closer. Could we possibly cuddle or just all sit on the blankets?" She spoke fast, as if embarrassed by asking to be near us.

I stood first before extending my hand to Leland, pulling him to stand, as well. He reached back to grab the spare blanket off his chair before joining Scout and I. "Just so you are both aware, I am a cuddler. I like to cuddle and be cuddled," I stated in my most serious tone.

Leland looked at me with an expression of mock surprise. "No! You, enjoy cuddling?" He clutched his hand to his chest. "Gat, you forget I have shared a bed with you. You are like a damn spider monkey in your sleep." He looked at Scout. "His own family won't share a bed with him because when you wake up, he is attached to you like a leech. Try being a teenage boy sporting morning wood and your best friend who you lowkey have a—" He stopped talking and shot me a look.

"Do tell, teddy bear. A lowkey what?" Scout giggled as she tried to say the words.

I bumped his shoulder with mine. "Oh yes, please share with us. You know they say, sharing is caring." He squinted at me, trying to look menacing, I think. I had known him for too long to be intimidated.

"Ok. Fine. I had a crush on you. There. I said it. And you know what," he looked at Scout again, "I had one on you, too. From the first time we met. But someone else did, also. They got up an hour earlier for months to go run. You might be thinking, *well, Leland, that's not odd.* No, it's not, but said person did it so they could run when someone else was sitting on their back porch at their bookstore." I blinked at my best friend. I can't believe he just gave me away. Then in his best game show voice, he continued, "But wait there's more! Plot twist, because the reason the person sat on their deck was because the other person ran that early."

"Well since we're spilling tea, I think it's only fair we bring up why a certain bakery owner started to have some grand excess of items that were the exact flavors a certain bookstore owner liked." I gave Leland my best gotcha look. "And that the certain bookstore owner started sitting out back because that's when a certain someone would come out for a breather." Scout's mouth dropped open as she looked at me then to Leland. I couldn't see, but I knew she had to be blushing.

She held her hand to her chest in faux outrage. "I cannot *believe* you would snitch on me. I hate to say it, two can play that game, or three, in our case." She giggled a little at her own joke. "Bumblebee, care to tell what the other reason you got up so early was? If I remember correctly, you and a certain teddy bear kept missing each other because your schedules were off. So what do those people do? Not tell each other, no. One gets up ridiculously early and the other timed their breaks at that exact time." She mimicked a mic drop.

I sat for a moment. How had we not all noticed this? We had, over the last year or so, been timing our lives around each other. How many other things had we changed or done in order to be closer to each other? We had all seen what we did for each other, but never thought about it being for another reason. I had always been antsy when Leland and I didn't get to hangout or catch up. When I started spending time with

Scout, she became a part of that. I needed the breakfast meetups. I looked forward to sitting and talking to them. It has been amazing having Scout here at the house because we were all together and it felt so right. I wanted to lighten the mood to say something that would make them laugh, but I wanted something else. I wanted to give them honesty and more.

"Come here, honeysuckle." I moved closer to Leland and patted the space between us. I relaxed back, Leland following my lead. Scout laid down on her back before rolling to her side and facing me. Leland grabbed her waist and pulled her close to him. I shifted closer to them both again, while still leaving a little space. I didn't want to pressure either of them. Some people didn't do a lot of physical touch. But I craved it. I especially wanted it from the two people in front of me. "Is this ok?" I ask, now sounding a bit unsure. Leland, being so big, reached over Scout and pulled me even closer. His fingers skated under the edge of my sweatshirt, finding bare skin. Goosebumps raced across my skin at the contact.

"The only thing that would make this better would be if we were naked," Scout spoke, catching me off guard with her words.

Leland's warm palm inched up the sweatshirt. "I mean, we don't have any close neighbors. Naked, outdoor cuddling would be fun."

I let out a shuttered breath. "I thought we were going to talk about things. Wasn't it the two of you who had things they wanted to talk about?" Scout stretched up, kissing the underside of my jaw. My brain short circuited, every thought that had just been there vanished. I let out a small whimper, that was completely manly and totally called for. *Holy sweet baby Jesus and all the wisemen.*

Scout continued to tease the column of my throat, nipping the skin then soothing the sting away with her tongue. Leland reached for her hand that was resting on my side, lacing their hands together with his palm covering the back of hers. He guided their hands down to rub the front of my pants. My dick was about to rip my pants open. They rubbed together, squeezing my hardening length.

"Oh, fuck. Yes, please," I shamelessly begged. I had been hard for what seemed like days—no, *years*. I needed release and damn, I needed it to be because of Leland and Scout.

I shifted my arm that had been draped across Scout to run my hand under the edge of her shirt. I paused, needing some sign that she wanted me to continue. She pulled her hand from Leland's to guide my hand higher. I cupped her through the bra, the thin material not hiding that her nipples were pebbled. I teased her momentarily before realizing that Leland hadn't started touching me again. "Leland, please touch me. Please." My voice was laced with want. He reached back down, the heat of his hand burning through my pants. I started to tweak Scout's nipples before kneading her breast. *Fuck this was so good.*

A sharp intake of breath had me opening my eyes. *When did I close them?* I didn't even know. I looked to see Scout's hand now running over Leland's impressive bulge. It was the hottest thing I had seen so far. It going to get a lot more intense if I had anything to do with it.

chapter 12

· · ·

leland

HOLY SHIT. *Was this actually happening?*

"Yes, Gat. Yes," Scout moaned before grinding her luscious ass back, firmly pushing on her palm. I see that Gatlin has rucked up the front of her shirt and pulled her bra up, exposing her beautiful, full chest. With her tit cupped in his hand, he pulls her nipple into his mouth, sucking the hardened point before taking it between his teeth and gently biting. Releasing the nipple, he pinched it between his thumb and forefinger. I could come just from watching them pleasure each other.

I run one finger inside the rim of Gatlin's pants, asking permission to touch him more. He responded by pushing further into my hand. I popped the button on the top of his pants, gently tugging the zipper down. I run my hand over his cock again, feeling the wet spot of precum. Fuck, he was leaking for us. He was leaking for *me*.

While I had been undoing his pants, he had turned his attention to doing the same to Scout. His hand now disappeared down the front of her pants.

"Is she wet for us, bee? Dripping and leaking like you are? Be a good boy and tell me about that greedy little pussy."

"Holy fuck, please keep talking like that," Scout spoke, her words clipped and breathy.

"That is hot as fuck." Gatlin's dick gave a twitch of agreement.

In response, I moved his briefs down, freeing him before grabbing and giving him a stroke. "Mmm you are so hard, baby." I ran the tip of my thumb over his head. "Look at all that precum, darling." Scout's eyes were glued to where I held Gatlin. "He is twitching like crazy, honeysuckle."

Gatlin let out a hiss when I rubbed over the tip again. He pushed involuntarily into my hand, chasing friction. He wasn't the only one, Scout was pushing her hips forward, crushing mine and Gatlin's hand together. I paused my slow teasing of Gat. "Bee, you haven't answered me. How wet is she? Could you just slide right in?" I punctuate the sentence with a squeeze of his dick.

"*Fuck*, yes she is dripping. Her panties—" His words were cut off when I licked my palm, bringing it back to his cock and began stroking him in slow, measured pulls.

"What was that? Use your words for me."

"Her panties are soaked." His words rushed out in a single breath.

Scout had now gotten my pants open and was starting her own ministrations of my cock. "Just like that. Fuck, I want to take you both in and do so many dirty things to you. Want to fucking claim you as mine." My filter was gone. I was going to tell them everything if I wasn't careful.

Scout let out a little cry before speaking, "Please. Please I want you both. Please, I need you." Our movements paused for a moment. Gatlin's gaze met mine over Scout.

"If we do this, there is no going back," Gatlin whispered, the slight notes of nervousness giving away his fears.

"As far as I'm concerned, we crossed that line earlier," I stated matter-of-factly. When you kiss and have basically a masturbation session, the line is long gone. Especially when feelings have long simmered beneath the surface. "Are you ok with this, bee? It's ok if you aren't ready."

"Fuck yes, I'm ready." To drive this point home, he pulled his hand from Scout's pants and stood. His pants clung to his muscular thighs, not allowing them to fall. "Let me dump sand on the fire and then we are going upstairs to continue this."

Within minutes, he had the fire out and had collected all the stuff from around the fire, speed walking toward the house. The cool down we were getting was not at all a bad thing. I had been on a knife's edge of coming. I pulled Scout to stand, not bothering with my buttoning up my pants, either. I bent to hook my arm under Scout's legs and scooped her up bridal style. "We better hurry, honeysuckle."

I leaned in to kiss her as we made our way to the house. Once inside, Gat dumped everything on the kitchen table and stepped in close. I let Scout down, sandwiching her between us. I turned her to face Gatlin and pulled her back into my chest. I left one hand on her waist, reaching the other and hooking it in Gat's belt loop to lock him in close to us. I leaned down next to her ear, my words coming as a low command. "Kiss him." They both immediately reacted to my words with a soft whimper of need. *Interesting.*

With both hands, she reached up, pulling Gatlin's hair down from the bun he had put it in. She combed her fingers through his caramel brown strands, the dim glow of the kitchen catching the streaks of blond. Tangling her hand, she maneuvered him where she wanted. Their lips met, the kiss starting like a slow fire. One of Gatlin's hands reached to clasp the back of Scout's neck, the other coming to rest on my hip. He snaked his hand under the edge of my shirt, his calloused fingers rubbing across my skin. The warmth of his touch caused a shiver to race up my spine. At that, I felt one of Scout's hands snake up and hook around the back of my neck. The things their touch did to me. It was hard to tell where one of us ended and the others began. There were hands touching and feeling everywhere. It was too much, but at the same time not enough.

They both pulled back for air, their chest rising and falling with heavy breaths. Scout's head rested on my chest as Gatlin looked at her then me, his expression blissed out. I shifted so I could reach down to take Scout's chin between my thumb and forefinger. I turned her face to mine, dominating the kiss from the moment our lips touched. On a gasp, I licked into her mouth, exploring every inch I could reach. The continuous assault on her mouth muffled her moans and whimpers. I felt more than saw Gatlin's gaze. His hand was now teasing the edge of my jeans and boxers. Enough of this kitchen foreplay.

I broke the kiss with Scout, taking her hand and spinning her to face me. Before she could react, I squatted slightly, wrapping a hand around the back of her thighs to throw over my shoulder. She let out a little squeak and then giggled. I reached back, grabbing Gatlin's hand. When his fingers laced with mine, he gave them a little squeeze. With Scout on my shoulder, I moved my hand and swatted her ass lightly. "Time to take this party somewhere more comfortable."

I was met with a *fuck yes* from both of them.

I couldn't agree more.

gatlin

As we made our way to the bedroom, my mind raced. I had no clue what I was doing when it came to being with a man. I knew how to be with women. I hadn't slept around per se, but I was no blushing virgin, either. I could say one thing without a doubt, though—bossy Leland was doing it for me. Combine that with Scout's sweet and open energy, I felt like I had died and gone to heaven. When we made it to Leland's door, I reached around to open it. He released my hand before he crossed the room, leaning down to let Scout gently fall from his shoulder. She landed on the bed, letting out a little puff of air. Her eyes glittered with happiness and excitement. *Me too, baby.*

"Before we continue, we need to talk about some things. I have been tested and I'm negative for everything. I can pull up my most recent results," Leland spoke, going from playful to serious.

Scout sobered. "I'm clean and I'm on birth control. While the IUD is a bitch to get in, I can't forget to take it."

Both their gazes fell to me. "I was tested about a two years ago, but I haven't been with anyone since." *Because the two of you have consumed my thoughts.* Locking that thought away, I looked between the two of them. "Now that we have all the boring business handled, we can have fun now, right?" I paused before adding, "Daddy?" throwing a wink to Scout.

Leland turned to me, looking more predator than man. He took one step forward. While I wasn't scared of Leland, I had no intention of making things easy on him. I shifted one foot back. Faster than I could have imagined, he snatched my wrist, using his strength to pull me to him. His other hand came up to cup my cheek. His intense gaze made me squirm. When he leaned in and kissed me softly, I was caught off guard. My body melted under his lips.

"Don't be a brat. If you run, I will chase you," another soft kiss, "I will catch you, and there will be a punishment."

Holy fucking fuck.

Our heads turn to the bed where Scout was reclined back on her elbows, watching us with want and need. She surprised us both with her words. "Strip each other." *Oh, bossy Scout, too.*

"Careful, honeysuckle, don't want to upset the bear by giving it orders." I snicker a little. The swat of Leland's hand on my ass had me sucking in a breath. *Was I into getting spanked?* My dick was trying to jailbreak from my boxers, so that would be a yes. Leland crowded toward me, forcing me to move closer to the bed. Once there, he didn't move away.

Without saying a word, he took his time giving me a full once-over. He reached to palm my cock before moving his hand away. He still didn't speak as he pulled the sweatshirt and shirt over my head. His mouth ghosted over my ear before he placed open mouthed kisses down my neck and to my chest. With one hand, he reached up to tweak my hardened nipple.

"We need to put on a good show for our girl. Don't hold back those sweet sounds. I want to hear how much you like my hands on you." With that, he latched his mouth onto my other nipple. I had never really had someone play with my chest, but damn it if it didn't feel amazing. I let out a low groan, my back arching with the new sensations. Taking the bud between his teeth, he bit down lightly before swirling his tongue and sucking it gently. If he didn't touch my dick soon, I was going to lose my mind. I wanted more, but knew it wouldn't take much more to make me come.

"Yes, Leland. Fuck that feels so good, baby." The endearment came out easily. My hands reached up to the sides of his head, trying to pull him, even closer if possible. A low rumble was his reply, the vibration moving through his mouth. He switched hands, moving his mouth to the other nipple. The cool air caused the moisture to chill, goosebumps covering my skin. With his right hand now free, he reached down to tug at my jeans. I drunkenly moved my hand down to help him push my pants to the floor. His warm hand started to stroke my rock-hard cock through my briefs. I have no words, only moans and whimpers for what his touch was doing. I did as he told me—I let every noise loose. The visible wet spot made it obvious how on board I was with what we were doing. Leland straightened, releasing my abused nipples. He hooked his fingers in the band of my briefs, pulling them down before letting them fall. He reached back to grab his shirt before pulling it over his head and tossing it to the side. With his pants still unbuttoned, it didn't take much for them and his boxers to puddle around his ankles.

Small is not the word you would use to describe Leland's body— and that included his dick. He was long and thick. For the first time in all the years of changing in front of each other, I truly looked at my best friend. I let my eyes trail over his body, truly appreciating the man. I was left speechless, which wasn't something that happened often. Leland stepped closer before placing a soft kiss on my lips.

His eyes locked with mine. "We take things slow. You are leading this." His hand was in mine, grounding me like he always had.

I still lacked the ability to form a full sentence and all I managed was a quiet, "Okay."

With that, he turned so my back rested against his chest, both of us facing the bed. If I was a teenage boy, I would have cummed everywhere, hands-free. Scout had moved up so she rested against the headboard; one hand under her shirt, the other doing dirty things in her pants. Even in the low light, the visible movement told what she was doing. I was even more turned on knowing that Scout had been watching. Our girl liked the little show.

"Is it ok for Leland to touch you, bee?"

"Yes, please." I barely got the words out as I felt Leland move our clasped hands to cross over my chest. His free hand came to rest on my stomach, the muscles twitching at the warm contact.

I was startled a little when Leland spoke, "Look how hard our sweet bee is. Should we give him a little relief?" His hand slid down, his finger grazing my throbbing dick, slowly tracing his fingers up and down my length. My body jerked forward slightly, my hips chasing the friction my cock craved. "Look at all that precum." He closed his hand around the swollen head, swiping his thumb across the tip. "Come here, honeysuckle. We need you." He continued to stroke me lazily until Scout stood before me.

Scout stripped her clothes slowly, almost teasingly. Between Leland's slow gentle strokes and Scout's teasing strip show, I was going to go mad. She finally pushed her bottoms and panties down before kicking them to the side. I let out a groan, feeling Leland's hot body against mine while watching the absolute goddess in front I needed more of.

As if hearing my silent plea, Scout dropped, batting Leland's hands away. With his hands now free, he roamed them over my body. Just as he moved back to my nipple, I felt Scout's warm, wet lips wrap around my tip. My hips jump slightly, pushing me further into her mouth. She reached one hand up to cup my balls as she bobbed up and down my length. She was taking me deeper than most women have. I was around average girth, but I have length that most don't. My hands tangled in her hair. She didn't need me to guide her—I needed to know this was really happening. Her mouth was fucking heaven.

I felt Leland's scruff rub the side up my neck before he kissed his way to my ear. Once there, he took the lobe, giving it a gentle suck before biting down. It sent an almost painful jolt of pleasure straight to my balls. "Open your eyes and look at our girl. She looks too good on her knees to miss." My eyes opened at the command to see Scout working me over. Fuck, was he right. This was what dreams were made of.

When our eyes met, she took me down her throat before pulling back. "Fuck, baby. Yes, please." She did it again, taking me deeper each time. Scout moved one hand to wrap around me. She was doing this twisting thing with her wrist every time she pulled off. By the second or third time, I could feel my balls starting to draw up. I didn't want this to end. I wanted them with me when I went over the edge. This was not something I was used to with intimate partners. I always tried to put my partners' needs before my own. If the girl I was with was happy and orgasming, then I was good. I got pleasure by giving it. Even though they were focusing their attention on me, I knew they were also enjoying this. But I needed more, I needed to give something to them.

I tugged Scout's hair back, gently signaling for her to pull off. She looked at me with concern at first. "If we keep going like that, I'm going to blow before we really get started." I stroked the side of her face before extending my hand to her. She kept eye contact as she stood, her pupils blown wide, the pink flush across her cheeks highlighting the spray of freckles across her nose. *She is beautiful.*

Looking at Scout and feeling Leland close at my back, there were so many things running through my mind. I knew I would have to sift through it all at some point, but I wanted this. That was something I knew with absolute certainty, I wanted them. *You always have,* the quiet voice whispered the words in my head.

"Gat, are you ok? We can stop," Scout spoke, her words low as her eyes searched my face. I gave a subtle shake of my head. I didn't want to stop. I leaned in to kiss her softly.

"I know you are both worried about me, but I trust you." I looked over my shoulder at Leland. "Both of you. I will tell you if I need to slow down or stop. I expect the same from both of you." I held both of their gazes for a moment.

Scout spoke first. "I stand by what I said earlier. I want you both." She punctuated her words with a squeeze of my hand.

I felt warm lips on my neck. My head fell back onto the firm chest of my best friend and soon to be lover.

Lover. The thought sent a shiver up my spine.

"I want nothing more than to be with the two of you." Leland's arms came around me. One stayed wrapped around my waist while the other reached for Scout. "So we are all on the same page?"

"Yes," Scout and I answered at the same time.

"Bee, lay down on the bed." I moved before he had time to finish the sentence. Every ounce of my being wanted to do what he told me. I propped myself up on my elbows, waiting for the next move. "As for you, honeysuckle, you did so good sucking his dick, I think he owes you a little something." He paused before he turned Scout to face the bed. "You are going to sit on his face and let him taste your needy pussy while I get to see how your amazing mouth feels."

Hot. Damn.

chapter 13

. . .

A WHIMPER ESCAPES my lips at his words. *Holy shit*. Bossy bedroom Leland had a mouth on him. I had already been dripping from watching them together and giving Gatlin head. This was by far the hottest thing I had ever done. As if he read my mind, Leland slid one hand down, running it gently through my folds. His finger lightly grazed my swollen clit. He moved easily through my wetness.

When he circled my clit with his finger, an audible cry forced its way out. "You are so wet, baby." He moved back and forth. "I could probably just slip right in."

I sucked in a breath as his finger breached me. "Fuuuck."

He thrust his finger before removing the digit and popping it into his mouth. "Oh, bee, she taste like heaven." He lightly swatted my ass, causing me to jump and let out a squeak. "Go give our boy a treat."

"Yes, sir." I moved quickly away, not looking to see if my words had an impact. If the sharp intake of breath said anything, they hit their mark.

I walked to the side of the bed, crawling up at Gatlin's side. His eyes tracked over every inch of my body. I kissed him briefly before turning my back to him and straddling him. With me on his chest, his hands wandered up the inside of my thighs, getting so close to my aching center, but not touching it. I leaned forward, opening myself to him. Losing patience, Gatlin locked his arms around my legs, pulling me to meet his awaiting mouth.

"Oh God, yes." I clenched as he licked and sucked at my pussy. He avoided focusing on my clit, causing me to shift. Leland stepped forward, running his fingers through my hair.

"Open for me. Tongue out."

I let my mouth fall open, my eyes staying locked on Leland's. He gave his cock a few lazy strokes before tapping it on my tongue. "Look at that. Such a good girl."

Gatlin chose that moment to latch on to my clit, sucking the bundle of nerves. My walls clenched around nothing. As he continued, my legs trembled with a building orgasm. He pulled back slightly, running his tongue through my folds. He let out a low groan, the vibrations and shock of pleasure had me clenching again. The way he devoured me was unlike any man had. Most of the men I had been with were turned off by the idea of going down on a woman. Not Gatlin. He treated it like a delicacy.

"Fuck. I want to live between your legs." His breath ghosted over my wetness. "You taste like fucking heaven, baby." He punctuated his words by diving back in. I gasped at the way he attacked my pussy. He was like a starved man and I was his first meal. My body was on fire having Gatlin between my legs and Leland watching all of this play out while he stroked himself, letting me get close enough to taste him, but nothing more. He was teasing me as much as himself. One of his big hands came up to stroke my cheek. I was so overwhelmed with pleasure. Slowly, he began to thrust his smooth length into my waiting mouth. His movements were slow and measured, never too deep.

"Bee, you should see what a good little cock sucker our girl is." Leland's filthy words brought me closer to the edge. "Look at how hard we are for you, honeysuckle. Bee is being so good, not even touching his cock." My gaze flicked down, seeing the bead of precum leaking from Gatlin's tip. When I clenched at the sight of it, it gave a twitch. Gatlin shifted, trying to move to reach between his legs. Leland spoke, causing Gatlin to pause. "Not yet, bee." Gatlin released a frustrated sound before deciding to take it out on me and my poor clit. We stayed in this position for a while, Leland thrusting slowly in and out of my mouth and Gatlin making out with my pussy. I needed to come more than air at this point. Even with Gatlin eating me out like a champ, I wanted more.

I popped off Leland's dick, stroking it as I moaned and ground my hips into Gatlin's face, before leaning in and licking Leland from root to tip. When I reached the tip, I pulled it back between my lips. Gatlin moved from just his mouth to working a finger into me. When he slipped a second finger in, I moaned around Leland. His hips gave an involuntary thrust. When he went to pull back, I wrapped my hands around his thighs, giving him a little tug. His cock slid down my throat. I tilted so I could look up and meet his gaze, holding the position until my eyes began to water.

"You want me to fuck that pretty face, baby?" He pulled back, his length falling from my mouth.

"Yes, sir."

Both men paused, a groaned *fuck* coming from both. "Tap my leg if it is too much." I gave a nod before opening my mouth back up for him. Leland wrapped my hair around his fist. He began to thrust his hips forward, Gatlin matching the rhythm with his fingers. My orgasm was barreling towards me like a train.

"I'm not going to last long, baby. Your mouth is fucking sinful." Leland's deep voice sounded even huskier than usual. "Bee, make our girl come all over your face and you will get a treat."

That one sentence turned Gatlin into a mad man. He curled his fingers, the tips searching for my g-spot. When he found the little sponged spot, I was a goner. Moving his mouth back to my clit, he massaged the spot until I was clenching around his fingers. *Fuck. Fuck. Fuck.*

I shattered, trying to keep my focus on Leland's dick as my walls pulsed. Gatlin continued to move and twist his fingers, working me through my climax. Leland stopped thrusting and pulled me off his cock, furiously stroking his length.

"Where do you want it, baby?" His words were strained by the need to release.

"Come on my tits. Mark me." *Well hello, Miss Horny Pants.*

Gatlin's talented mouth was driving me closer to another climax. "Yes, bee. Fuck, you are going to make me come again," I whimpered. "So good, baby." As my orgasm began, I let out a pleasurable scream, my body shaking. "Oh fuuuuck. Fuck yes. I'm coming." I felt Leland's warm cum paint my skin, some getting on my face while most landed on my chest. He let out a low, guttural groan as he pulled the last drops from his orgasm.

Gatlin's hips gave a little thrust, his cock seeking friction. I raised up and moved off of him, releasing his hands from where they had been trapped. He immediately moved to squeeze the base of his dick. Turning to me, he reached over to grab my shoulders, giving me a gentle push back. I fell back on the bed, his body covering mine. He leaned forward, taking my mouth in a hard kiss. Releasing my lips, he moved down to my neck, sucking and biting the skin before he did something that shocked both Leland and I. When he reached my chest, he paused for a moment before leaning down and licking Leland's cum from my skin.

"Holy shit, bee." Leland had moved to sit on the edge of the bed beside us. Slowly reaching out one of his hands, he ran his fingertips along my arm, the touch leaving goosebumps in its wake. He then moved to gently comb them through Gatlin's hair and down his back. He touched Gatlin's hip, nudging him to move off me. "It's your turn, sweetheart. If you just want Scout this time, that's ok. There is no rush." Our sweet teddy bear, always looking out for his people.

"No. No. Please I need..." Gatlin closed his eyes as if trying to collect his thoughts. "No, need you both. Want you both to touch me." His words were low and almost pleading.

gatlin

I didn't know what was going to happen next, but I knew what my body was screaming for. There was no way I was only getting one of them. That was not what this was. Leland stood and walked back to the foot of the bed. He reached up and grabbed my calves, pulling me to the edge of the bed. An unexpected laugh came out at the sudden movement. Scout turned so her head was facing the end of the bed. I raised myself up on my elbows to watch them. When soft lips landed on my hip bone, my head fell back, releasing a sigh. Another set of lips kissed the other side. Hands moved across my skin, running over my stomach and legs, but never touching my cock. I thrusted my hip up, trying to tell them in a not so subtle manner where I needed them to be. Scout shifted again, piling pillows up at my back then sandwiching herself between me and them.

"Lean back on me, bee." She kissed my shoulder. "We have you." She moved my hair and kissed my neck. My lids fell closed again.

"Look at me." My eyes popped open, connecting with Leland's heated gaze. "I want you to watch who is worshiping your cock." I gave a shaky nod, full of anticipation. "Words, sweetheart."

"I don't think I will be able to look away." I tried to infuse every ounce of conviction I felt into my words. I couldn't say I was exactly nervous, but this was new for me. I appreciated them taking their time and checking in with me, but now I needed action. "Please, I need to come."

Leland's pupils grew darker, his heat-filled expression not hiding the paper thin control he had over his lust. His big hand reached up to circle my cock, tilting the tip toward his mouth. With our eyes locked and Scout's plush lips kissing over my neck, my best friend lowered to take my tip in his mouth. *Jesus, Mary, Joseph, and all the wisemen.*

"Oh God, bear." My hands reached to grip his head as he took more of me into his warm, wet mouth. My fingers tangled in the longer hair on top of his head. He hollowed out his cheeks as he bobbed his head up and down my length. *Shit.* I wanted to last, but there was no way.

"Mm look at our big strong man sucking your dick. Does it feel good, baby?" Scout spoke low in my ear.

"It's so good—Oh *God*, yes bear. Fuck."

Scout reached around to tweak my nipple, sending a spark straight to my groin. My hips gave a little thrust. My eyes were still glued to Leland as he moved even lower, my cock hitting the back of his throat. He slid one hand up my thigh, resting on the hand I had on his head. Without pulling off, he told me what he wanted me to do. He wanted to *deepthroat* me. I mean, that was what he was currently doing, but he wanted *more. Yes. Yes. Yes,* my inner voice screamed and boy, did I agree.

Scout's warm breath ghosted over my ear when she spoke, "Do you want to come down his throat?" She ran her tongue over the shell of my ear while she pinched my nipple. Leland had started to move again before he pulled off.

"You are going to fuck my throat with that beautiful cock and then come down my throat." His big hand was stroking and squeezing my dick. "Because you want to be good for me, right? If I need to stop, I'll tap your leg." He gave a little twist of his wrist at my tip. I nodded furiously. "Words," he commanded.

Holy shit.

Was I dead? I had to be, right? "Yes, I want to be good for you and fuck your throat and—" My words were cut off when Scout raked her teeth down my neck. "Please. Please let me fuck your throat. I want to come." Leland's reply came in the form of taking me to the back of his throat. "Oh fucking fuck." His hand moved off mine, which spurred me to start thrusting. I did as I was told, taking his throat with deep thrusts. I came to three realizations:

First, Scout had unlocked nipple play for me.

Second, having both of them was exactly where I was meant to be.

And third, Leland had no gag reflex.

When I felt a tug on my balls, I was so close to blowing. "More. Need more," I panted out the words. He ran his hand back up to my cock, gathering some of the spit at my base. The same hand returned, only this time, below my sack. He massaged my rim with his moistened finger without breaching my entrance. "I'm not going to last." His finger continued to rub and apply pressure while Scout pinched and tweaked my sensitive nipple. Leland moaned as Scout once again spoke low in my ear.

"Come, baby. Coat his throat."

"Yes. Fuck, I'm coming." I drove deep, releasing most of my load down his throat. Before I finished, Leland moved off, collecting the last spurts in his mouth. *That is so hot.* When he popped off my dick, he leaned over me, one hand resting on the bed with the other wrapped around the back of Scout's neck, pulling her to him in a hard kiss. He opened, sharing my release with her. If I had any cum left in me, I would be blowing again. He broke the kiss with Scout, turning to me before giving me the same treatment. He dominated my mouth. The mix of flavors was almost overwhelming. Pulling back and taking my chin between his thumb and forefinger, he turned me to Scout. We didn't fight for control, we just sunk into the kiss. Our tongues tangled for a moment before we were pulling back.

"Did I die? Is this heaven?" My body was completely sated, causing my words to be sluggish.

Leland let out a low chuckle before he spoke as Scout kissed my shoulder. "No, bee, you are definitely very much alive."

"Good. But damn, that would have been a way to go." I shifted off the bed, reaching a hand out for Scout. "So clean up and cuddle, right?"

Scout let out a happy little sigh. "Yes, please."

With that, we moved to the bathroom before all piling in the bed. Scout laid between myself and Leland, her back pulled close to his chest. I moved in close to her front, reaching up a hand to stroke her hair before moving my hand to find Leland. Moving one of his hands to my hip connected us all. And it felt *perfect.*

chapter 14

· · ·

leland

WHEN I WAKE the next morning, I realized last night was not a dream. I had Scout's warm body pulled close while Gatlin's fingers were laced with mine, where they rested on her hip. I took a moment to study both of them. They were both beautiful in their own way. Scout with her doll-like features and fair skin. Then Gatlin, tan with the sprinkle of freckles across his nose. They looked almost angelic with their hair fanned across the pillows. I could look at them every minute of the day and I would still be in awe of them.

I shifted slightly, trying to untangle myself. While I would love to stay here with them, my bladder was screaming for the bathroom. I watched their faces, trying to make sure I didn't wake them. Gatlin's arm wrapped around Scout's waist, pulling her closer. His chin now rested above her head, her face now buried in his neck. I took one last look before heading to the bathroom. I would fight for this. For them and us. If they wanted there to be an us, then I would make damn sure it happened.

ONCE I LET MUD OUT, I got everything together to make food. I thankfully had enough time to make breakfast and was just moving to the coffee maker when I heard footsteps coming down the hall. I turned to see a shirtless Gatlin walking in. He still looked half asleep as he combed his fingers through his hair, pulling it in a low bun, his gym shorts hung low on his hips. The sculpted muscles of his torso on full display. He had a trail of hair disappearing into the waistband. Which I now knew led straight to his dick surrounded by the same colored hair.

That fucking cock.

If I would have died last night, it would have been after the best sex of my life. My wet dreams had nothing in reality. I *craved* more of it. I could pound nails with how hard I was. The sounds and sights of last night ran through my mind like a movie. It was completely unplanned, but totally welcome.

I turned to grab the mugs of coffee and told him good morning when I felt his hard chest press into my back. The warmth from his body seeped through my shirt, heating my skin. He turned his head to the side, his cheek resting at my shoulder. "Good Morning." Gatlin's voice was still sleepy and rough. "Why are you up? It's the weekend and you don't have to work."

I set the mugs back on the counter and turned so we were chest to chest. When he reached around me, my arms did the same. Gatlin had always been physically affectionate, not to this extent, but still more than other guys. It was one thing that, in my younger years, kept the flames of my crush alive. Once I got a bit older, I shoved those feelings down. Now the little spark I thought long extinguished was becoming a raging forest fire. He was like this with most people he knew, just dialed back. *Besides Scout.*

"Good morning, I woke up and decided to make breakfast. Is Scout awake?" My voice came out a little rougher from not speaking yet.

As if realizing there was breakfast, he began to perk up. "Breakfast!

And yes, she is." He turned toward the stove, turning his back to me. "Are those Nan's biscuits and gravy?"

I was too captivated by his back and exposed neck to reply. *Fuck it, time for a risk.*

Circling his waist, I pulled him back against me. A surprised puff of air escaped his lips. I leaned close to his neck, running my nose over the sensitive skin. Once I reached his ear, I kissed the same path before returning to his ear. I sucked his lobe between my teeth, giving it a nip. The only noise I heard come from the man in my arms was a sharp intake of breath. I ran the hand that was wrapped around him lower, not touching his dick, but resting just over his abdomen. His body became even more relaxed. "That's it, lean into me. Eyes closed and keep them that way."

I caught movement out of the corner of my eye. Scout stood at the entrance of the hallway. I nodded for her to join. Without a word, she crossed the kitchen, coming to stand in front of Gatlin. She ran her hands up to his chest before bringing them to his waist. I spread my legs a little wider and leaned more heavily on the counter. With a tug, Gatlin was pressed against my groin. Reaching around Gatlin, I grabbed Scout, pulling her until she was flush with him. She leaned forward to place kisses over his chest. I watched her for a moment and listened to the soft noises coming from Gatlin.

I leaned around Gatlin just slightly then take his chin, using it to turn his face to mine. His eyes were still closed. I covered his mouth with mine. He opened immediately, granting me access to his mouth. Our tongues moved against each other for a moment before a small hand reached to turn Gatlin's head to hers. They exchanged the sexiest kiss I had ever witnessed before breaking free. Then Scout leaned to give me the same treatment.

"Well, that is a *very* good morning," Scout spoke, her voice lower and filled with lust. "I want more, but I am also starving and I require coffee." She leaned against Gatlin, his body weight pressing him closer to me. "We don't want the dark side Scout to come out," she joked, but it was honestly true. Scout probably bled coffee. She pulled back and moved to grab a mug of coffee. Gatlin gave a little chuckle before he took his coffee. I immediately missed the weight and warmth of them.

"We can't have that. It's a good thing Papa bear is always taking care of us." Gatlin's usual ribbing let me know that he was ok. We needed to talk about all of this. That was the only way we can make a go of this.

Scout giggled before her eyes meet mine. "What did you make us for breakfast, Papa bear?" A smile stretched across her face. Those two picked up that nickname up from Seb, and now they pulled it out to poke at me. The only thing was, it rang a little true for me. Ok, maybe more than a little. When Seb said it, my body did not have the same reaction. Out of their mouths, a whole new side of me tried to push out.

I didn't think I was a Daddy dom, but I liked to take care of them. *Liar.* Ok, so I *was* a Daddy dom. It just fit with how I operated. I didn't want that dynamic in day-to-day life, but I did like taking care of my people. Even before this, I looked out for them and their needs. Now those needs were of a different variety.

Focus, Leland!

I cleared my throat before speaking. "Biscuits and gravy," I confirmed. "There is more coffee in the pot."

"I could just kiss you." Scout paused for a moment. "Oh wait, I did that already," she said, giggling at her own joke. "I'm going to grab my medicine to take. You guys go ahead and start."

Gatlin and I both shook our heads. "We can wait on you," I added. No way were we going to dip our plates and start eating without her.

She gave us both a soft smile before disappearing back down the hall.

Once she returned, we loaded up our plates and grabbed our coffee mugs before digging in. We ate in comfortable silence, just enjoying being together. I was not the talkative twin. I always left the talking to Oakland. Most people were not comfortable with sitting in silence. To find not one, but two people who were comfortable to just sit in silence and take in moments was something I would never take for granted. I knew this couldn't last because we needed to talk things out. After yesterday's revelations, not talking wasn't an option. With breakfast done, it's time to have one of *the talks*.

Please let them want this.

gatlin

I could see it on Leland's face before he said a word that he wanted to talk about last night. I prayed, for his safety, that he had let that bullshit go from yesterday. There were so many thoughts rattling around in my head. I didn't want to spiral down, but this was an area I knew little to nothing about. *Relationships.* I knew how to treat my partners, but this was new and different. I stared at him, trying to see into his mind. "Just know that if you start this talk with some shit like you did yesterday, I'm not going to hold Scout back," I said, trying as always to lighten the mood.

"I won't go easy on you, either. So be advised," Scout added in.

We waited for what felt like hours when it was actually mere seconds. "I'm not, and honestly, it is the complete opposite of what I was saying last night. I'm sorry for all that I said. Just know that it was nothing to do with either of you. It was things that I had convinced myself of." Leland paused for a moment. "I thought about it a lot last night and this morning. What if we did this?" I gave what I hoped was a curious look. Surely, he didn't mean like us together past the bedroom? *Right?*

"What do you mean?" Scout spoke first, her words almost hesitant.

Leland cleared his throat before laying it all out there. "I want you. Both." He looked between us. "I'm not talking about just for sex and fun. I want us."

Holy fucking fuck.

"I understand this isn't conventional, but I don't care about that. Last night was the best night of my life." He looked down to his lap. "I don't want to mess up what we have, but I can't ignore what I am feeling." He looked back up, the sincerity and openness showing on his face.

I let out a shaky breath before asking, "You want there to be an *us*? Like me and Scout, and you and Scout?" I needed to confirm that he did in fact want me like I wanted him. The knot in my stomach tightened painfully, dread and hope mixing. My hands were clenched into fist on the table. I knew he said both, but both to me right now had too little detail. My thoughts were raging. Time had basically stopped between what he said and now.

Scout reached for my hand, taking it with a soft smile. My brain immediately quieted. She gently squeezed my hand and turned back to Leland. "Is that what you mean? Us? Are you just sharing me *or*...?"

His head snapped up, the words rushing from him. "No, I mean the three of us together, as one. I want to *be* with both of you. I underst—"

"Yes," Scout and I answered at the same time. Before he had time to register what was said, we rounded the table to him. We collide with a still sitting Leland sandwiched between us. Scout turned his face to hers, kissing him. When she pulled back, I did the same. Then Scout and I leaned around him, to share our on kiss.

We pulled apart, smiling like fools. "So we are dating? Like the three of us?" Scout looked between us.

"Hell yes, we are!" I said, adding a fist pump.

Leland let out a chuckle. "You're a dork."

"He is, but he is our dork," Scout added to the teasing.

Theirs. I really liked that.

chapter 15

. . .

scout

I WAS STILL in shock on Monday because of the events of the weekend. I was dating two hot guys. Other than some heavy make out sessions, we had not gone any farther. I wasn't complaining, because it was hot as hell. I also loved seeing how they were with each other. There had been an invisible divide that was gone. It wasn't even the physical displays, the things they did in "secret" were out in the open. With being friends already, there wasn't a lot we didn't know about each other, but we took time to talk about what we wanted in our relationship. One thing being that we didn't have to all be present to be together or with each other. We all agreed that there was absolutely no jealousy between us when it came to each other. I had been in relationships with guys who had no clue how to talk things through. That was the other major point, talking openly and honestly about what was going on. Gatlin had lovingly told Leland he could not shut down and push things down. While it was not his intention, his comments had hurt Gatlin and me. With the air cleared, we bummed around watching movies, talking, and making out. A lot. I may have been masking some beard burn with this morning's makeup.

The back door opening pulled my attention from thoughts of the weekend. "Spill it," Lettie said as she entered the office. The store had been open for a few hours, but she had offered to come in so I could do administrative work and orders.

"No *good morning*? Geez, the least you could give me is a *hello, how was your weekend*?" I looked at her with a little smirk. I had sent her a very vague message about the developments of the weekend.

She gave me a deadpan stare, daring me to keep going. "I need the details. I understand that sarcasm and torture are your love language, but as your best friend, spare me this once. Did you get a double dicking or not? The beard burn you are trying to conceal says there was a little action. So I say again. Spill."

Coffee shot out my nose at her words. I grabbed napkins out of my desk drawer. "Really, Lettie?"

"Yes, Scout. Really." She gave me a moment to clean myself up then stared at me. She knew I wouldn't hold out.

"No, not technically. I mean, we made out most of the weekend, but that's as far as it went. Does oral count as double dicking?"

She let out a frustrated groan. "What must I do to be blessed in this way? To have two men wanting to do dirty things to me. Is there a god or goddess that requires a sacrifice?"

I let out a snort. This was why I loved her. There was no judgment, maybe a little jealousy, but mostly just happiness for me. I wanted to tell her everything, but it didn't feel right to share that Gatlin and Leland were intimate. She wouldn't think anything of Gatlin's sexuality, but that was for him to decide to share or not. A knock on the door halted our conversation. Finch, or rather Fin, stood, looking unsure and a little flustered.

"Well, hello there." Lettie turned on a megawatt smile upon seeing him. "What brings you here on this beautiful day, handsome?"

His expression was unreadable as usual. "You know why I'm here. You called in an order. The front of the bakery is swamped."

Lettie's eyes twinkled with mischief. She and Seb had joined forces to either soften Fin up or drive him to commit murder. I'm honestly not sure which will happen first. "They put you on delivery duty?" I asked him. His eyes never left Lettie though.

"Yes, ma'am."

She gave him a complete once over. "You are always such a gentleman, Finch. Thank you for bringing my order over. I wouldn't want to get hangry."

With a nod and a quiet, "You're welcome, Colette," he was gone, heading out to the front of the store.

I turn my gaze to Lettie. She was not looking at me, instead she watched Fin as he left. *Well, well, well.*

I cleared my throat and it caused her to jump. "Something you would like to share with the class, *Colette*?"

Snatching the bag off the desk, she took a massive bite of the cherry cream cheese Danish. She gave a hopeless shrug and said, "Oh no, my mouth is full. Can't talk. You know how rude that would be. Any who, gotta go, bye," briskly leaving my office. If she thought we were done talking about all that, she didn't know me well.

I WAS mid-email when my phone chimed.

> Bee: 12:05 p.m. Can you come over to the store?

> Me: 12:05 p.m. Of course. Is everything ok?

> Bee: 12:06 p.m. If I say no, would that make you come over faster?"

> Papa bear: 12:07 p.m. Bee.

> Bee: 12:08 p.m. Ok, ok, everything is fine. I promise.

> Me: 12:08 p.m. Coming.

Grabbing my keys, I headed for the door. Mud raised his head before laying it back down. "I'll be back, sweet boy."

I walked over to the back door of Gatlin's store and let myself in. I thought they would be in the back, but I didn't see them as I walked through. "Hello?"

"Up front." I heard Leland's deep voice call from somewhere in the store.

Just as I passed by one of the big changing rooms, an arm reached around me, pulling me in. My scream came out muffled when a warm palm landed over my mouth. I quickly realized that it was not just one person, but two. The hand moves away from my mouth, and the heated gazes of my two guys fill my vision. "What are you two doing? You almost gave me a heart attack."

Instead of words, their response came as action. I was pressed between their bodies, their mouths running over my neck. "We can't do this here. What if someone catches us?"

Leland pulled back slightly. "You'll need to be really quiet."

And there goes my panties.

Had I ever wanted to have sex in public? No. Did I want to now? Abofuckinglutely.

Gatlin took my mouth in a deep kiss, his tongue dancing with mine as a moan worked its way up my throat. I felt Leland's hand move down my body to the top of my pants. I went for slouchy business casual today in one of my favorite old-man sweater vests with a tank under it, wide-leg capris, and a pair of sneakers. A shiver moved over me when his warm fingers made contact with my bare stomach.

Gatlin pulled back from the kiss. I chased him for a moment when he spoke, "So needy. Are you wet thinking about getting caught? Do you want bear to check?"

"Please."

Leland's mouth was beside my ear when he whispered, "Please what, honeysuckle?"

"Touch me. Please."

Spinning me so my back rested against his chest, he undid my pants, but didn't move to pull them down. He instead slipped his hand down the front of my panties. A low groan left his lips when he found my dripping center. "She is fucking soaked." Leland's words came out as a low groan.

Gatlin moved in front of me, lifting my sweater and tank to reveal my bra. "Look at those gorgeous tits." He hooked his finger in the cups and pulled them down, setting both my breasts free. His hands kneaded them before he moved to my nipples, taking both the hardened points in his fingers and pinching them lightly.

"Oh fuck." My words came out louder than I intended.

With his free hand, Leland turned my face so he could bring his mouth to mine. He took over the kiss, melting my brain with how he moved his mouth. When Gatlin pulled my right nipple into his mouth, the sounds I made were muffled by the kiss.

My clit throbbed at the light contact Leland gave it. I needed to come. I jerked my head away from Leland's mouth, panting, "I need to come. Please." I didn't care at this point how needy or whiny I sounded. I felt Gatlin switch nipples, taking the other in his mouth to suck.

A bolt of heat rushed to my core when Leland pressed on my clit. He began to rub slow circles. This was not going to take long. Gatlin stood and took over kissing me while Leland worked me closer to climax.

"Are you going to come for us?" Leland spoke, low in my ear. He slipped one finger in, now grinding his palm against the swollen, sensitive flesh.

Gatlin latched back onto my nipples, sucking and licking them while Leland added a second finger before starting to pump. I was so close to going over. Gatlin took my nipple between his teeth, biting down gently and I came apart. "Yes, yes. I'm coming." My legs shook from how hard and fast the orgasm hit me.

My eyes were hooded when I noticed Gatlin reaching down to where Leland's hand was still in my ruined panties. Grabbing his wrist, he pulled the bigger man's hand from my pants before wrapping his mouth around the soaked digits.

"Dammit, bee. That's fucking hot." Leland stared at Gatlin who was licking him clean. When he was done, he pulled Leland to him, kissing him and sharing the taste of my release with him. The ease and comfort they had in their friendship stayed even as more developed between them. It was something that made it easier for me to be open with them and explore what this was.

"Let me take care of y'all." I went to kneel in front of them, still speaking in a low whisper.

Leland stopped me before Gatlin kissed me softly, shaking his head. "This was about you, honeysuckle." He ran his finger across my cheek and down my neck.

Leland kissed my neck before speaking at a normal volume, opening the door to the fitting room. "Also, the store is empty and locked." I gasped quietly at the realization. "There are only three people who get to hear the sounds you both make when you come apart, and they are standing right here." Oh, hot and bothered Scout really liked possessive Leland, and from the bulge tenting Gatlin's, pants he did, too.

"Plus, what kind gentlemen would we be? The first time we fully worship you, it will not be in the changing room of my store," Gatlin added with a quick peck to my lips. "Now, let's eat lunch so our man doesn't scare the youth and elderly with his horse dick." When he turned, Leland reached out and swatted his ass. Gatlin paused and smirked at him. "Next time, harder, please. *Sir*." He jumped out of Leland's reach, laughing as he moved through the store.

I snorted a little laugh before adding, "I think we should tie him up and teach him a lesson." It was said as a joke, but the squeeze Leland gave my hips where his hand still rested told me that he would very much enjoy the idea.

"I won't tell him until after we're done that it was your idea." He popped my butt with a swat as he passed me before following Gatlin.

Uh oh. Mouth, I believe you remember my foot.

I might have just gotten myself in the best kind of trouble.

leland

Ideas ran through my head at light speed. The whole time we ate, I thought of all the things I wanted to do to them. I had a few relationships in the past that had given me some experience with tying up my partners. I didn't do all the knots and ropes, but I had educated myself of the safety of using anything to bind someone. I wanted to be sure that what was going on wouldn't cause harm. While I had dated some assholes, no one deserved for their trust and safety to be at risk. With all that in mind, there were some things we would need to discuss.

While we had not gone past oral and hand jobs. I needed to know where Gatlin stood on the physical side of things with me. I knew he had penetrative sex with women, but what was his opinion about it with a man? I didn't mind either way—what we had done so far had been amazing and I genuinely didn't need more. In most of my relationships, I had topped. Not that I didn't like to bottom, it's just that most people saw a big, beefy guy and thought that I wouldn't want to be on the receiving end. The same went for Scout. If she never wanted to have penetrative sex, that would be completely good with me. I never understood the pressure people had for what was "sex" and what was not. I was getting to be near the two people I was head over heels for. What else could a man ask for?

After lunch and a quick but steamy kiss from Gatlin, Scout I headed back to the bakery. I would be leaving when Scout was ready to head home, while Gat would be staying later. The campout was in a few weeks, and he was going into full prep mode. Tonight, he would be at the store late for parents to drop final packets off, which meant he would be answering a million questions and wouldn't be home until late. An idea sparked. I pulled my phone out and fired off a message to Scout.

> Me: 1:15 p.m. Want to drive our bumblebee wild?

> Honeysuckle: 1:15 p.m. What did you have in mind?

Me: 1:16 p.m. I guess you'll have to see. XO

Honeysuckle: 1:17 p.m. (typing)

Honeysuckle: 1:18 p.m. That is not very nice, Papa bear.

Me: 1:18 p.m. See you soon, love.

With that, I put my phone up and got back to work.

WHEN THE BUZZER on the back door went off and Scout walked in, I did a double take. Glancing at the clock on the wall, it read well after five o'clock. I had gotten so caught up in preparing orders and trying some new recipes that I lost track of time. She crossed the room to where I was working.

She came to a stop as I turned to face her. I reached to tuck a loose strand of hair behind her ear as I pressed a soft kiss to her lips. "Hi, honeysuckle." My words ghosted across her lips. Her hands reached to grab the front of my apron, holding me in place as she sealed her lips more firmly to mine. She pulled back a moment later, her cheeks flushed pink. *Fucking adorable.*

She let out a contented sigh before leaning back to look at me. "Hi. How was your day?"

"Better now. Always brighter and better with you and bee around. I'm pretty much done if we want to head out." I kissed her one more time before stepping back and taking off the dirty apron.

"That sounds good." She moved with me toward the office for me to grab my stuff. "Oh, did you talk to Oakland? She said she messaged you earlier."

I grabbed my phone and saw I had a missed call from her and a few messages.

Oaktree: 2:07 p.m. THE LIGHT OF YOUR LIFE IS CALLING.

Oaktree: 2:10 p.m. Well, I see where I stand.

Oaktree: 3:45 p.m. Since you aren't answering, I called Scout. She gave me the ok to come over tonight and hang out with you guys. Glad she still loves me…Love you, bristle butt

Me: 5:46 p.m. We are about to leave the bakery. You will be permitted entry if you bring food.

Oaktree: 5:47 p.m. *Rolls eyes* Like I would forget. I'm also bringing some wine.

Me: 5:48 p.m. Disgusting. But fine, we'll see you at the house. Love you, oakleaf

Well, that changed my plans for the evening. I couldn't be mad, though. I loved spending time with my sister, really all my family. It had been a while since we had hung out.

"I guess we will have company tonight."

"Yeah, I think she is having a rough time at work. She was telling me the other week about a higher-up that has been micromanaging her team." Scout sat on the couch, waiting for me to finish packing up. "Sounds like the guy is a real piece of work."

The dude either had a death wish or was an idiot. My sister was the last person to try and step up against. Especially if she felt her team had been wronged. "Damn. I know that's hard on her. Hopefully he will move along." I turned to face Scout and asked with a smile, "Ready?"

She returned the smile before she replied, "Definitely."

chapter 16

· · ·

I GOT HOME from the store much later than anticipated. When I walked into the living room, Scout was curled up against Leland. Oakland and Leland were talking quietly. I loved Oakland, but I really wanted to kiss my people, curl up, and sleep. The weeks before the campout were nothing but preparing kids and parents. There was paperwork, a packing list, and endless questions. We had a handful of siblings that had done the trip and knew the drill. The new kids and parents had a learning curve when it came to the big trip. I was dead on my feet.

When I went to pass by the couch, Leland snagged my arm, his thumb rubbing across the underside of my wrist. He looked at me like he was expecting something. I leaned down, brushing a kiss across his full lips. A low moan rumbled up his chest. When we pulled apart, he had a small smile. Unable to stop myself, I pressed another kiss to his mouth. *God, I needed this.*

"There are some leftovers in the fridge if you are hungry." His eyes bore into mine, studying me. "Get you some and then come relax. You look exhausted."

"Dammit. I'm going to owe that old bat even more money now." Oakland's words broke through the moment. "And neither one of you better tell her I called her that. Also I'm *so* here for this." She gave an excited little shoulder wiggle.

I gently kissed Scout's head before I spoke to Oakland. "We would never snitch on you, oakleaf. Unless she offers me home cooked food—then you are on your own. There are only two people safe under those terms." I gave Leland's shoulder a light squeeze.

Once I had eaten and was settled into the couch, it didn't take long for my eyes to grow heavy. The low hum of Leland and Oakland talking lulled me to sleep.

I was tucked into Leland's big bed when I woke up later. I was curled around Scout's back with Leland at my back. I had always liked to be the little spoon, it was just never something the girls I had been with wanted. They were always the ones getting cuddled. Though nothing compared to this. It was so much more because of who it was spooning me, and I them.

I pushed farther back into his chest and his groin. I had given a lot of thought to that over the last few days. Hell, who was I kidding? I had thought about it more than that. There had been a few—scratch that, *many*—times over the years when I had slipped a finger in my back door when jacking off. I had even used a small prostate stimulator. Talk about a fucking orgasm. Those events were more frequent once the dreams of Leland and Scout started. I was curious to say the least. "Bee, I am going to be rock hard if you keep doing that." Leland's rough, sleepy voice was low in my ear.

What he had failed to realize was that Scout was also awake and grinding back into me. I couldn't stop even if I wanted to, which I definitely did not. She rolled over to face me, kissing up my neck and jaw. "I think that is what he wants, bear. He is getting so hard."

Their hands met at the band of my boxers. Scout grabbed the front, pulling it down for Leland. His hand slid in, his warm, rough palm sliding over my dick. The contrast between the smooth and rough only drove me higher. "Yes, please, that feels so good." He ran his thumb over my dripping head, collecting the precum and rubbing it into my skin.

He slowly jacked my cock, my hips involuntarily pumping into his hand. I was getting close to the edge when he stopped squeezing my base, stopping my climax. "Ugh no, please."

"Shh, baby. It will be worth it, I promise." Scout shifted. I felt her hands moving around my cock before she lifted her leg up and hooked it over my hip. Leland's fist wrapped around my length and helped guide it into her warm, wet pussy.

"Oooh fuck." I was doing everything in my power not to slam up into her.

Leland moved my hair away from my neck, kissing his way down to my shoulder. "Does she feel good, bee? Is that sweet pussy gripping you?" He pulled his hand that had been between us, running it down my side as Scout and I rocked together.

"She is so tight." My hips thrust forward when Scout tightened around me. "Dammit, I just want to fuck you into the mattress."

A breathy moan escaped her lips. "We can do that, but not right now. We have a plan for you, bee." She continued to rock, bringing me closer and closer to the edge.

"What do you want, bee? What do you need?" Leland whispered into my ear.

I didn't need time to think of an answer. I needed them both. I wanted them both. "Need both. Touch me, bear." I sounded almost whiny, but I could care less. I would beg if need be.

"Anyone says stop, we stop. Got it?" Our bear was always protecting us. We both gave our agreement. "Have you ever been restrained or tied up?"

His question threw me for a second. Scout rolled her hips again, causing me to moan. "No, but I have thought about it. Oh fuck, baby, you are so tight." At my statement, she clenched around me.

Leland rolled over and grabbed a tie from the floor. "Would you want to try something? You can say no."

"Oh hell yes, I want to. Please." I was buried deep in the woman I was falling for and the man I had unknowingly been in love with was going to tie me up. *Someone pinch me. I must be dreaming.*

Scout paused her movements while I moved my hands. Leland took my wrist in his hand and gently tied the tie around them. Once he was done, there was still enough for him to tie them to—*wait, what was he tying them to?* It was a fucking ring. Did Leland have a sex bed? We would be talking about this later. "Is that ok? Not to tight?" I shook my head. "Words."

"It's not too tight," I let out a breath before adding a quiet, "sir." Where it was normally a joke, I wanted to say it to him in that moment. I wanted him to hear me say it seriously. Scout had said it and I had seen the reaction he had. I wanted to give him that as well.

He kissed me while gliding his fingertips down to where my dick was still buried in Scout's dripping center. His fingers teased her clit, causing her to clench around me. *Dammit, that's so good.* "One more question, love. Be honest with me. Has anyone ever played with your hole but me the other night?"

My face flamed. It was one thing to do in the privacy of my room. *No. Honesty, Gatlin.* "Just my fingers and a prostate stimulator." I didn't think I could get any hotter.

"Holy shit that is hot." Leland trailed his fingers down my spine. "I'm going to worship both of you. Scout, take over, nice and slow. I want to do something special for our boy."

"Yes, sir." Her words were breathy.

Leland groaned low before moving, taking the covers with him, leaving Scout and I both uncovered. He reached over, turning the bedside lamp on and dimming it down. He grabbed a small bottle of what I assumed was lube and moved farther down the bed. He tapped my leg. "Shift your leg up, let me see." I followed his command. This position exposed where Scout and I were connected. We were both lying on our side, with one of Scout's legs thrown over my hip, he had a front-row view of everything. When his hot breath coasted across my skin, I almost blew right then. I couldn't see how he was lying, but I could feel the brush of his lips over one of my ass cheeks. "Fuck, this is so fucking hot. Seeing where the two of you are coming together." His fingers trailed over Scout's stretched lips, brushing my base in the process.

"Yes, keep talking, please. Tell us what my pussy looks like stretching around bee's cock." *Fucking. Fuck.*

I thrusted forward at the feel of Leland moving between our legs, pausing my movement while I tried to figure out what he is doing. When he flattened his tongue to run over where Scout and I connect, my brain short circuited. "You both taste like heaven." His words were low as he spoke. I thrusted into Scout at his words. He watched as I moved in and out of her tight heat. His hands never stopped touching and caressing us. "Fuck, I need more. Scout, love, lay on me and wrap those pretty lips around my dick." This new position put them in the 69 position. With Leland being so much taller, he wasn't close to being able to eat her out. My dick jerked at the absence of her warm, wet walls. I knew whatever was coming next was going to rock my world.

I was lost in thought when Leland spoke again. "Bee." My eyes snapped to him. "Want to try something new?"

"I mean as far as new things, this was all kind of new." I tried to bring my usual humor, but even I heard the nerves in my voice. When I found my words again, the answer was simple. "Yes, please."

"I'm going to untie your hands from the headboard, and you are going to sit on my face and let our girl fuck herself on you. I want to taste that sweet ass of yours. Do not cum until I say so. Do you understand?" There was nothing but pure heat in his eyes. I fucking loved it.

My body gave a shiver in anticipation. I held myself up slightly, not wanting to put all my weight down. I had told women before to put their weight on me, but it was a different ball game to be the one hovering. As my dick found its home back in Scout, Leland didn't hold back. He gripped Scout's hips and pulled back. "When I said sit on my face, I didn't mean hover." Without the full use of my hands, I was at their mercy. With a final tug, he had me where he wanted me. The first pass of his tongue over the tight ring of muscles had me tensing. He brought a hand up to my leg as Scout began to move. I didn't know how, but they were moving in sync and I was about to blow.

"Oh God, you fill me up so good." Scout's words came out on a moan. "How does he taste, bear?"

Leland lifted me just enough to speak. "So fucking good. Want more, sweetheart?"

Sweetheart. I like that.

I was now actively trying to rock and move. "Yes, fuck yes, please." He dove back in like a starved man. I never had someone eat me out before, but hot damn. As he worked me over, I felt myself relaxing. I could see Scout's head bobbing on Leland's cock as she fucked herself on me. I sunk further into my pleasure. My climax was approaching and I needed them to come. Sensing the coming release, Leland speared his tongue, driving it into my now relaxed hole. My movements grew jerky.

"Can I come? Please, *please* let me come." My words were gasping pleas as Scout continued to ride me all while Leland was making me see stars.

Scout was the first to start over the edge. "I'm coming! Yes, fuck. Don't stop." The words were rushed. I felt Leland lift me slightly where he could speak, "Come now," then he dove back in. When her walls tightened around me, I was done for. The warm mouth on my ass didn't stop. I could feel the scratch of his stubble against my skin. He licked and sucked the ring of muscles before he moved to run his finger over my hole. I could feel the tip of his finger teasing my opening, then it was replaced with his tongue. This continued while Scout continued to fuck herself on me. It wasn't long before I was also going over the edge with a shout. Scout sucked Leland until he, too, was shooting his release into her waiting mouth.

When the last drops of cum spilled, I felt close to blacking out. That was the most mind blowing thing I had ever done. "Holy shit, that was amazing." My words were laced with awe as we moved to get off Leland. Scout untied my hands, kissing my wrist.

"That was the best sex I have ever had," Scout admitted.

Leland replied with, "Same."

We laid in a tangled pile, catching our breath. My brain started to think of all the other things I wanted to do.

I bolted upright, remembering something. "Leland Boone, do you have a sex bed? And also, is that the tie you wore to prom?" As I sat looking at the tie, I knew it was. The man never wore dress clothes, especially not ties. I had seen him in exactly one tie and it was the one he wore to prom. The very same one that he used to bind my hands.

Scout started to giggle. "I told you he would notice."

"Yes, the bed is a sex bed...*now*. It didn't start out that way," he said mischievously. "Also, yes, that is the tie I wore to prom. It is the only one

I own. We thought you might like it. Was Scout, I mean, *we* correct to assume?"

I looked at between them. Both looked like they were trying to hide a smile. "Is this true, my sweet honeysuckle?"

Scout stayed silent for a moment, trying to fight a giggle before she pressed her lips together and then opened them to speak. "Yes, that might be true." Her face turned serious for a moment. "Did you enjoy it? It's ok if it isn't really your thing."

I laid back down, taking a moment to check in with myself. This was something that my therapist had me do. I tended to act and speak before thinking through what I truly wanted. I want to do it again and more.

"Yes, it was amazing." We grew quiet again, just being with each other. My brain was starting to race again. I thought of all the things in and out of the bedroom I wanted with them. I wanted hot and steamy sex, but I also wanted mushy, lovey things. I dreamed of cuddling in bed and having lazy days off to big holidays with our families. Flashes of the future played out in my mind, all of what hopefully would come to fruition.

"I want you to take my virginity." It was quiet for a moment before I realized how that sounded. "Oh shit. Fuck a duck. No, I'm not a virgin, I mean I want you to take my anal virginity." The words flew out of my mouth before I had a chance to stop them. *Shit.*

The sound of silence greeted me. *Fucking crickets.* At this point, I didn't know how I hadn't kept the women away with how smooth of a talker I was. *Hello, God, it's me. Odd time to get in touch, but if you could just cease my existence, that would be great. Thanks, and keep up the good work.*

I hadn't even thought about the fact that Leland might not want that. *Double fuck a duck. Or maybe don't.*

My thoughts came screeching to a halt when a throat cleared. *Here we go.*

"I mean, I don't exactly pack the right parts biologically, but silicone can be a girl's best friend." Instead of Leland's deep voice, it was Scout who was speaking. Shock at her words caused a laugh to burst through my lips.

Once the laughter had died away, Leland raised so he was looking at me and Scout. "I want both of you in whatever way I can have you. I will never pressure you to do something. If penetration was completely off the table, that would be ok. If you want to top me, that's ok, too. If you want me on top, that's fine." He paused for a moment. "Hell, we can do both." His eyes moved between us. "I mean shit, honeysuckle, if you wanted to get in on some pegging action, I say let's go for it." He had moved now, but was still holding one of our hands each. "What matters to me the most is that the two of you are taken care of. I find my pleasure in making you feel pleasure. I have been told I get bossy in bed. If it was too much, I will try to change how I am in this period. I know I can get kind of Daddy dom, but for you, I would try to tone it down."

"Please don't stop being bossy. It is so fucking hot, and the dirty talk? I think I could have come just from that." Scout dramatically fanned herself. "Also, I am not really interested in the pegging stuff. There is nothing wrong with it, but it just isn't for me. It would have been hot to see, but right now, I'm glad that we are getting some of this stuff out and in the open. And I'm in, too. I know we need to discuss and sort out things, but this feels right," Scout finished, giving both of our hands a gentle squeeze.

I was trying to suck down the emotions clogging my throat. I had never felt that I clicked in relationships. The only people that things felt right with were in the bed with me. "I want all that." I steeled myself for what I planned to confess next. Honesty, that was what we were giving. No reason to feel embarrassed. "I have a prostate massager. I have used it for the last couple of years regularly." I could feel my cheeks growing warm. I turned my head away, not wanting to see what they thought of my words or what I was about to say. "I had dreams, I guess more fantasies about, well, the three of us. Together."

"Don't look away." The command in Leland's voice caused my cock to twitch, my gaze moved back to them. "I had them, as well."

"Me too," Scout added. "They pale in comparison to actually being with you both, but they got me through some lonely nights." She gave me a soft smile. This was why they were my people. "My question is, when are we going to make all our fantasies a reality?" Her heated gaze moved over both of us before she slid out of bed. "Be right back. I have an idea." With a wink, she left the room. I wanted to know what she had planned, but was also slightly nervous.

She returned not even a minute later, holding three boxes. It took me a moment to realize what they were. "Are those sex toys, ma'am?" I gave her a questioning look.

She laid them on the bed for us to view. "Yes, bee, they are. They haven't been used or anything. Lettie and Oakland have the same sense of humor." I looked to Leland who was looking at the toys with interest. Picking up one of the boxes, she opened and pulled out two anal plugs, both on the smaller side. The second box contained a silicone dildo. It wasn't large, but also wasn't small. Last was a bigger, vibrating dildo. "This one apparently does a lot of movement." As if to demonstrate, she clicked it on.

"Holy shit." The thing moved and vibrated. "That is the Swiss army knife of toys." I stared at the moving dick. The plugs caught my eye and I reached to pick up the smaller of the two. While we had been sitting here talking, I had started to recover—and from the looks of it, so had Leland. I wanted this, but I was nervous. What if I didn't actually like having a dick up my ass? I knew he said he wouldn't be disappointed, but I would feel like I was letting them down. He reached his hand over to remove the plug from my hand.

"How about you top me first? I haven't gotten to be inside our girl's sweet pussy yet. Plus, I have dreamed about taking your dick in my ass since we were teenagers." *Fuck yes.* He scooped the toys up, leaning to set them on the nightstand.

Scout climbed back on the bed, sitting beside Leland. They both looked at me, waiting for what my reply would be. "Leland, move up the bed. Scout, distract him while I get him ready to take me." Scout gave a shiver at my tone. Leland let out a low groan. The minute he was situated, Scout began to kiss his neck and jaw before moving to his lips. I watched for a moment as they took pleasure in each other's kisses. I moved down and put my body between Leland's spread legs. Knowing what I wanted, he bent his legs, exposing his ass to me. I just stared at it for a moment. I couldn't believe this was happening. My thoughts were interrupted.

"I can prep myself if you want," Leland commented softly. There was no judgment or mocking in his words.

I shook my head. "Absolutely not. I have done anal before. Of course, when we start, if you don't like something, tell me, but I want to do this for you." I grabbed the small bottle of lube that Scout had laid down with the toys. "Remember, sweet honeysuckle, nice and distracted." I slicked my fingers, rubbing one over his rim. Scout's lips muffled his groan. I watched him as I continued to rub, wanting to make him feel good. Scout reached down to wrap her hand around his cock, stroking him slowly as she kissed him. It was the hottest fucking thing I had ever seen. "Ready for more?"

He pulled his mouth away from their kiss. "Yes, please."

I slid the tip of one finger in, pausing before easing my way in more once I felt him relax. My moves were slow, allowing him to adjust. I didn't know how many times he had done this, but from how tight he was, I might die when it was my dick and not my finger. This went on for a few minutes before he began to move.

"More."

I looked up at him, my eyes connecting with his as I added the second finger. I worked on it just as slowly as the first. Scout had moved now, she was kissing down his chest. She moved to one nipple, taking it between her teeth. Leland hissed and then groaned as my fingers rubbed across his prostate. She continued down his body until she was looking me in the eye. She gave me a mischievous look before she licked a stripe up his cock, right as I thrusted in, hitting his prostate.

"OH FUCK!" Leland shouted.

Scout winked at me. "Does that feel good? Having bee's finger rubbing you in all the right spots? He is so good at it." She leaned back down to suck the tip of his cock into her mouth before pulling off. "God, bee, he is just so big, I don't think I can handle all this on my own. Want to share?"

I felt Leland clench around my slow, thrusting fingers. He liked that idea. Instead of saying anything, I leaned forward to suck one of his balls into my mouth. I had no clue how to give head to a guy, but I loved to have my balls played with. I moved to the other before pulling back. "I think he liked that. Look at all that precum." I had moved my hand from Leland's leg to wrap around his cock and Scout's smaller hand. The head of his cock was shiny with precum. I leaned forward, my eyes locked on Leland's gaze as I tilted his dick to me. The sheer look of pleasure on his face as I ran the flat of my tongue over his slit collecting his precum was so satisfying.

He whimpered, his chest rising and falling as we continued to lick and suck his dick, all while my fingers continued to work in and out of him. I scissored my fingers, continuing to open him up.

His control snapped when Scout began to bob her head up and down while I sucked on his balls. "Enough. I'm ready. Fuck. Me. Now."

I pulled my fingers from him. Getting off the bed, I walked over and grabbed a condom. When I turned back to the bed, I held it up. "I know it can make it easier—"

Before I could continue, he was shaking his head. "No, I don't want anything between us." His eyes went almost misty. "I have wanted you for so long. Please."

How could I deny this man? I had already taken Scout bare. I couldn't imagine not giving the same thing to Leland. I grabbed a pillow and tapped his hip. "Lift your hips." He did as he was told and I placed it under him. I grabbed the bottle of lube and applied a generous amount to my cock. Scout watched as I moved back between Leland's legs. I notched my dick against his hole. "Relax, bear. It's just us here, let us in." He took a slow breath before he nodded. When I felt him bear down, I pushed the tip in, pausing for him to signal me to continue. Once he took a few deep breaths, I was able to move.

Our pace was slow until skin met skin. I gently rocked in and out, each time pushing a little further. That was when Scout moved to straddle him. Grabbing his dick, she guided him to her warm, wet center. "So big. You both fill me up so good." She rocked and circled her hips. We started to move in almost a slow dance before the speed changed. Scout began to ride him earnestly. I picked up my thrusts, the sounds of groans and moans filling the room. Sweat began to coat my brow as I started to really fuck into Leland.

"Yes, bee. Fuck yes. Don't stop. Fill me up." Leland's words were spoken on a moan.

Scout continued to bounce on him. "I'm so close. I want to come with you both. Please. Fuck, please."

Her words were a battering ram to my restraint. I fucked hard as she slammed down on Leland. His hand gripped her waist hard enough that I was sure there would be bruises. Leland gave a guttural moan. "Oh God, I'm coming. Fuuuck." His words were cut off by Scout's release, her body tensing. She fell forward, her palms planted on Leland's chest. She twitched as the orgasm continued to work through her body.

Leland clenched around me, causing stars to burst behind my eyes. My climax rolled over me, my dick twitching as I shot my hot release into Leland. Scout had slumped forward, kissing Leland before she straightened and leaned her back against my chest. She tilted her head so I could lean around and kiss her as well. The sounds of heavy breathing filled the room as we all tried to catch our breath.

Scout slid off Leland before I slowly pulled out, as well. I moved to the bathroom and grabbed three washcloths and wetted them. I walked back to the bed, wiped myself off, then tossed the first rag in the hamper. When they both reached for the rags, I shook my head. "Let me." Leland relaxed back, a sigh escaping his lips as I wiped him off with one rag before switching and doing the same to Scout. I knew we would need a shower, and Scout would need to use the bathroom. The fact that women could avoid potential problems post-sex by just going to the bathroom was amazing to me. But a quick cleanup for now would do.

ONCE WE WERE all settled back in the bed, the weight of my feelings hit me. I was falling for them. Honestly, I think I was already there. The realization was freeing, but terrifying. I had been one way my whole life, or so I thought, and now all this had come in and flipped my world. I ran my fingers through Scout's hair, where she practically laid on myself and Leland. Leland's arm was draped over her, his palm resting on my side, his finger rubbing circles on my skin.

"I really love this. Us." Her words were sleepy and slow. "I never thought I would find this." She let out a big yawn. Her breathing evened out. My eyes grew heavy as I laid there, warm and connected to the two most important people to me. I was just dozing when I thought I heard Leland speak.

"I am never letting you two go. I love you both more than words can describe." His words were hushed. He said them like a secret prayer.

This was the best dream I never wanted to wake up from.

I love you, my big teddy bear and sweet honeysuckle.

chapter 17

· · ·

SOFT LIPS PRESSED a kiss to my forehead woke me enough to hear Leland. "I'm heading to the bakery. Message me when you get up." I was still half asleep, but heard the same words repeated to Gat, who was still in bed. He was working from home today while I had a couple of meetings, then needed to check on the work in the apartment. I had been slacking on tracking progress, because honestly, I loved being here with the guys. I enjoyed my alone time, but I had spent a lot of time that way. Having people to come home to was such a nice change.

When Gatlin's arms tightened around me, I drifted back to sleep.

I WOKE LATER to lips kissing down my chest and stomach. Young me would be freaking out at the idea of someone seeing the slight stretch marks that were on my stomach and legs. Current me, though, had learned that my body was beautiful, stretch marks and all. I had to remind myself sometimes, but quieting those thoughts with age had gotten easier. A moan worked its way up my throat. He moved between my legs, running his tongue through my wet folds. I spread my legs, giving him better access. He took full advantage. His mouth moved over my pussy, sucking my clit gently before licking into my opening. He continued to use that talented mouth until I was tipping over the edge. He was with me through the whole orgasm. When he moved back up the bed, his face was covered in my release.

"That was quite a good morning alarm to wake up to." I reached around his neck, pulling him closer, his body covering mine. I pressed my lips to his, tasting myself mixed with him. His response was a low moan.

We kissed lazily for a few minutes before pulling apart. "I would have loved to do more, but didn't want to in case you were sore."

This man.

I was fast-tracking toward the big feelings. I had loved them as friends, but we were on a course to full-on love at lightning speed. Not that I was complaining. "Thank you. I actually am a little sore." At his look of concern, I added, "In the best way. This sore was so good." I moved my hand toward his morning wood. "That doesn't mean I don't want to say good morning." I rolled us over and worked my way down his body. I felt a twinge of guilt that we had not gotten to do this to Leland. We would just have to make it up to him. *Make-up blowjobs were a thing, right?*

When my lips wrapped around his hard length, he sucked in a breath. "I'm not going to last long, baby." I felt Gatlin's hand come to rest on my head, holding me in place. With that, I went to work, hollowing out my cheeks and bobbing up and down. I reached up with one hand to massage his balls. When I took him to the back of my throat and gave his balls a tug, he spoke again. "Baby, pull off or you are going to get a mouth full." No way was I pulling off. I redoubled my efforts and was rewarded when I felt him lengthen before his release shot in my mouth. Pulling off slightly, I caught some of it on my tongue. Once he was licked clean, I moved up the bed. Gatlin reached for me and crushed his lips to mine. We made out, sharing the taste of him that still lingered in my mouth.

We broke apart from kissing. "That was fucking amazing." Gatlin sighed. "Best morning wake up to date." I snorted a laugh before cuddling into his side. "But seriously, sweetheart, if you get too sore, tell us, please. You know bear would say the same." With a squeezed hug and a peck on my lips, he shifted and moved to get out of bed. "Want some coffee while you get ready?"

"Yes, please." I smiled at him before also climbing out of bed. A girl could get used to this.

The first meeting ran longer than expected, but it was not unwelcome. My grandparents formed a partnership with some local groups who provided books to displaced children and teens. Some of the books went to kids who were in the foster system, others were given after a natural disaster or house fires. The group expanded to now not only give books, but other resources. We had been able to build a network that not only helped kids, but also adults. I knew giving a book probably wasn't a top priority for most, but sometimes reality sucked and that book was a tiny escape. This had been important to my family growing up, so it was a given I would continue it once I took over the store. Not that I was complaining; I had been able to meet some amazing people.

I also wasn't upset about our meeting location. I shut my notebook and looked up to catch a glimpse of my teddy bear. I still could not believe that we were dating. Warmth spread over me, thinking about the three of us. Last night had been mind-blowing, to say the least. The connection that I felt to them was like nothing I had ever known.

"Do you want a napkin for your drool?" Sebastian plopped down in the chair across from me.

I jumped, bumping the table and sending my notebook and paper to the floor. "Lord love a duck, Seb!" I clutched my heart, looking at him. He snickered as he helped me collect my stuff from the floor. "And my drooling over the level of fineness my men contain is not to be judged. Also, are you all secret ninjas? You are all way too sneaky. Do you have a secret club or something?"

He shook his head, giving another little laugh. "Listen, I will not argue the hotness of Papa bear and Gat. Anyone with eyes can see they are flaming hot and head over heels for you and each other." He raised his hands in mock surrender. "Honestly, I just don't want the elderly to slip on the pool of drool on the floor."

I leaned around the table, quickly scanning the floor for said pool of liquid. "Shut up, there is not. Besides, I have seen you drool over a few certain someone or should I say *someones*." I eyed him, watching the pink tint cross his cheeks. Seb had become a good friend over the years he had worked at the bakery. "Oh, and on that note, try not to drive Fin insane. I know you and Lettie are sunshine reborn, but not all of us are blessed with the gene of unlimited sunshine and rainbows."

"You know we are as innocent as lambs." He reached to clutch his non-existent pearls.

I rolled my eyes at his antics. Lettie had drunkenly confessed to being attracted to Sebastian and Finch. I told her to go for it, but she then started casually dating a guy. I honestly didn't really like him. He gave weird vibes. I learned to trust my gut a long time ago, and he didn't pass the vibe check. I thanked the cosmos that she ended up breaking it off with the guy. She could do so much better. "And I am the Queen of England." We both started laughing, drawing the attention of a few customers and the sexy as fuck owner. When our eyes met, a smile lit up his whole expression. Once his hands were wiped, he walked over to where we sat.

He leaned down, placing a kiss on my temple before he moved his lips to my ear. "I hear you had a good morning."

A shiver ran over my body. My thighs were squeezed tightly together. "It was a very good morning. Only one thing would have made it better." I turned to take his mouth in a slow, passionate kiss. "If I would have had both my men there." *My men.*

When a low groan came from Leland, I almost came from the possessive and needy sound alone. "On that note, I'm going to go climb in the oven." Seb straightened, muttering under his breath. "Blegh, it's like listening to your parents talk about having sex." He walked toward the swinging doors that led to the back and pushed through.

We both gave a laugh at Seb's antics before Leland sat across from me. "I have a plan. I need you to help me, my sweet honeysuckle. Bee has a special gift coming Friday. You also have a little something, too." I looked at him curiously.

"What is it?"

He winked before kissing me again. "You will just have to see."

Damn these men and their teasing.

WHEN FRIDAY CAME, I was death glaring the clock by lunch, willing it to speed up. The week had been busier than usual with the camp out being the next week. Leland was prepping stuff for the bakery to run without him and Gatlin was prepping for the trip. They had a meeting yesterday with the parents, kids, and volunteers, which meant they didn't get home until after I had passed out. I was pulled from sleep by their warm bodies snuggling close to me.

"Earth to Scout." Lettie waved her hand in front of my face. "Go to lunch before your scowling scares the kids." Like a mature adult, I naturally replied by sticking my tongue out at her. "What has put that look on your face, anyway? I figured double dicking would make for a very happy woman." She placed her hand on her full hips, squinting at me. "Spill. Is it not good double doozy dicking?"

"Double doozy dicking? What are you, a child?"

"Only at heart. So share about the DD."

"Are you having a stroke or something? What DD?"

My brain came fully online, but not before a voice answered, that was not in fact Lettie's, "*Double dicking*, dear. Keep up. Are they not satisfying you? I'll have to give them a talking to." Nan stood off to the side of the desk.

My face flamed, eyes going wide. I was going to murder my best friend. I mouthed, "*You're dead*," before facing Nan. "No, ma'am, no need to do that. I was just thinking about—" My mind went blank. *Shit.* "Some. Um."

"Dicks? Well, double dicks?" I squealed at another voice joining in. I turned to see Sebastian standing with a bag and coffee in hand.

What in the hell was going on?

Sebastian set the bag and coffee on the counter and reached for

Nan's books. "Nan, don't tell me that you read these? And if so, how did I not know?" He winked at her. He was such a charmer. But he was so genuine in his interest in people that you couldn't help but like him.

Nan passed the books over, playfully smacking his arm. "You know, these have some great information and suggestions. For all types of relationship pairings." She eyed Sebastian, but his smile never wavered. The front doorbell chimed, and a man entered the store. He glanced around the store before spotting us. Lettie stiffened and then went to the back of the store. I then realized who the dude was.

Fucking Franklin.

To say I didn't like this man would be an understatement. I hated this man. He and Lettie had dated and broken up ages ago, but he never gave up. He was like glitter. Or herpes. Never really going away. He would show up, playing the nice guy who just wanted to stay friends. I didn't buy it. I had heard some of the things that were said when they were together and then post break up. He was a grade A asshole.

"Well, it seems like everyone is taking the day off. Didn't realize these small places did well enough for taking breaks." He laughed at his own attempt at humor. "I came to take Lettie to grab a bite to eat. Seems like she has the time now."

Nan looked him up and down before she rolled her eyes. "I think her lunch period is already occupied. It isn't very gentlemanly to expect a young busy woman to drop her plans for," she gave him a once over before finishing, "well, you."

Damn Nan.

Franklin scoffed as if the thought of Lettie having plans was impossible. "Busy." He lifted his hands up, doing finger quotes on the word. "She doesn't have plans, I'm sure." The level of conviction he said it with made me want to throw a book at his head. I had plenty of heavy books close by. One to head would do perfectly.

"Well damn, I guess a blind squirrel doesn't always find the acorn, because you would be wrong," Sebastian said in his usual, calm tone. If you didn't know him, you would think he was joking. The way his jaw clenched, however, gave him away. Seb was close to Gatlin's size, maybe a touch leaner. He was an avid runner and swimmer, and his body was built for it. "She in fact has plans with me." He stood casually with his hands tucked in his pockets, his usual carefree smile now forced.

"Sure she does." Franklin leaned, trying to peer into the back room. "Seriously, though, I don't have time to wait. Be a friend and run and grab her for me. I'm sure she will be happy to see me." He gave a flick of his hand at Seb.

Nan cough-whispered, "Doubt it."

"Listen—" He turned to Nan.

"Franklin, watch what comes out of your mouth next." My eyes were laser focused on him. "If Lettie's actions have not made it clear, then I will. Do not come back to my store. Do not come near Lettie again. You are a condescending asshole that is not welcome, nor wanted. Now leave."

It was like a switch flipped in him. "I won't be told what to do by some *bitch*," he sneered.

Movement caught my eye before the sound of a fist met flesh. "Watch what you say, motherfucker. That's our girlfriend." Leland stood next to Gatlin, who shook his hand from the punch. I didn't know them defending my honor would be so hot, but it was doing things.

Clean up on aisle three, horny woman soaked her panties. Again.

Franklin fell on his ass. He took a moment then jumped to his feet, touching his jaw where Gatlin had made contact. He shifted toward Gatlin then realized that he was outnumbered and outmatched in size. "Keep her fat ass. Not even worth wetting my dick." With those parting words, he turned to leave.

"Listen here, you fucking sack of crusty dog shit." Seb started to lunge forward, but arms banded around him.

"No, bluebird." Fin held him tight against his broad chest. I had never realized that he and Leland were built similarly. "Let the dickhead go, he isn't the important one." He didn't let Sebastian go, but turned him towards the back where Lettie had gone. Realizing he had just escaped a having his ass handed to him, Franklin scurred out like the rat he was.

"See you next Tuesday!" Nan yelled at his retreating form. "Well, I'm going to go have a sit with Cleo and have a coffee," Nan declared before walking out of the store. Leland shook his head at his grand-mother, a smile pulling across his face as she left.

I moved to my guys and was immediately sandwiched between them. "Is your hand ok?" I lifted Gatlin's hand to look at his knucks.

A smirk lifted the corner of his mouth. "It's ok, I guess, but you and bear can always kiss it better later." He winked at me. I giggled when I heard Leland give a low groan.

"I think we can arrange that.

chapter 18

. . .

gatlin

"ICE PACK," Leland said, handing me a small bag of ice. It wasn't the first time I had punched someone, but I also wasn't a twenty something anymore. Scout had decided to close the store down for the day and send Lettie home. This was not the first time Franklin had shown up at the store, but it better be his last. We were now sitting at home, winding down. I had things for the campout that probably needed to be done, but I had barely been home, and I missed Leland and Scout.

My phone pinged. Unlocking it, I saw a message from Orrin.

Oreo: 4:06 p.m. Sooo I have some bad news.

Oreo: 4:07 p.m. My parents are coming to town week after the camp out. I tried to get them here next week so you could avoid them all together, but of course that doesn't align with their schedule. I wanted to give you a heads up, but also Leland because they will insist on coming downtown. *Aggressive eye roll*

> Me: 4:08 p.m. I have not talked to Mom, but I'll call her. Thanks, man, I'll let him know. If he says anything though, it will be me he deals with.

> Oreo: 4:09 p.m. Me too. I have already dropped to low contact and he knows he is close to getting cut off completely. We need to meet up when you get back next week.

> Me: 4:09 p.m. Definitely! I'll message when we're back. Maybe we can do a cookout and get you away from the parents for a bit.

> Oreo: 4:10 p.m. Be safe next week!

I clicked my phone off and tossed it to the side. I really did not want to see my aunt and uncle. The breath I didn't realize I was holding escaped in a sigh as I rested my head back on the couch. *Shit.* Over the years, I had avoided any contact with most of my mom's family, as had my parents. I would need to tell Leland and Scout. I wish I could believe my uncle wouldn't go looking for trouble, but he would.

I felt someone move behind the couch. "Why the big sigh?" Scout leaned down to kiss my forehead. When she straightened, I got lost looking at her. She was gorgeous. She literally took my breath away. It was so odd to feel this bone deep attraction for two people who were opposite in every way appearance wise. Scout was soft and feminine. Her features were delicate and cute. Then Leland was all man, strong and so handsome. When Scout rounded the arm of the couch, I took in every inch of her. My mouth watered looking at her hourglass shape. She may have been dressed in her comfy clothes, but it did nothing to hide her amazing ass and legs.

I pulled her to my lap, giving her room to get comfortable before wrapping my arms around her waist. I didn't want to have to go through it twice, so I called for Leland. Within a minute, he came into the living room. "Orrin just messaged." I looked at Leland, knowing that my face was probably telling him everything he needed to know.

"When and how long?" His expression was a careful mask of calm.

I patted the couch next to where Scout and I sat. "Week after next." I took his hand, lacing our fingers together. "Orrin tried to get them to come next week, but they, of course, refused. They know when we do the campout. They also know Mom and Dad have helped before. It may just be a coincidence they can't come while we're gone, or they may be doing it on purpose." We had shared pieces with Scout, but it had been years since they had come back here.

Scout looked between us when understanding settled over her face. "Orrin's parents?"

I nodded. The guilt of being connected to them ate at me like usual. "We have told you some about them, but since they are coming, we need to tell you everything." I looked away, trying to figure out where to start before turning back to look at Scout. "So you know my uncle is a homophobic asshat. Well, there is a bit more to it."

Leland took over, seeing I was struggling. "He tried to get me shut down after he came in, making a slew of shitty claims. When they still lived here, and when they would visit anytime, he saw us and he made comments. Nasty things that I won't repeat, but nothing I hadn't heard. Seb was joking at the bakery one day, the usual Papa bear stuff."

"Being Seb," Scout added with a soft smile. This part was not going to be something she wanted to hear.

Leland let out a little chuckle. "Well, Thomas, Orrin's dad, was in the bakery. He never came in, but of course, had that day. He heard Seb making jokes about liking a bossy man and that everyone needs a Daddy. Thomas was the only one in the bakery, which I guess made him brave enough to say something. Basically said that we both deserved to have our asses kicked, and if we were back in the good old days that people like us wouldn't just be out and about. He said more, but honestly, it isn't worth repeating." He shook his head and looked at me with sadness, but also anger in his beautiful eyes. "I banned him from the store and told him if he ever came back, I would call the cops. He didn't outright threaten us, but saying shit to me was one thing. I wouldn't stand for him making passive threats at Seb. That was the last time they came to town."

I had not looked at Scout while Leland talked. I was ashamed I shared blood with people who thought the way they did. I honestly didn't know why they were coming to begin with. My mom and dad didn't talk to them and Orrin kept the lowest contact possible, just enough to know when they would be here. I chanced a look at Scout, expecting her to have a look of disgust. Instead, her jaw was clenched tight. She was angry. She stood abruptly and paced away. My heart began to pound. Leland turned to face where she stood, pressing his shoulder to mine, grounding me.

Please don't leave. The statement was meant for both of them.

She spun back to face us. "How dare he? I mean, honestly, to think like that. I just want to punch him in his stupid face." She walked back to the couch. "Well, it makes sense why no one is pleased they are coming here." She sat half on me and half on Leland before leaning back into our chests. "So, do we avoid them the best we can? Leave town for the week?" Under her breath she added, "Hire a hitman?" Leland and I both chuckled.

"No hitmen, and we can't leave town after just getting back, unfortunately. Avoiding them will be the best option." I kissed her head where it rested on my chest, then turned to Leland. "Orrin wanted to give you a heads up. I know it isn't my apology to give, but I am sorry that I am related to him."

He shifted so he could place a soft kiss on my lips. "You have nothing to apologize for, bee. I could care less what he or anyone else thinks about me or the relationships I'm in. I have the two of you and no one can tarnish or dim the feelings I have for you both." He kissed Scout's head before relaxing his head back on the couch.

I'm in love with them.

SATURDAY WAS SPENT GETTING equipment together and double checking that everything was ready. Scout offered to come help get things organized, but when Lettie showed up to the store, it was obvious where she was needed. Scout had messaged that she was going to hang out and would message later. Over the years of being next door to them and getting to know Scout, we have also gotten to know Lettie. She was badass that gave as good as she took. If that jackass was willing to say all that in front of people, I can't imagine how he acted behind closed doors. Scout gave us a bit of backstory once we had gotten home. After hearing some of the things Scout had witnessed or heard, I wanted to find the guy and cancel his birth certificate. Of course, I knew that wouldn't help Lettie. *It would make me feel better, though.*

I grabbed some crates from the second floor. Anything that was used for the trips and nature tours I did was kept upstairs. I was thankful to have a second set of hands. Especially when those hands were attached to the big beefy man I enjoyed admiring. I stumbled slightly, the awkward weight of the items shifting.

"Here, let me get one of those." Leland pulled the top crate. "Are there more that need to come down?" He motioned his head toward the stairs. I stared at his arms flexing as he took the weight of the supply box before setting it down. "Bee?"

"Oh no, this is it." I looked over the boxes on the table. "I brought most of it down already." My eyes caught on his chest and the way his shirt was stretched across the broad expanse. I knew under that shirt was hard muscle covered by thick chest hair. That hair led down his soft but strong stomach, to that absolutely amazing dick. I could see the outline of said dick and it looked like it was getting hard. Since giving my brain permission to have these thoughts, it was like the dam on my horny thoughts burst. I thought about Leland and Scout constantly. I lived in a state of semi erect. I was ready, willing, and able for sexual activities at all times. A throat cleared and ripped me back to reality. *Whoops, horny Gatlin strikes again.*

"Like what you see?" Leland looked at me, one eyebrow raised. His tone was teasing, but there was an undercurrent of pleasure that told me he liked the way I looked at him. I nodded at him, not trusting my voice to not come out like a pubescent teen. "Come here, bee." He leaned his weight back on the table.

Glad those are sturdy worktables.

I moved closer, our slight height difference feeling more noticeable. I had never trusted a partner to take control, but I knew Leland would always take care of myself and Scout. Honestly, letting him or Scout take over sounded like the most freeing thing. It's something I would be interested to talk about and maybe explore with them more. Currently, though, there was a hot man standing in front of me hard as a rock and looking at me like he could devour me. I let my eyes fall to the visible bulge in his pants. His hand reached up to pull the hair tie from where I tried to get my hair out of my face. With his usual gentleness, he removed it, letting my hair fall before running his fingers up the back of my neck to grip the loose strands. With a tug back, I met his gaze. He slanted his mouth over mine, taking control of the kiss. There was no gentleness to the way he was kissing me. His tongue invaded my mouth, licking into every corner. We both knew who was in control of this kiss.

Fuck.

Leland groaned into the kiss, pulling my hair and causing pinpricks of pain across my scalp. He moved his lips down my jaw and to my neck. He gently nipped and bit at the sensitive skin. His free hand pulled me closer, our hips now flush. A whimper left my throat at the pressure of my hard length against his. My hips moved, trying to get any relief. A bone deep need settled into every part of my body. "Look at you, so needy. So hungry. What do you want, bee?" His breath ghosted across my ear as he spoke. "Do you want me on my knees for you?"

I wanted to say no, that I wanted to be on my knees, but I had never given a blowjob on my own, at least. I wanted to worship his glorious dick. The nervous butterflies beat around in my stomach and had me pausing. I don't want to do a piss poor job the first time I went solo. There was a whole list of things I wanted to do. All of them I wanted Leland and Scout to enjoy. When I was silent for too long, Leland pulled back slightly so he could see my face. "I have an idea." He reached down to unzip my pants, then his. Once he has freed us both, he grabbed his wallet, pulling out a small pack of lube. I jumped slightly at the cool liquid running over my hot skin. He didn't give me time to recover before circling his hand around both our lengths.

"Oh, fuck."

He squeezed, then glided his hand up and down until I was about to lose my mind. "How does that feel, baby?" He punctuated the question with another squeeze. I nodded my head, not being able to form a coherent thought, much less words. "So good for me." He wrapped his other hand around us, alternating between jacking our dicks and running his palm over the tips. "So much precum. I think you like having my hands on you."

My head fell back on a groan, my hips thrusting into his fist. "I need to come, please. Please let me come." I thrusted up again.

Leland slanted his lips over mine, taking what he wanted. Taking what I was so willing to give. When he pulled back, I chased his lips. "You want to come?" I nodded like a bobblehead on a car dash. "Since you asked so nicely. I want you to fuck my fist and then paint my dick with your release." I didn't need to be told twice. His grip tightened, getting a better hold on us. Once his hands were still, I couldn't stop myself. Everything felt like too much and not enough. My thrusts grew frenzied and rough as I barreled toward my orgasm.

"Gonna come." The words left my mouth the moment I exploded. Burst of light erupted behind my eyes as ropes of hot cum ran over Leland's hand and dick. He pumped a few more times before he was also spilling his load, our combined releases mixing and running down our dicks. When he let us fall from his hand, my head fell to his chest as I tried to catch my breath. "That was fucking amazing." He wiped his hands on a rag he had in his pocket. His arms came around my waist, pulling me flush to his chest. I held the sides of his shirt in a tight grip like I was afraid he would slip away or this would all be a dream.

He pressed a kiss to my head before chuckling. "Agreed." He gave another chuckle.

"What?" I looked up to meet his gaze.

"I was just thinking if past us could see us now. Together and with the most amazing woman." I honestly didn't know what past me would think. I would hope it would make me get my head out of my ass faster. Even then, some deep part of me knew that Leland was more to me. The same thing happened with Scout. I knew she was supposed to be more. A little part of me was always jealous of the people they dated. I would try to convince myself that it was because I missed getting to spend time with them. Now, my brain and heart were on the same page, and it was obvious.

I leaned up to press a soft kiss to his lips. "Want to have a little fun?" Leland looked at me with a raised eyebrow. I reached around him, stretching to grab his phone. With my clean hand, I snapped a picture of the mess we had made. Turning the phone, I showed it to him.

"Fuck, that's hot. I didn't know you were such a tease. Send it." I sent the message in our group chat and then set his phone back down.

"I think we should clean up, finish up here, and grab our girl." I wanted to do other things, but those were for home. A plan started forming in my head for what I wanted to do once we got home. I have been keeping a little secret from Scout and Leland. Tonight, I will hopefully get to give the big reveal.

chapter 19

. . .

leland

BY THE TIME we finished cleaning up, we didn't have to find our girl because she found us. She walked in the back of the store with Mud trailing behind her. Since she had moved in, he stuck to her like glue. Normally, he split his time between the bookstore and Gatlin's store. As much as I loved having our boy around, he couldn't come into the bakery. Like him, I also wanted to spend all my time with Gat and Scout.

Gatlin met her as she crossed the room while I hung back, just watching them together. They shared a slow, sweet kiss before she made a grabby hand to me. I let out a low chuckle, moving to where they stood. With Gat's hair piled on top of his head again, it gave me open access to his neck. I placed a soft kiss on his nape, his body shivering slightly against my chest. He broke from Scout, letting out a sigh before shifting so I could get to her. The soft press of her lips to mine had me semi-hard and pushing against my zipper. Getting off with Gatlin had just stoked every present spark they set in me. I couldn't be in a room with them and not want to touch them or just be near them. They had woven their way under my skin, and now there was no me without them. "We missed you today, honeysuckle. Is Lettie ok?"

The way she gave a little sigh told us that Lettie was in fact not ok. "That jackass got drunk and called her multiple times last night, and then started to text. When that didn't work, he showed up at her apartment. A few years ago, there was this guy who stalked her. He never did anything to her physically, but the mental games were awful. Long story short, it really messed with her sense of safety. I don't think Franklin was trying to do anything, but it really freaked her out." Gatlin smoothed his hand across her cheek when she began to chew the inside of her mouth.

As much as I wanted to take the two of them home, Lettie was important to Scout. And if she needed to support her friend, Gatlin and I would never stand in the way of that. "If you need to hang out with her, it's ok, love. We would never come between you and her," Gatlin spoke, taking the words right out of my mouth. Nan was right—we were an old married couple; or had spent so much time with each other we just had hive mind.

"You know we care about Lettie, and if she doesn't want to be left alone, we get it completely. She is always welcome to crash at the house, if that would help." I ran my fingers through her hair, letting the soft strands fall back to her back.

"Well, it's funny you should say that...Did you know Fin moved in with Seb?"

"No, I did not know that. When? And how has Fin not murdered him yet? I consider myself a morning person, but I can't handle early morning Sebastian regularly. It's like someone vomited rainbows and sunshine, and it became a human," I said, the surprise apparent in my tone. I had been missing being able to really talk to Sebastian. When we did talk, it was all work. Business had been crazy the last few weeks, not to mention I had been spending a lot of time with Scout and Gatlin. I would need to text Seb and find out what had been going on. I had a very close group I cared to keep up with. My work family was in that circle.

"Wait, what do you mean *funny you should say that*?" Gat's question made little alarms go off in my head.

"I'm not trying to gossip about them, and I don't know all the details with Finch. However, Seb came over to the store and told Lettie they would be going by her house to grab things, and she could stay with him and Finch. Of course, she tried to say that she didn't want to be a bother, but Seb wasn't having it. I knew they were friends in a *we work beside each other* kind of way."

Gatlin sneakered before collecting himself. "They do not just want to be friends. They want to be the bestest of friends that give special hugs and do all kinds of naughty things to each other." We were silent for a moment before erupting into laughter.

"Does that make us the bestest of friends? Because I definitely have naughty ideas that include very special hugs." Scout's voice was a mix of teasing and desire.

"Oh, honeysuckle, we are well past just being the bestest of friends." I gave her ass a squeeze before swatting Gatlin's and walking away from them, giggling.

AFTER WE HAD COLLECTED ourselves and belongings, we grabbed Mud and headed home. With Gat and I leaving for the week with the kids, we had planned on dinner and relaxing on the couch. Scout had offered to cook, and normally, I would help. Tonight, however, I needed a shower before anything else. I wanted to pull Scout and Gatlin to the shower and get clean and dirty at the same time. Hot shower sex sounded like a great way to kick off our evening.

"I'm going to run through the shower really quick. Super smelly. Be back in a few," Gatlin called over his shoulder as he walked toward what used to be his room. The man was moving like his ass was on fire. Since we had decided to be together, we had not slept a night apart. This usually meant we all ended up in my room, due to me having a massive bed. Big man equals big bed.

I wanted to grab Scout and go after him, but something stopped me. I felt Scout's warm body press to my back, her arms wrapped around my waist. There had been times in my life when I had been self-conscious about my size or the soft layer of fat around my middle. This was not the case now, especially not when her hands started to make their way down my body to my pants. I walked a little taller when I felt her or Gatlin looking at me. As she reached my zipper, a groan worked its way up my throat.

"You know, I had to wait so long today after I got that picture." Scout used the palm of her hand to apply pressure to my groin. "I was dripping just thinking about the two of you. All I wanted was to come over to the store and lick you both clean."

"*Fuck.*"

She continued talking, running her hand up and down my straining cock. "Would you have put us on our knees to clean you?" A noise close to a growl was the only sound I could manage. Before she could say another word, I turned until we were face to face. She gasped at the sudden change in position. I grabbed under her perfect ass, lifting so she could wrap her legs around me. My mouth crashed down on hers. The kiss was punishing compared to most we have shared.

"Fuck, I need to shower, but I need to know how wet you are now." I walked to the couch and set Scout down before coming to rest between her legs. "Do you want me to taste that sweet pussy, baby?" She squirmed and shifted, then nodded as her hips rolled, trying to find relief. "Good, I'm going to need you to be loud, honeysuckle. Don't hide any of your sweet sounds from me. I want you to drive bee wild." With that, I helped her shimmy out of her pants and underwear. Once her bottom half was bare, she let her legs fall open, revealing her glistening center. I leaned in, not breaking eye contact, and licked a long strip between her folds.

"Oh fuck. *Yes.*" Her words came out more of a whimper that morphed into a deep moan when I moved to her clit. Using my tongue, I swirled the little bud around before gently sucking it between my lips. When she began to thrust her hips up, I moved one arm to press her waist down. This effectively pinned her hips to the couch.

I leaned back slightly. "Be good and don't move while I have my desert." One jerky nod was all I got before her hands grabbed my face, trying to move me back to where she wanted me. With that, I dove in, eating her out like she was the finest treat. With my free hand, I slid one finger into her, curling it to stroke over that place inside I knew would send her over the edge. This was not the time for slow build-up. I wanted her to come fast, hard, and loud.

When she began to meet my thrusts, I added a second finger and focused on her clit. "I want you to come for me. Be greedy, baby. Take what you need and soak my face in your juices." I leaned back in, thrusting and licking her. I felt her spasming around me, her cries growing louder the closer she got to release.

"I'm coming. Yes, don't stop." She clenched around me so hard I thought she would break my fingers. I continued to slowly thrust, nipping and licking her through the rest of her release before removing my fingers. I licked one long strip up her folds, a pleasured *hmm* vibrating up my throat. I sat back, my graze moving over her face, taking in the flush of her cheeks. Her eyes glazed over with a blissed out expression. To know that I had brought that look to her face made me puff out my chest out in pride. Any amount of pleasure I brought to Scout or Gatlin gave me a little boost. I was addicted to seeing their faces as they came. I always wanted more.

"God, that was so fucking hot. I didn't know we were doing dessert before dinner." Scout looked up to where Gatlin had walked into the room, crossing to where I still squatted between her legs. He lowered so he was also eye level with the most beautiful pussy I had ever seen. "God, I want to devour you." Scout's hips moved as if begging him to do just that. Instead, he grabbed my hand, bringing the fingers that had just been buried in Scout to his lips. Swirling his tongue around my digits, he cleaned them before popping them from his lips. The heat in his expression burned as our mouths met, lighting the short fuse of myself control. For a moment, he controlled the kiss, licking into my mouth before nipping my bottom lip. The heat and tension that had retreated had climbed back to a volcanic level. "Mmm, I love the way you taste together." He hummed against my mouth before pulling away.

Holy shit balls. They are both so fucking hot.

"Christ on a cracker, you two are going to be the death of me. Why are you both so hot?" Scout spoke as she shifted back on the couch, grabbing a blanket to cover her lower half. I stood, extending a hand to Gatlin before hauling him up.

"The same thing just crossed my mind," I said with a low chuckle. I moved away from them, needing to put a little distance between us. "Before I drag you both to bed and we fuck six ways to Sunday, I am going to go shower." With that, I turned and headed for the shower. My nickname may be teddy bear, but at this rate, I was going to turn into a damn polar bear with all the freezing showers in my future.

THE SHOWER DID nothing to dampen my need. Cold showers only smothered my longing for them until I was out. Once I was warm again, it was like a snake charmer came out. I would return to full mast. I couldn't complain, but it was a bit troublesome. I adjusted myself, trying to make an attempt at concealing my straining erection. I came back to the kitchen to find Scout and Gatlin huddled together at the kitchen island. I stood in the doorway, watching them. The flush that currently covered Gat's cheeks told me I was *very* interested to know what they are talking about. I moved closer and Scout caught my gaze and winked. Now I really needed to know.

"Honeysuckle, what did you say that has our sweet bumblebee blushing?" Gatlin spun around, his cheeks growing a shade darker. *Interesting*. I moved to stand behind Scout, caging her between my arms and the island. I looked at Gatlin who had now found the ceiling fascinating. When Scout turned to face me, I looked down to meet her gaze. Her leafy green eyes sparkled with humor. My eyes flicked to Gatlin and back. He was now staring daggers at the back of her head like he was willing her not to speak. His cheeks were still tinted pink.

"All I will tell you, is that it's a surprise." She pulled her lower lip between her teeth. Scout couldn't lie to save her life. She would give you truth nuggets, but no lies.

"A surprise? When do I get to know what this surprise is?"

Scout patted my chest as she moved from between my arms. "Patience, Papa bear. Patience. I promise you are going to be very pleased." She and Gatlin both started to move about the kitchen, getting dinner ready. Meanwhile, my dick was yet again hard to the point of pain. *Fucking fuck.* I might lose my mind by the time we finished dinner. Or all my blood would continue south and I would pass out. I wanted neither option.

My assessment of my sanity being gone was not far off when we finished eating. I also did, in fact, feel like if some of my circulation didn't make it to the rest of my body, I would hit the floor. I was vibrating with need. Every cell in my body wanted to go upstairs and not leave until I pulled every orgasm from my two partners. I abruptly pushed back from the table to stand. My chair made an awful noise as it slid. Gatlin stopped mid-sentence, both he and Scout turning to me. Gatlin's mouth was still open while Scout looked at me wide-eyed. If the look on my face and the bulge in my pants didn't let them know dinner was over, I was about to.

"You both have to the count of three to get your asses upstairs and naked." They both sat, unmoving. "One." Scout was the first out of her seat. I heard her giggle as she darted toward my room. I looked at Gatlin. "Two." His mouth morphed into a cocky, little smirk. Moving around to stand behind his chair, I leaned down so my mouth rested beside his ear. "My sweet bumblebee, good boys get come and enjoy that sweet pussy upstairs. Brats get to watch and wait." He shivered as my words ghosted over his skin. I pulled the lobe of his ear between my teeth, biting hard enough to cause him to suck in a sharp breath. I released his skin and kissed his neck. "I'll give you one more chance." I straightened, giving him the space to move. He and I both knew he would go, but not before throwing me into a tailspin.

"I'm going." He reached, grabbing my bulge through my jeans. I let out a hiss at the grip of his hand. "I expect my brattiness will soon be forgotten." Before I could question him, he was off like a shot. I took a few slow breaths in an attempt to calm my racing heart, then walked toward my room.

Time for some fun.

scout

Once in the bedroom, I started to shed my clothes. While Gatlin and I had planned this, we had no way of knowing that Leland would take the bait and go all bossy on us. We both enjoyed pushing our teddy bear's buttons, but also giving him and each other pleasure. I had not had this in past relationships—the give and take of lovemaking. When it boiled down to it, this all stemmed from our love for each other.

When we got home, I could tell something was going on with Gat. He had been off the last few days. There would be times that he would be fine and then suddenly leave the room like his ass was on fire. It turns out, it kind of was. Well, maybe not on fire. but his ass was feeling some kind of way. While Leland showered, I grilled him until he finally told me what was going on. He had been slowly stretching himself with butt plugs. While his cheeks were tinted pink with embarrassment, mine was boiling hot with arousal. Watching the two men I cared for pleasure each other was something I didn't know was such a turn on. This was one of the many things I had discovered I enjoyed in the last few weeks. I also wanted to try things in the bedroom, but those could wait. We had time to explore all of the naughty things that crossed our minds.

I heard Gatlin before I saw him. He came into the room half naked where he had discarded his clothes as he came down the hall. With a pull of his zipper, his pants were dropping to the floor. As he stepped out of them, our eyes locked before his hungry gaze moved over my body. I had chosen to wear a bra and panty set in hopes of getting to show them off. They were a little fancier than what I normally wore. I only had a few sets, opting most of the time for whatever my hand landed on.

"Holy shit, honey, you are a fucking dream."

There had been very few times before I met Gat and Leland that anyone had made me feel as beautiful and wanted as they did. I stood, letting him take in every inch of exposed skin. He moved across the room, crowding me toward the bed. The backs of my knees hit the bed, causing us to tumble backward. As my back hit the bed, our mouths met in a crash of teeth. This kiss was feral, full of want and need. My hips moved of their own accord, craving friction and release. The sound of a belt undoing had us pulling apart. Leland stood in the doorway, slowly undressing as he watched us on the bed. His hard cock pushed at his briefs, the tip peeking out the top of the band. Still frozen, we watched him kick his pants to the side and prowl towards us. The predatory look in his eyes had moisture and heat pooling low in my stomach.

He stopped at the side of the bed, looking down at us. "I want to know what this surprise is."

I looked to Gatlin. My hand squeezed his arm gently where I had been holding him. The vulnerability in his expression showed how nervous this made him. He had admitted that he was nervous, and even questioned whether Leland would even want to take his "anal v-card." Of course, I told him that Leland would think it was the greatest honor to be his first. I also reassured him that both Leland and I would never push him, and just to be honest with us. With a curt nod, he slid off me and stood at the end of the bed. I shifted over on the bed to be closer to where Leland stood.

I looked up to him, his eyes finding mine. "Close your eyes, bear." My words came out low and breathy. He followed my order, his eyes snapping shut. When I looked back to Gatlin, he was sliding his briefs down his legs. He climbed back on the bed, making us both now eye level with Leland's still very hard but clothed dick. I hooked my fingers in the band of his underwear, tugging them down his legs. Once free, I leaned forward, kissing the tip of his dick.

"*Fuck,*" Leland almost growled out.

I wrapped my hand around his base, taking the tip into my mouth. My head bobbed a few times before hearing a sharp intake of breath as I hollowed out my cheeks. When I popped off, Gatlin took my place. He licked a long strip up the underside of Leland's heavy cock then swirled his tongue around the head, my hand still circling the Leland's base.

"Open your eyes, baby," I told Leland just as Gatlin took more of his throbbing length into his mouth.

His eyes flew open, a gasp left his mouth at what he saw. This was just part one of his little surprise. "Shit, yes just like that. Oh God."

Leland combed his fingers through Gat's hair as the latter continued to pleasure his dick. I stroked him in time to the same rhythm, bringing him closer to the edge. With his free hand, Leland guided my face back toward his groin with Gat. I chuckle lightly at him, still being the bossy one. For the next few minutes, we made out around his dick, sucking and slurping until we were all ready to burst.

gatlin

I started slowly, taking Leland into my mouth. I loved to be bratty, as he says, and push his buttons, but at my core, I wanted to be good for him. From a very young age, I knew there wasn't much I wouldn't do to make him proud. I hollowed out my checks, trying to do things that I knew I enjoyed. I took as much of him as I could before pulling back to lap at his tip. While I continued, Scout had raised up to her knees to kiss Leland, the sounds of their pleasure only making me work harder.

"Oh fuck. That's so good, baby. Look at you sucking my cock. Look at him, Scout. Isn't he beautiful taking my dick?"

"Mmm, such a good boy for us."

Scout moved back down to where I was working to pleasure Leland with me. Within a few seconds of our joined efforts, Leland spoke. "Enough. Fuck. I am going to come if you two don't stop." Leland's voice was strained as he stepped out of our reach. I tried to keep a tight rein on my control, but I was right there with him. We both sat back on the bed, waiting for what was coming next. "Honeysuckle, as beautiful as that bra and panty set is, I want to see all that's mine."

Scout, like me, enjoyed teasing Leland. While she did as she was told, she made it torturously slow. Unclasping her bra at a leisurely pace. I could tell that Leland was as ready as I was to drink in her whole body. I moved, deciding to give her a helping hand. I kissed up her stomach, but stupidly forgot what was lodged in my ass. A moan escaped my lips as it rubbed across my prostate. In my haste to move, Leland glanced at the very visible plug in my ass.

Well, secret's out now.

chapter 20

· · ·

gatlin

SHIT.SHIT.SHIT.

    This was not the plan. Not that there was a concrete plan, other than me blurting out, *"Leland, I want you to stick your monster dick in my ass. Look, I was even super prepared and have been stretching! Aren't you so proud?"* Obviously, I would have tried to be smoother about it, but accidently showing him was not on the bingo card. Judging by the look on Leland's face, though, I would say that the reveal is being very well received either way. Instead of saying anything, I raised my ass up while keeping my head and chest between Scout's legs. She was still sitting up, her eyes dancing across my face. One of her eyebrows quirked as she silently questioned if I was ok. Before I could react, I felt a big warm body press against my ass.

    "What is this, bee? You are both so needy." Leland ran his hand down my back before swatting my ass. I sucked in a sharp breath at the sting. The impact had me clenching around the plug. "Do you want me to play with your needy hole, baby?" His feather-light touch moved down my crack and skated across the plug. I released a whimper that escaped my throat at his teasing caress. "Mmm, so needy. If you want me to make you feel good, then you better take care of our sweet honey-suckle. She is dripping for us." I looked at Scout's glistening folds, her hips thrusting slightly under my gaze. My tongue darted out to wet my lips. Movement to my left caused me to turn to where Leland now squatted beside my head. I looked at his handsome face. I thought, not for the first time, that I had been in love with this man for most of my life. I could kick past Gatlin's ass for not truly seeing this man sooner as more. My eyes moved from his face as I tried to hide the guilt and regret I'm sure was showing. "Gatlin, look at me." My eyes snapped to his at the use of my actual name.

"Yes, sir?"

His pupils dilated at my words. *Gotcha. Sir, it is. In the bedroom, at least.*

Scout giggled above us before sobering at the look Leland gave me. "How far do you want to go? Even if we get going, if you say stop, that's it." His care and the conviction in his expression was such a fucking turn-on. Scout and I both found protective Leland hot as fuck. We had discussed it in length. Gossiping like two hens, or a hen and a rooster, about our man.

"I want you to fuck me. I want your cock in my ass while I fuck our girl." I looked away, my cheeks flaming as the words tumbled out of my mouth. I knew what I wanted, but asking for it was a different story.

"Is that what you want as well, honey?"

"*God*, yes. I want to feel you fucking bee while he fucks into me."

Holy shit, that was a hot image that I needed to be a reality right *now*. I shifted, the plug moving across my prostate. I let out a needy whine. I had never felt like this with anyone. I felt like, for the first time, I could drop all the walls and truly show what I wanted and needed.

"Please," I basically whispered the words. "Please, I need you both." The seconds felt like a lifetime. Maybe Leland didn't want this tonight —or at all. He has said he did, but that could have changed. I could feel embarrassment trying to work its way into my mind.

"Baby, breathe." Scout's thumb rubbed across my cheek. Her expression was soft and loving.

I fucking love her.

I wanted to scream the words, but they were stuck behind the knot currently clogging my throat. My eyes stung like I was about to cry. I realized that I had never said *I love you* to someone I had sex with. It was always biological, not emotional. For the first time, I would not just be with someone to mutually scratch an itch. As that reality sunk in, I could feel everything trying to bubble to the surface. *Hold it together. For now, at least.*

I felt lips press to my temple, and my lids fell shut.

"Breathe, love. You get our girl ready, and I will make you feel so good."

Leland moved back behind me. He ran his hand down my back to my ass, caressing me like I was precious, before leaning in to place a kiss on my right cheek. I looked back to Scout, not breaking eye contact as I kissed my way down the inside of her left thigh. When I reached her dripping center, I moved to the other thigh, skipping over where I knew she wanted me. Her groan of frustration was barely out when I flicked my tongue over her clit.

"Oh yes, more." Her fingers tangled in my hair, trying to tug me closer.

I pulled her clit between my lips, lightly sucking the sensitive bundle of nerves. We both moaned in pleasure as I felt Leland gently moving the plug. He was working the plug gently, back and forth. I had been wearing this one on and off for a few days, so I was more open than normal. The plug wasn't as big as Leland, but it would definitely make things easier. I refocused on my task and began to work Scout up to her first orgasm of the night.

"Are you ready to take it out?" Leland gave a little tug on the toy.

"Yes, sir."

He laid his free hand on my lower back. "Ok, bee, breathe and bear down for me." I did as I was told. There was a slight burn as widest part moved past the tight ring of muscles. "You are doing so good. I bet you are both dripping for me." I let out a breath as the plug slipped free. My hole instinctively clenched, missing the fullness. "Ready for more?" I thought he meant his monster dick. I was about to protest when I felt his hot breath on my skin.

"Oh, fucking *fuck*," I gasped as he spread my cheeks before leaning to lick across my clenching hole. After that one lick, he went to town.

Leland ate me out like a possessed man. He then teased me with his tongue, working it in. I followed suit and dove back into Scout. I moved from her clit to her entrance, thrusting my tongue in and out. Her warm walls clenched around me. I tried to match the rhythm Leland set. He worked me closer and closer to the edge. Every time I was at the tipping point, he pulled back. This continued until Scout and I were both twitching messes.

"I'm going to cum." Scout's strangled words spurred me on. I kept pushing her closer to the edge of release. Her grip tightened painfully in my hair as she squeezed my head between her glorious thighs. "Yes. Yes. Yes." She ground her pussy on my face, soaking me in her release. I continued to gently lick and suck her sensitive flesh. When I felt cool liquid dripping down my crack, I tense momentarily. I was more than ready to take this next step, but this was the first time I was being prepped to take a man's dick. Leland ran his fingers up and down my lower back. He moved to massage my lower back before moving to my ass cheeks, kneading them. I relaxed under his hands. I moaned into Scout when I felt Leland press a single finger against my hole. It was just pressure, like he was not trying to push in, but more massage the outer ring of muscles. Between the lube and spit, it didn't take a lot for the tip of his finger to slip in. He started out slow, pausing with just the tip. Then, he began to work the single digit in and out. Scout moved back when she came down from her climax. My head dropped to the bed as I moaned. It was one finger, but thinking about it being Leland had my pleasure climbing.

"More. Please more.""

I reached for Scout when she moved, letting out a disgruntled noise. "Shh, I'm not going far. Raise up." She slid under me when I did, putting us in a 69 position. "Be good and don't come." I lost all sense of reality when her wet lips wrapped around me. Leland worked two fingers in, spreading and scissoring them. I felt my body barreling toward the end. My body hummed with what felt like electricity. Every nerve crackled under the surface.

"I'm ready. I need you both. Now." I heard the desperation in my voice. The demand to have them surrounding me. For the first time, I felt like I could truly be open with what I need and want. I liked giving control to them and letting my mind quiet. Scout's body moved from under me, bringing me out of my thoughts. I raised up to give her room, coming to my knees before setting back on my heels.

"Gatlin."

My name caused me to turn to Leland. His face was flushed pink, causing his freckles to stand out. My eyes trailed over his body. He was just so big everywhere. His broad, strong chest was covered in soft chest hair. The trail of hair led down over his softer stomach to his cock, which stood long and proud. I continued down his strong legs before looking back up to his eyes. The brilliant blue of his eyes were blown out by his pupils. He looked over my face, searching for something. "Sir?" I was poking a very horny, on edge bear, but I couldn't stop myself. A rumble was the only sound for a moment. I watched Leland clench his jaw, the muscle ticking. He let out a breath before settling on the bed. Scout snuggled in.

"You truly want this? I'm sorry if my asking is frustrating, but I will always put the two of you over anything. So, I need you to be absolutely positive." He reached out to tangle his fingers with mine and then Scout's.

"Yes, I want this." I looked to Scout, pressing a kiss to her lips before turning back to Leland. "Make us yours."

leland

"Make us yours."

His words spurred me into action. I stood up, moving off the bed. I was so hard it was almost painful. I had never wanted two people more in my life. I had found everything I thought was just a pipe dream. *Make us yours.*

They were already mine.

My best friends. My loves. My forever.

Gatlin turned to face where I stood at the end of the bed, shifting his feet out from under him. I reached out and grabbed them, yanking him toward the end of the bed. I leaned over him, taking his lips in a hard kiss. I licked into his mouth, showing him that I was in control of this. He didn't fight me, but gave in beautifully. I nipped his bottom lip before raising up. I looked at Scout, her gaze fixed while she slowly circled her clit with her fingers. We have found out that Scout got very turned on watching Gat and me together.

"Come here."

She moved without hesitation. I gave her lips the same treatment I gave Gatlin's. She moaned into my mouth when I pushed my tongue in her waiting mouth. I could kiss the two of them until I died. I pulled back enough to look at her lust-blown eyes.

"I know you said that you wanted it from behind." I look to Gatlin. "But I want to see your face the first time I push into your sweet little ass."

"Yes, please. I want that."

Scout reached up toward the head of the bed, grabbing a pillow. "Here, lift your hips and put this under them." She moved the pillow under Gatlin, helping him get it situated. "There, that will make it more enjoyable." My heart melted even more at the exchange between them. Even though Gatlin had done the same thing for me, seeing Scout return the gesture caused a tightness in my chest.

I set up between Gatlin's legs, trailing my fingers over his legs. I grabbed the lube from the bed, pouring a generous amount on my cock. He watched the movement, his eyes tracking as I grabbed my dick. Scout ran her finger over his skin before leaning in to kiss across his chest. I moved the tip of my dick to his entrance. I applied the slightest pressure, but Gatlin was holding his breath in anticipation.

"Breath, bumblebee. You have to relax, love. Bear down on me just like with the plug. It may not feel great or even good to start. We go as slow as you need. You say stop, that's it."

I watched as he released a breath before taking another lung full of air and releasing it, as well. When I felt him relax, I applied more pressure. I ran soothing hands over his legs. Just as Scout moved to his nipple, my tip slipped in. She sucked gently on the hardened bud while I gave him a moment to adjust. The sound of his gasp and moans reached my ears. It made me want to pound into him hard and fast, but that was not happening tonight, though. His hips began to shift, trying to pull me in. I took that as my sign to begin to work myself in.

"So fucking tight. I feel you squeezing me, trying to pull me deeper. Such a greedy little hole." I continued to work myself in, Scout teasing him the whole time. By the time our hips were flush, there was nothing but continuous moans and gasps. I paused again, letting him adjust. I was also walking the knife's edge of my control. I needed the moment to get myself under control. "Are you ready, honey, to ride our sweet bee?"

"Fuck yes."

She climbed over Gatlin, her knees resting beside his hips. I reached up to her hips, helping guide her. His dick laid hard against his stomach, twitching and leaking precum. It had softened when I started to push in, but had returned to its full, glorious length. Lowering herself, she spread her pussy lips, sliding up and down his length, soaking him with her juices. Reaching a hand behind her, she grabbed Gat's cock, lining it up with her entrance. As she began to lower herself, Gatlin tightened around me. At this rate, his was going to cut the circulation off my dick.

We all let out a collective groan when she was fully seated. I could die here. Connected to the people I loved.

God, I am madly in love with them.

"I'm ready. Please fuck us."

Leaving one hand on Scout, I moved the other to rest on Gatlin's leg, needing to feel that this was real. I started to slowly thrust as Scout lifted herself up and down Gat's cock. The view I had of both of them had my slow rhythm accelerating. The slap of skin mixed with the sounds of pleasure. I wanted to draw this out. This was what I had dreamed of for so long. Not just the physical, but the emotions and connection. This is what I have craved with partners.

"Yes, just like that." Scout was grinding down on Gatlin, moving her hips in a circle. Gatlin's low moan was the only reply.

"You like it when I ride you? Squeeze all the cum from you?"

Scout's dirty talk would drive me over the edge to soon if I didn't start moving. I began to thrust faster, sawing in and out of Gat's warm, tight hole.

"Yes, bear, fuck my needy hole. Love getting fucked by both of you. Fucking ruin me."

I fucked into Gatlin. Scout was riding him like a professional bull rider. She fell forward, slamming their hips together as she fucked herself on his hard dick.

"Fucking mine. Both of you are mine." I claimed them, brutally thrusting into Gatlin, one of my hands squeezing Scout's hips. "Who do you belong to?"

"You. I belong to both of you," Scout panted out, pounding down on Gatlin. "God so good."

"Yours. I'm yours. Both of yours."

I continued hammering every word home. "My fucking heart and soul. *Mine.*" It was very caveman of me, but fuck, they brought something primal out in me.

"Not gonna last long." Gatlin gritted out the words. He gripped Scout's hips, helping her to continue her movement. I felt Gatlin clench around me this time, harder than any other time. I knew he was close. I shifted so my next thrust hit that sweet spot inside him. The low groan he released told me that I found my mark. The fact that this was happening was still unbelievable to me, but I continued to drive my hips forward, pegging his prostate with every thrust. The sounds of our moans of pleasure echoed around the room. I leaned forward, my chest resting against Scout's back. We were all damp with sweat, our bodies sliding as we moved. I kissed her exposed neck before scrapping my teeth over the delicate skin.

"Oh God, oh fuck, I'm coming." Scout lost her rhythm, slamming down to keep driving her higher. "Yes, yes, yes. I'm coming." Her legs shook as she ground down onto Gatlin. I straightened and held Scout's hips as an anchor to pound into Gat. My thrusts were punishing, but the noises of Scout coming again had me continuing. I was like a feral animal, driven by carnal need. At that moment, my only goal was to get as deep as possible in Gatlin. I needed to fill him with my cum. I wanted to hear him cry out with pleasure.

"Shhiittt. I'm coming. Fuck yeah, honey, milk that cock."

I could see where Gatlin's fingers dug into Scout's soft hips. Their words drove me over the edge. When I felt my climax coming, my thrusts became jerk and uncontrolled. I slammed my dick to the hilt, wanting to be as deep as possible. My head fell back, every muscle in my body locking up with my orgasm. When I came, it was their names on my tongue. My hot cum filled Gatlin as his walls contracted around me.

"Oh God, it's so hot. It feels like you are setting me on fire from the inside. I fucking love it. Love feeling your hot cum in me."

At Gatlin's words, my cock gave a few final twitches, sending the final spurts of cum into him. As my climax faded, I continued to lazily thrust as I watched the aftershocks move through both of them. Scout fell forward, laying chest to chest on Gatlin. His hands were banded around her, holding her to him. I gently pulled out, immediately wanting to be inside one of them again. I stepped into the bathroom, grabbed a few damp cloths, and returned to the bedroom. I was met with the soft, even breathing that only meant sleep. I walked over and kissed Scout's temple. Her eyes blinked open at me, blissed out and content. A sweet smile crossed her face.

"Sweetheart, let me help you off and then you can pee and clean up." I rubbed her back before helping her up. She moved to the bathroom. Having a twin sister who believed because we shared a womb, there was no TMI, was a curse and a blessing. Finding out that women needed to pee after sex was one of the positive things. Finding out that the reason Oakland knew this was from too much sex and not enough peeing—her words, not mine—was not ideal.

I turned to a sleeping Gatlin. Just like with Scout, he took my breath away. His golden skin was on full display. My eyes tracked over his whole body. His long lashes touched his slightly reddened cheeks. He hadn't trimmed his bread, so it has grown out a little. My eyes caught on his full lips. They were slightly puffy from all the kissing. At this thought, my dick gave a little twitch. *Calm down, dude. We aren't teenagers.*

"He is gorgeous, isn't he?"

"Both of you are absolutely stunning." I turned to look where Scout stood beside me, winking at her. I moved over to Gatlin, smoothing his hair away from his face. Scout grabbed the rag from my hand and wiped him off. He had to have been absolutely drained, because he didn't move the whole time we cleaned him up. He ran himself ragged before any trip. Whether it was the Nature Nuggets or a store client, it didn't matter. Once I had cleaned his backside, I tossed the rags in in laundry bin.

I easily shifted him up the bed where his head was now on a pillow, getting him covered.

"That is so hot. The way you can just move him like he weighs nothing. Well, honestly, both of us." Scout walked towards me, every inch of her body on display. Her smile turned teasing as she trailed her hand over me.

I grabbed her hand, kissing her fingers before turning her toward the bed. "Bedtime."

She climbed in, snuggling into Gatlin. Laying her head on his chest, I followed her in, sandwiching her between us. Without waking completely, Gat reached his hand, covering Scout's where it rested on his chest. I reached my arm over and covered their hand with mine. Tiredness started to pull me under.

"Mmm, I love you both so much." Gatlin's soft words filtered into my mind. When I woke up the next morning, I couldn't be sure if they were real or just a very good dream.

chapter 21

. . .

scout

"ARE you sure you don't want to come? We have plenty of room in our tent." Gatlin was loading stuff up in his truck behind his store. He and Leland were leaving for the Nature Nugget trip this morning. Normally, I would be all about going, but this year was just too busy at home.

"You know I would love to, but Amos wants my opinion on some stuff in the apartment. My mom also wanted to do a family dinner. I also made plans with Lettie. We haven't gotten to really hang out. I'm sorry, bee." I felt like I was letting him down by not going. I could try and move things around to go. I could call my parents to get them to cover for me. They have occasionally filled in at the shop over the years. My thoughts were spinning as I tried to work out how to do everything when I felt a warm hand band around my waist from behind.

"Stop," Leland breathed the word into my ear. "Take a breath." My body reacted to his low, commanding tone. I drew a deep lung full of air, then released, my body melting back into Leland's chest. Gatlin walked over to cup my check. The gold fleck in his topaz eyes caught in the early morning light.

"It's ok, Scout. We are not upset that you need to stay here. Of course, we would love for you to be able to go, but it's ok. I promise you." His eyes pierced straight into my soul.

"We will have to plan a trip for just us for later. Yeah?" Leland gave me a little squeeze before kissing the top of my head.

"Definitely."

Gatlin's soft smile melted away the last of my worries. With a soft kiss, he turned toward the store. "I'm going to wrangle the kids up and start dividing them up. You're not leaving, are you, honey?"

"No, I was going to see you guys off and then do some work. Amos should be here soon." I snuggled closer to Leland as we watched Gatlin.

"Ok, good. We can't leave without kissing our girl goodbye." He winked and then walked through the door.

"Try and relax some while we are gone. Nan brought some new books by the bakery the other day. I left them in the bedroom if you want to read any of them." He turned me, so I was now facing him. Because of our height difference, I was looking up to him. "I'm going to help bee so we can head out. I saw something about some rain moving in, I don't want to be setting up during it."

"That would not be fun." I leaned up on my toes, wrapping my hand around his neck and pulled him to me. The kiss was tame, but I couldn't stop myself when they were around. Touching and kissing was a must.

"I know I speak for both of us. We are going to miss you."

"I will miss you guys, too. But just think of all the great sex we will get to have once you are home."

ONCE THE GUYS HEADED OUT, I went into the store. I didn't really have much to do, but it was better to hang out here and get a little social interaction than sitting at home. Plus, owning your own business meant a lot of time spent doing the not fun things. I was in my office when Amos found me. He knocked lightly on my door.

"Busy?"

"Nope, I'm just doing busy work." I turned to face him with a smile.

I haven't been up to the apartment recently, so I was not exactly sure how much had been done or what was left. I trusted Amos to do what needed to be done. He was a Godsend after the revolving door of contractors that had quoted the job. I didn't know him, but he knew Cleo somehow—I think through her brother. She recommended him and I hired him on the spot. He has given me sound advice on building and renovating and tried to do his best to get this job done.

We stepped into the apartment, and I was honestly in shock by how much was done. The hole that had to be cut was gone. The water damaged walls and floor have been replaced. Everything looked amazing. I was so happy to be close to it being done, but a pang of sadness made my chest tighten. I have loved living with the guys. I had people to come home to and have meals with. I will miss being under the same roof when I move back here. My brain registers that Amos had been talking and I hadn't heard any of it. I realized that I had blindly moved into the apartment during the time I had spaced out.

"I'm sorry, Amos. What did you say? I completely missed it." I felt my cheeks warm with embarrassment.

He smiled softly. "I was saying that you should be good to move back in. The only thing left for us to do is finish painting the last rooms then it's all yours.

My stomach dropped.

"Ready to move back in? So soon?" My breathing was starting to pick up. I had lived alone for years by this point I should be excited to get my own space back. The apartment I had put so much money into. I felt nothing but dread.

"Well we are a bit behind, so it's not that soon. But yeah, we were able to really knock a lot out during the last few weeks. I guess it helps when the bossman has insomnia and works all hours." He gave a little self-deprecating laugh. "So yeah, you can move in, I would say, within the next week."

Next week.

The ball of dread kept growing. I felt my heart rate starting to climb. I loved the apartment. Truly, I did, but I also didn't want to think about being back here alone. I started to pick at my fingers, trying to stave off the panic. I swallowed around the lump in my throat. I really shouldn't be freaking out. It's not like we wouldn't all still see each other. We're dating, for heaven's sake. For some reason, though, moving back here just feels so wrong.

"Th-Thank you, Amos." I forced a smile. "I really appreciate how hard you guys worked and it looks amazing in here." I look away from him, trying to disguise it as taking in the room. I drew in shallow breaths. *Get it together, Scout.*

"It really did turn out well. If you ever wanted to rent this place out, we could always close in the steps and create its own exit. It would be perfect to rent out. Little extra income, and depending on who it is, you could trust them to watch over the store at night." He looked at me out of the corner of his eye. The look he gave me told me I had not been covert in my panic. "You know, it's just food for thought, I guess. Nothing wrong with wanting to be close to the people you love." I turned back to him. His face showed understanding for what I was feeling. I didn't know Amos well, but he seemed like a nice guy.

I thought about what he had said about renting the place out. I didn't know if Leland and Gatlin would want me even to stay permanently. We had been friends before dating, but moving in together may seem like too much. It was something to talk to them about. "I will keep that in mind. Especially about the separating the entrance. I didn't realize that was a possibility." With that, we moved around the apartment, going over various things that had to be changed or fixed.

When we finished, we had been upstairs for close to an hour, deciding on final colors and discussing the back stairs and what that could look like. Walking back down the steps, my phone pinged with a message.

> Papa bear: 9:00 a.m. We made it, honeysuckle. Cell signal is spotty, but we will message or call when we can. XOXO

> Bumblebee: 9:01 a.m. *Sent a photo*

Bumblebee: 9:02 a.m. Look how hot lumberjack teddy bear is. 🥵

I clicked the photo to make it bigger. Leland was squatted down next to a fire ring, stacking wood to start a fire. His jeans were stretched to their limit on his thick thighs. He was wearing a flannel shirt with the sleeves rolled up and a t-shirt under it. The t-shirt stretched across his chest, showing off the strong muscle beneath. His hat was flipped backward like usual. His face had a bit of a beard growth, completing the whole look. He was focused on the fire and not paying attention to Gatlin taking a photo. He looked so hot.

Me: 9:05 a.m. Another pair of panties ruined.

Bumblebee: 9:07 a.m. Mmm sounds like you need help with that.

Me: 9:08 a.m. If only my two boyfriends weren't off doing manly things… jk I hope you guys have fun. Message when you can. XX

Papa bear: 9:08 a.m. I cannot with you two.

Papa bear: 9:08 a.m. We will. Remember to relax a little sweetheart. XX

Bumblebee: 9:10 a.m. I'll try to get more photos for us. 😉 XX

I click my phone off and set it down on my desk. I had gotten so used to having one or both of them close that their being gone was odd. I tried to shake off the weird mood and focus on lining up some new books to add to the teen and young adult section. I lost track of time reading about the various books when I saw a coffee on the edge of my desk. I turn to find Lettie standing beside my desk.

"Good morning, sunshine! Did the men folk make it ok?" She sipped her coffee while waiting.

"Yeah, I was just messaging them a little while ago. The signal is spotty, so I probably won't hear much from them." A feeling twisted in my stomach. I forced it away, not wanting to inspect it to closely.

"Good! Ok so what's the plan for the week?" She looked at me expectantly.

"Well, I have dinner with my parents tonight and then probably hang around the house. Would you want to come over and do a movie girls' night?"

"Of course, we are doing movie night! I have a thing on Wednesday so we could do it Thursday. Neither of us open the store on Friday, so we could have a slumber party!" Her excitement was infectious, and even though that feeling still lingered, I was excited to get to hang out with my best friend.

"Awesome, I'm glad we are getting to hangout." I smiled at her. "What do you have going on Wednesday?"

"Oh, well it's a date. Or dates, I guess?" She turned her head, her darker complexion hiding any blush. *Dates?*

"Ma'am, don't look away now! Give me the details! Dates? Like plural?" Before she could answer any of my questions, the bell chimed over the door.

"Oh shoot, look at that! Better get up front. Wouldn't want the boss to catch me slacking." She hurried from the office.

I squinted at her in frustration. "I can guarantee the boss would not care!" I yelled to her as she headed out front. I heard her laughter echo back. I so want to know what she meant, but I guess it can wait until later.

LATER DOESN'T END up coming. By the time I was leaving, the store had been busier than normal and Lettie had been running around. I decided to let her off the hook and head to my parents' house. Giving her a quick goodbye, I grabbed my stuff and headed to my car. It felt odd to be leaving the store alone without the guys. The one silver lining was that I had Mud with me.

"Come on, sweet boy." Mud got to his feet, bumping into my leg lovingly.

Driving down the familiar road to my parents', I was hit with the same feeling from earlier. When I pulled into the driveway, I put the car in park and grabbed my phone. Before I got out of the car, I sent a message in our group chat.

> Me 5:52 p.m. Miss you guys! I hope you are having fun. Be safe XXX

I watched the screen for any sign they may reply. After a few minutes, I put my phone away and got out of the car to head into the house. I gave a knock as I unlocked the door. I let Mud go ahead of me. He moved through the house like he owned it.

"Hello, Mom? Dad?"

"In the kitchen!" I heard my mom call from the back of the house.

As I passed the steps, my brother came down to meet me. "Hey, sis! Sorry, I was coming down to get the door, but you beat me to it. I thought you had Mud?" He looked disheveled. Almost like he had been making out, or worse, having sex. *Nope, not going there.*

I moved to give him a hug. "Hey, Atty, he went into the kitchen to mooch. How's school going?"

Flint, my brother's roommate, came down the steps, looking just as out of sorts. *Hmm, that's an interesting development.* Flint was a big guy compared to my brother. I think he played football or something at their college. My brother played soccer for the college and was fit, but he was built like a runner. Muscled, but not bulk. Flint walked over and slung an arm around my brother's shoulder. "Yeah, Atty, how is school going?"

Atticus smacked his stomach before shoving his arm off. "Shut it if you don't want me to start spilling secrets, puddles."

Before I could blink, Flint had my brother in a headlock and they were roughhousing. My mom poked her head around the corner. "Hey, baby, come on into the kitchen. Boys, stop fighting in the house like you aren't legal adults."

As we headed back to the kitchen, there was a chorus of "Yes, ma'am," from them both. "I swear, men all have a child buried that only emerged when they are with their best friend. How are you, sweetheart?" She grabbed a coffee mug, filling it before sliding the mug across to me. Not only did I look like the younger version of my mom, but I also inherited my love of coffee from her. We both started drinking coffee in the morning and didn't stop until the night.

"I have been good, just working and hanging out with the guys." I had maybe forgotten to mention that I was dating both Leland and Gatlin. I know they wouldn't care. It came down to wanting to tell them face to face and this was the first chance I had to come over. "About the guys, we are together." My dad walked into the kitchen. He kissed my head, giving me a little squeeze.

"Hey, Scoot, sorry I interrupted." My dad walked over to my mom, snatching her into a kiss. They broke apart, smiling at each other. It melted my heart. I had watched them my whole life love each other, always wanting to find the same. That thought gave me the strength to tell them.

"Hey, Dad, I was just telling Mom that—well, me, Gatlin, and Leland are together." I looked at them, waiting for a reaction. Nothing. Maybe they didn't understand. "You know, like we are dating together. The three of us are in a relationship." Still nothing. What the hell? "Um, guys? I know it's not conventional and people will not understand, but I care about them and they care about me." They just stood there, smiling at me. "Ok, listen, I didn't expect you guys to freak out, but this feels very anti-climactic. Have you been replaced with clones? Are you having a synchronized medical emergency? It's like you aren't even surprised."

My dad laughed at that. "Scout, baby, why would this surprise us? The three of you have been slowly orbiting each other for the last few years, getting closer and closer. It's more surprising it hasn't happened sooner than this. This also means your brother owes me."

My mom looked at my dad in surprise. "He owes me, too. What did you bet with him?"

"I owe who what?" My brother appeared at the door of the kitchen.

"You apparently owe our parents money or something because of a bet. What exactly was this bet?" I turned to look at him before glancing at my parents.

"Oh shit, you told them about you and your men?"

"Language, young man," my mother scolded him.

"*My men?* I mean, I told them that Leland, Gatlin, and I are together."

Flint laughed coming into the kitchen, pointing to my brother. "He bet you would chicken out and not say anything."

"Hey, douche canoe, whose side are you own?" My brother's faux outrage laced his tone.

Flint clutched his heart and looked to my brother. "My heart. Do you question my loyalty? I am wounded, sir."

While the two of them bickered, my mom reached across the kitchen island to squeeze my hand. "We just want you to be happy and be with someone, or in this case *someones*, that treat you well."

Emotion clogged my throat at my mom's words. I blinked back the tears that threatened to spill. They were tears of pure happiness and relief. I was not sure I wanted to do this right now or alone, for that matter. I was honestly glad I pushed through and did this on my own. "Thank you, guys. Really, I know you would be ok with it, but thank you either way."

"Of course! We will always be there for you and your brother," my dad told us, tears pooling at the corner of his eyes. "Ok, right. Let's eat dinner and then maybe play a board game or watch a movie."

The rest of the evening passed with jokes and laughs. I missed doing this with my family. Since taking over the bookstore, I lost a bit of the connection with my parents and brother. I planned to change that in the coming months.

When I went to leave my parents', it was lightly raining. When I reached home, it was coming down in buckets. I thought about the guys and checked my weather app. I know about where they should be, so checking the weather was not a hard task. When the radar loaded, it looked like they are getting pounded with water. I silently prayed for them and everybody with them to be safe.

Please, be safe. Please.

I didn't hear from them until the next morning before they headed out for a hike. I was thankful that I had Mud, because the house and work were so quiet without the two of them. Even before we had crossed the line into dating, we were always hanging out. At least with Mud around, there was still some company and cuddling. Tuesday and Wednesday passed in a blur of busy days at the store and then hanging out at home. I had gotten a message from the guys just checking in. I knew the cell service was trash where they were. It was great for disconnecting the kids and adults and getting in nature. I wanted them to have a blast but also safe.

When I didn't get to join, though, I hated not hearing from Gatlin or Leland. I was a worrier. They were a part of my inner circle, and I liked keeping that circle of people close. When Thursday came around, I was ready for movies and hanging out with Lettie. I checked my phone one last time to see if the guys had messaged before the girls would arrive at the house. There was nothing. The message I had gotten that morning said that the two of them were going hiking alone this morning to check a trail, but would be back down before lunch and would let me know they were back. The kids were going to be doing stuff around the camp with some of the volunteers. Anxiety had started to creep in when the day wore on and I still had not heard from them. I had called Oakland earlier that week and invited her to girls' night. I had also invited Cleo, but she already had plans. When I met Oakland and Cleo, they just became a part of the girls. It had been Lettie and I for so long. Not that I was complaining.

Oakland and Lettie arrived at the same time. I took a breath before opening the door, pushing all the anxiety to the back of my mind. They were fine. Bad cell service. They just got busy with the kids, no big deal. They were fine. It just wasn't like them not to message. Everything is fine though.

So why does the knot in my stomach say otherwise?

chapter 22

· · ·

gatlin

THE TRIP WAS GOING AMAZING. The little bit of rain didn't even dampen the mood. It was now Thursday and Leland and I were heading to check one of the harder trails. This one headed to the lake and was usually the final hike of the trip. I was finishing packing my bag when a warm body pressed into me.

We had kept the touching to a minimum, only in the tent we were sharing. By the end of the day, though, we were so tired that we crawled into our sleeping bag, yes, one very big sleeping bag, and passed out. We had done nothing more than cuddling and a quick kiss. I was slowly losing my mind. I missed Scout and I missed touching my boyfriend whenever I wanted.

"You about ready to head out?" Leland asked before pressing a soft kiss to my temple.

I clipped the flap over on my bag and shifted around to face him. Being out in the woods for a few days, his beard had turned from a shadow to actual scruff. His freckles were also standing out from being in the sun. He looked hot as hell in a t-shirt that hugged his barrel chest and a flannel over the top. The sleeves, of course, were rolled up, exposing his forearms. I had realized rather quickly I really liked his arms. Leland had always been as strong as an ox, but there was something about his forearms. A throat clearing had me looking back to his face. He leaned in, running his fingers up the back of my neck and tangling them in my hair. I had not pulled it back yet, so it gave him something to grab onto. He hauled me closer, crashing our mouths together. We met in a hard clash of teeth. I moaned into the kiss, shifting my hips closer, trying to find release for my aching cock. Leland controlled the kiss, his tongue dominating my mouth. I didn't know where he learned to kiss the way he did, but damn, was I thankful.

He moved from my lips, kissing and nipping his way down my jaw. With my hair still wrapped around his hand, I had no choice but to let him move me. Working his way back up, he nipped the lobe of my ear. His warm breath coasted across my skin, causing me to shiver.

"If you keep looking at me like that, we won't be hiking to the lake. Instead, I am going to find a tree and bend you over it."

Holy shit. Yes, please.

"Ngh." My words are a whimper. "Please—I'm so hard. Need you."

"My greedy little bumblebee. Gets his hole played with a couple of times and now that's all he can think about." He moved one hand around to my lower back and slid it down my pants. His warm fingers traced the top of my crack before removing his hand. He pulled back, bringing his hand around to my mouth. I didn't even question him when his finger slid between my lips. Removing his finger, he slid back down my ass, going farther than before. "Is this where you need me, baby?" His finger grazed my hole. I swear, I was about to crawl out of my own skin. I was too hot and shaking with need. "Mmm, I bet I could make you come without even touching yourself." Between the kisses to my neck and the pressure Leland's finger applied, I could most definitely come hands free. I was wound tighter than an eight-day clock. "Imagine if our girl was here. We could take turns fucking her, or if you were really good, she might even let you fuck her throat."

I wished Scout was here. Fuck, I wished she was here and there were no kids. Then we could fuck all over this mountain. What I wouldn't give to hear her and Leland's noises of pleasure echoing around me. If I think too much on the subject of them coming and finding pleasure, I'm going to blow.

Leland removed his hand from my hair. He knew I was not going anywhere. Reaching around, he undid the front of my pants, pushing my boxers down to reveal my rock-hard dick. A bead of precum hung on the tip. Not one to miss an opportunity to tease, he trailed his finger up the underside of my shaft, collecting the precum and bringing it to his mouth. He sucked the finger until it was clean. Damnit, I wanted that finger to be my dick. He reached back down, gripping my cock before slowly working his fist up and down, coating me in precum.

"Bear, please. Please make me come." I was not above begging at this point. I could hear the rest of the camp starting to stir. We were camping a little apart from the kids. The adults set a perimeter of tents around the kids. I knew we shouldn't be fooling around, and I would feel guilty about it later. Right now, I just wanted his hands on me. It wouldn't be long before I had to go out and be a responsible adult. In response to my pleas, he hummed into my skin. His finger rubbed circles around the tight ring of muscles. He pushed just the tip in. I sucked in a breath, clenching down on the intrusion, but loving the feel. I could feel my balls start to pull up. I felt like a fucking teenager with a hair trigger. A few words from Leland and I would be a goner. Of course, my man delivered with words and more.

"You hear that, baby? The camp is starting to wake up. If they only knew what you were in here, begging for. Look at how much you are leaking." My eyes glanced down to the angry, flushed tip of my shaft. "I think the next trip, it should just be me, you, and our sweet honey-suckle. Take her hiking and then push her up against a tree. We could fuck her right on the trail where anybody could walk up on us." My groan was muffled by Leland's big hand. "It seems like you like the idea of getting caught. If you were able to hold off coming, you could even shove that hard dick into me while I took our girl. You did seem to enjoy fucking into me."

I couldn't hold it back as he focused on my tip, giving a little twist as he squeezed with a little more force. I leaned forward, burying my face in his neck as the first spurts of cum left my dick. I fought back the urge to shout as the climax continued. My body was jerking with aftershocks when I felt it safe to move out of Leland's neck. I looked to see his hand is covered in my release. I pulled back to look into his eyes. They were still clouded with lust, but also pride at giving me pleasure. Without looking away, he brought his hand to his mouth, cleaning each finger. My dick gave a twitch, trying in vain to harden. *Cool it, dude.*

"Mmm, that was quite the morning treat." Once his fingers were clean, he leaned back in, kissing me before grabbing a pack of wipes and cleaning his hand off. My brain had gone offline and didn't reboot until I felt the cool wipe on my shaft. I hissed at the contact. "Sorry, bee, but not good to leave it on all day."

"Yeah, I know, just sensitive. That was hot as fuck. We should have videoed for Scout." I could just imagine her using that vibrator to come while she watched her two boyfriends get off. Speaking of getting off. I reached for the button on Leland's pants, wanting to return the favor. He gently took my hands in his. He lifted my right hand, turning it to kiss the inside of my wrist.

"We will have time for that later. I can hear a few of the kids outside."

Shit. I was supposed to be the leader of this and I'm in my tent with my dick out. Leland must have seen the guilt cross my face. He touched my cheek, bringing my eyes to focus on him. "Bee, it's ok. They haven't been up long. I promise. I know we need to set up the activities before we head out." I wordlessly nodded before he leaned in, kissing me one more time. He moved aside to let me go out first. "After you, sweetheart."

I don't know what I did in my past life to deserve him and Scout, but damn, I was a lucky man. Two more days and we would be home with our girl.

Two more days, honeysuckle.

"ALRIGHT GUYS, while me and Mr. Leland are gone, you guys have your choice of a few activities. Each one of these will put you towards leveling up. Some of the awesome adults with us have volunteered to do these with you guys, so be respectful of the time they are taking to be here." I looked out over the group of kids we had this year. The Nature Nuggets was a co-ed group that ranged in age and background. Some of the kids came from great homes, others not so much. We also had teen volunteers who also helped our adults. We tried to make the group an open and accepting place for anyone, and thankfully were able to achieve it, mostly. "Ok, I am going to give you time to eat breakfast and decide what you want to do, and then we will divide up. Sound good to everybody?"

"Yes, sir," the chorus of voices responded back.

Everyone started to disperse to get their breakfast when one of the volunteers approached where I stood with a mom of two of the kids.

"Hey, um, Mr. Gatlin? Can I talk to you?"

I turned to find Miles, a guy who had just graduated high school. He had been a part of the group as a kid and then just kept coming. From what I have learned, his home life was not the best. He spent most of his time with his grandparents. He was able to move in with them before high school permanently. They were the ones that got him involved in Nature Nuggets as a kid. His grandmother had confided that it was, so they had an excuse for him to be with them more than with his parents. From what Nan knows about the family, his parents were neglectful and borderline abusive. We had some parents who stepped in to be surrogate parents for him and others like him. I was always thankful when they did, because these kids deserved it.

"Of course. What can I do for you, Miles?" I took in the young man who had been almost too skinny the first time we met when he was around seven or eight. He was still a smaller guy, but he had found his own style. I tried to encourage all the kids that being outdoors wasn't for one kind of person. The first time Miles came with his fingernails painted at twelve, I realized we had done right for all the kids. Not one of them or the volunteers batted an eye. Some of the kids complimented him on the color, asking if he could help them and what colors he had. It warmed my heart because that was not the case for him in his everyday life.

"I'm leaving early for school. Like when we get back. I was going to wait, but Mom is back. My grandparents are worried she will try to start something. I just don't want to see her." He had a distant look as he took in the forest around us. I knew what that meant, and he didn't need to explain. "I wanted to let you know that I really appreciate everything you and the other adults have done for me. I know I wasn't the easiest when I was younger, but having all of you really made my life better. So yeah, that's all, I guess." He continued to look away, but I could see that he had started to blink like he was trying to stop the tears that were trying to fall.

"I know you will be busy with school, but you are always welcome to come back and join us. Thank you for volunteering and always helping out. If you ever need anything, you know you can always call or text." I didn't want to cause the kid to cry in front of everyone. I did want to let him know that he had me in his corner. He was a good kid. He let out a slow breath before giving me a relieved smile.

"I will." He started to turn away, but I had one more thing I needed to say.

"Oh, and Miles?"

"Yeah?'

"I'm proud of you, kid." He returned my smile before walking over to help with breakfast. I looked around at all the kids and the beautiful scenery, just taking it in for a minute. I was thankful that Miles was actually going to the same school as Atticus, because I will admit that I had asked him to keep an eye out for him. Not many people had looked out for him, but that didn't mean it always had to be that way.

"Everything ok?" Leland came to stand beside me, offering me a cup of instant coffee.

"Yeah, just enjoying the day and thankful I get to share it with you."

leland

The sun had been out as we left camp, but of course as we worked our way over the lake, it began to sprinkle. Within a few minutes, it was a downpour. We had rain gear on, but we huddled under a rock formation to keep from getting completely soaked. There was just enough room under it for both of us to sit. We sat in companionable silence, drinking water and eating the snacks we had brought. Being out in nature always seemed to calm Gatlin. It was like his brain would quiet down. When we met Scout, it was one of the things they bonded over. I enjoyed the peace of nature, but the two of them almost needed to be in the open air. I had come out of the bakery more than once to see them working or just sitting on the back porch of Scout's store. They did it rain or shine, in the heat of the freezing temperatures of winter. Usually, they would be drinking coffee or eating something from the bakery. I was never jealous of this; I knew they wouldn't bat an eye if I walked over. Sometimes, I did. There would be other times I would just watch them, taking in all the little things I could. Now was another one of those times when we just got to be together.

At around the two-hour mark, the heavy rain started to slack off to a sprinkle and then nothing. The sun came back out like nothing had happened. With all the rain we had gotten over the last few weeks, the trail was a mess. This was one of the reasons we scouted the trail before we brought the kids on it. It was not a long hike, but it had some tricky parts that Gatlin always liked to check ahead of time. When we moved from under the formation, both of our phones pinged. I pulled mine from my pocket, seeing some emails, other notifications, and a message from Scout.

> Honeysuckle: 10:02 a.m. I hope you guys are having a great day. Be safe! I miss you both!! XX

I smiled down at my phone then looked to see Gatlin mirroring the same expression. "Hey, c'mere." He reached for my hand, tugging it until I moved closer. Standing in front of me, he turned his phone to take a selfie of us. At the last moment, I kissed his cheek, causing both of us to laugh. Being with Scout and Gatlin made me feel like a teen with his first love. Everything is new, but comfortable. The separation we kept as friends had dissolved away. I remained standing close to Gatlin when we looked at the photo. Gat let out a happy sigh. "You are so damn cute. Now to send it to our sweet honeysuckle."

> Bumblebee: 10:14 a.m. *Sent a photo*

> Bumblebee: 10:14 a.m. Got a little service and I was attacked by a bear! We miss you, honeysuckle, and can't wait to see you. XX

We waited a moment for the message to go through before Gatlin looked at me with a megawatt smile. "Ready?" I nodded, getting my bag settled into place. I followed behind Gatlin as we headed out.

Normally, we would take our time and enjoy the hike, but we needed to get to the lake and back. The rainstorm blowing through had put us behind. We normally would have been to the halfway point by this time. Instead, we were just getting to the first point Gat liked to check. The rock on this part could shift easily, especially after heavy rain. Fortunately, the rain must not have been enough to cause issues, which was a major relief. There had been years in the past when we had to skip this hike. It was always a major disappointment for the kids and the adults, if I was honest. The highlight of the week had always been swimming in the lake at the end of the week. It was always a little cooler in the mountains, but still got hot during the day. After being out in the elements, it was a nice way to relax and end the trip.

It had turned into a beautiful day now that the rain had cleared. I was really looking forward to getting to the lake. If we had time, I hoped to either bend Gatlin over or be bent over a tree before we headed back. I was distracted by my thoughts of sex when Gatlin suddenly stopped. I stumbled, almost running into his back. We were on a narrower part of the trial with a steep drop on one side. The wind was blowing the leaves on the trees that surrounded us.

"What–?" I started to ask when I was silenced by Gatlin putting his hand up. I listened, not hearing anything at first. Then I heard a cracking. *What the hell?* Gatlin was looking ahead and then to the edge below. It was not terribly high, twenty to twenty-five feet, but it was steep and covered in trees and large rocks. There was nothing for a moment, then before either of us could get out of the way, one of the bigger trees above us gave. The roots pulled up from the ground. I grabbed Gatlin, jerking him backward into my chest. He fell into me, the momentum pushing me closer to the edge. The tree landed in front of where we stood on the narrow trail. I still had a hold of Gatlin when the side of the trail gave way. There was no way I was going over the edge and taking him with me. I shoved him forward onto the trail in a last-ditch effort to keep Gatlin from going over. There was no stopping the inevitable, though. I hit hard against the ground, my pack causing me to be top-heavy. I reached blindly, trying to find something to grab and stop me before I hit the rocks that were closer to the bottom. I snagged what I could only assume was a tree. There was a sickening pop before pain radiated from my right shoulder and elbow. The scream that left me was cut short by the wind being knocked out of me. I landed back first against another tree, my pack taking the brunt of the impact. While trying to suck in air, I watched in slow motion as the trail continued to give way, the tree shifting as Gatlin tried to find purchase. I saw what was going to happen, panic and bile rising.

"GATLIN!!" Was the last sound before the tree slid the ground under him, causing him to lose his balance. The tree sent debris down the side. When something hit my arm, my vision started to darken. Fuck. I couldn't pass out. I tried to force my eyes to stay open. The pain radiating up my arm wouldn't be subdued. This couldn't be it. I hadn't gotten to love them long enough. Please let me love them longer. The last thing I saw before the world went dark was Gatlin falling.

This can't be it. I need more time with them.

chapter 23

· · ·

"HE IS LITERALLY TRYING to take my job. Like seriously." Oakland took a swig of her wine. She has been telling us about the new guy that is working under her. The guy was brought in under Oakland, but was acting like he was the boss. "The other day, I seriously caught him ordering my assistant around. He has also made multiple people on my team cry. Not to mention he has made some seriously unprofessional comments to female staff and me. I have tried to talk to my Mr. Loveless but he is useless." She took a breath then another drink of wine. "Ok, sorry I'm done. It's just so frustrating. I work with mostly men who are not all that bad, but this guy somehow has them wrapped around his finger, including Loveless." She looked down at her lap, her expression defeated. I placed a hand on her arm, giving it a gentle squeeze. Oakland was loyal to her people, so it was easy to see how hard this was on her. Especially if she felt like she had no way to fix the situation. "Anyways, off the petty party train on to more interesting topics." She turned her gaze, locking on me. "How are things going with my brother and my not-blood-brother?"

At the mention of my men, butterflies started up in my stomach.

"Oh my gosh, look at her face! She is all dreamy-eyed." Lettie reached over to poke my rib.

"Hey! Stop it or I will bite you." She jerked her hand back, knowing that I was being completely serious. I would bite. I had before when she didn't take me seriously. That time it had been over a donut. But the point still stood. "It's going really well. I mean, we have been friends for a few years, so the shift to more was not too bad."

"Ok so the real question: have you done the dirty with them at the same time? You know, two hotdogs in one bun?" Lettie waggled her eyebrows.

"No. Nope. Do not under any circumstance answer that question. I do not want to hear about my brothers' sex life. Blegh." I laughed at the face Oakland was making, Lettie joined in and eventually Oakland. "Seriously though, it's going good?"

"Yeah, truthfully, I am in love with them. I know it with everything in me. We have had things to work past. I didn't want to get in the way of the connection they had already. Gatlin was trying to figure out his sexuality when it came to Leland. Then Leland thought we would be better without him." They already knew all of this, of course. We were not shy with our physical affection, so people knew. Gatlin considered the Boone family his second family, so they were the third group of people he came out to. He still didn't really like to label himself, which is completely fine. As long as he was happy, that was what mattered. "I honestly can't believe it sometimes—that we are together. After the past fails, I was fine with just me, but instead, I got two amazing men who are my best friends and boyfriends."

"That is too freaking sweet. I'm jealous. I want hunky mean to want me. Preferably multiple men." Lettie huffed before crossing her arms over her chest. "I mean geez, is that too hard to find?"

"I would take just one guy that was really good at se—" Oakland's phone started ringing. Flipping it over, I caught the flash of the screen. "Hey, Mom, I'm–" She paused I could hear her mom's muffled voice through the phone. She was talking in a rush. From the words I could make out, it sounded like she was maybe crying. "When? Like how long?" She waited again before her eyes met mine. Her face had drained of its color. "Ok. Love you both. We'll see you in a few." She disconnected the call and took my hand.

"Oakland, what is it?" I felt bile start to rise up in my throat. The edges of my vision started to darken. *Breathe, dammit.*

Before she could answer, there was a knock at the door. I jumped to my feet, running to the door. Mud started barking, running excitedly to the door. He was supposed to be with the guys, but when it was time to go, he refused to get in the truck. Throwing it open, my parents stood there with Flint. Mud pressed into my side. I laid one hand on his head, looking at my family with complete confusion. *What? Why are they here?*

"Uh, hey, guys? Why are y'all here?" I asked before moving to let them in. Before I closed the door, I saw two other cars pull in. I waited for Leland and Gatlin's parents to get out of their cars. Nan passed them and came straight to me.

"Nan? What is going on? I don't mind you all coming over, but what is wrong?"

She looped her small arm through mine, using that to turn me back to the house. "Let's get back inside, dear." We walked to the living room. Oakland sat with Lettie on one end of the couch, my parents sat at the other. Atticus was sitting in one of the armchairs with Flint perched on the arm of the chair, his arm draped across the top. They sat close, Atticus almost leaning into his side. No one was talking, which meant something was really wrong. I was just about to open my mouth and demand answers when Georgia, Leland's mom, came in with Birch, or Big B, his dad, so I waited. They were followed by Gatlin's mom, Hadley, who was gripping Gatlin's dad, Memphis, like she was about to faint. Between the know that was currently cutting off my air and the amount of people in the house, I was going to hyperventilate.

I can't breathe. Oh, fuck, I can't breathe. I'm going to pass out.

A warm hand touched my arm. I sucked in a sharp breath at the contact. "Scout, honey, let's sit down, ok?" Nan gently guided me around the couch, sitting beside me. My dad got up, making room on the couch.

I tried to swallow around the lump that was logged in my throat. "Can someone please start talking? Please?" The *please* came out as a whisper. I blinked back the tears that started to form. My eyes and throat started to burn with the need to let them fall. I swallowed hard, forcing myself to take short breaths. I couldn't pass out. Leland's mom came around the couch to squat down in front of me. Her eyes were red and puffy like she had been crying. I didn't even notice that my mom had moved to my side. I glanced at her then focused on Georgia.

"Scout, sweetheart, we got a call from one of the volunteers for the Nature Nuggets. Earlier, Leland and Gatlin went to hike up the lake trail. You know bee, he always likes to check that trail before the kids go on it." She gave a soft smile before she sobered and continued. "They were supposed to be back at around lunch. They haven't come back." Mud pushed his way into the gap between Leland's mom and me. His weight settled on my feet as Georgia's words sank in.

"What do you mean, *they haven't come back*?" I looked at my watch, it was close to 9:30 at night. My eyes began to blur with tears. Another figure was squatting in front of me, I wasn't sure who it was at first until they spoke.

"The volunteers had to load the kids up and bring them back. They didn't have enough signal to call until they were off the mountain. By that point, it was almost five o'clock." Hadley's words were soft.

"Why did they wait so long?" Anger at the volunteers bled into my tone. "Why would they wait so long to do anything?" Nan squeezed my thigh reassuringly. Any other time I would welcome it, but right now I just wanted to throw her hand off, and find Leland and Gatlin.

Georgia wiped away the tears sliding down her cheeks. "There was some rain, so they figured it delayed them, which would have made them move slower. They also left a bit later than intended. While one volunteer called the rangers, two of the others called Birch and Memphis. They tried to call you first, but they called us when it went to voicemail. I'm so sorry, honey. When they told us what was going on, Memphis called your parents. We wanted to be here with you in case they called back, or you heard the voicemail."

"My phone is on the charger in our room. It was going dead." I went to stand when Atticus threw his hand up and jumped up.

"I got it."

He jogged back, handing me my phone before going back to his chair. I touched the screen to unlock it. There were four missed calls and two text message. I clicked the calls, figuring it was the volunteer. They didn't leave a voicemail, so I clicked out and went to my text messages. My eyes filled with tears. There was unread messages in our group chat. My thumb shook as I clicked the message. A photo popped up of the guys. Gatlin was smiling from ear to ear, his cheeks flushed pink. Leland had his arm around Gatlin's chest and was leaning around to kiss his cheek.

> Bumblebee: 10:14 a.m. *Sent a photo*

> Bumblebee: 10:14 a.m. Got a little service and was attacked by a bear! We miss you, honeysuckle, and can't wait to see you. XX

The screen blurred, tears now coming freely. They landed on the screen. I turned into my mom's chest, tears soaking through her shirt. My phone slipped from my hand, landing with a thud. They left me to cry for a moment. My mom's perfume and dad's cologne mixed and soothed like when I was a child. This was a nightmare I wished their arms could protect my from. When I felt I could, I straightened, taking the tissue Nan offered. She was also dabbing her eyes. Everyone in the room was silent, waiting for what came next.

"So what now? We have to find them. Are they looking? Is there something we can do?" My questions were growing more frantic.

"Right now, we have to wait. The rangers are out looking. They think they may have gotten stuck somewhere on the trail. They had to cut some small trees that had fallen at the start of the trail," Gatlin's dad spoke from where he stood beside Birch.

I can't just sit here. I have to find them. They have to be ok. Please be ok. I still have so many things I want ot say. Please.

"SCOUT, HONEY?" Nan reached out, taking one of my hands. I looked down to see that I had picked my skin raw. She gently rubbed circles on the back of my hand. "Did you know that teddy bear broke his nose?" I shook my head almost robotically. "He sure did. Well, he wasn't the one to break it, exactly." Her warm fingers massaged my palm, triggering my body to start to relax. For her age, she was surprisingly strong. "I was in the house one afternoon, I guess the boys would have been around twelve or thirteen. They came barreling into the kitchen. At first, I thought bumblebee was hurt. He was red faced from crying and look on the verge of a panic attack. He was inconsolable and also shirtless." Everyone was listening, pulled in by the simple story and welcoming the distraction. "Bear moved the fabric from his face and blood began to pour out of his nose. Well, this set Gat off again. Sweet teddy grabbed the rag and held it to his nose before going over to comfort his best friend. I stood there, watching them for a moment. Leland comforting him and assuring him that it was an accident. When bee's tears dried, he jumped into action. He put an ice bag together, got a clean rag, and helped Leland get cleaned up and comfortable. It turns out Gat had tried to hold a branch out of the way, but when it slipped from his hand, it cracked Leland directly in the nose. We figured out rather quickly that his nose was broken, which caused it to hump just slightly. For the next two weeks, Gatlin did everything for Leland. It drove Leland insane because he like to be the one to do things, but he saw that bee needed to take care of him. That was bear's way of taking care of Gat." She squeezed my hand, drawing my eyes up to meet hers. "The point of this is, those two have been taking care of each other since they first met. They take care of each other and you, and then you take care of them. They will fight the devil himself to get back to you." Her expression was earnest and full of conviction. She was right, though. We did take care of each other and would always fight to be together.

The shrill ringing of Oakland's phone startled everyone. She pulled her phone out of her pocket. All of my hope that it might have been one of the guys calling was shot down by the look on Oakland's face. She was pale, and her hands were visibly shaking as she answered the call and placed it on speaker.

"Is this Ms. Oakland Boone? And are you the sister of a Mr. Leland Boone?"

"Yes, I am. Who is this?" Nan once again squeezed my hand, grounding me as the seconds ticked by. We waited for the person to answer Oakland.

"This is Ann, I am calling from Mountain Creek Hospital. Your brother is en route to the hospital now."

"Just my brother? Is Gatlin Ford with him? Are they both hurt? Can you tell me how bad it is? Is it just one of them? I have you on speaker and Gatlin's parents are here." Oakland fired questions at who I assumed was a nurse.

"This is Memphis Ford. I am Gatlin's father. If there is anything you can share, we would greatly appreciate it. Is my son with Leland?"

"I do know they are both in the ambulance. Unfortunately, I can't tell you much about who is injured or who is more severe. The reception is poor where they are coming from, even the radio signal is spotty out there. I would advise you to make your way to the hospital. Just in case."

Just in case. Just in case what?

A ringing in my ears plunged the whole room into silence. I could feel bile start to rise up my throat. I was going to be sick. I tried to breathe through my nose, to stop the revolt my stomach was currently throwing. I needed to move. I had to get to the hospital. I would be there when they arrived. I wanted to reach through the phone and shake Ann the nurse for not being able to tell us more. I wanted to scream at them for not having good service. It was no one's fault, but my mind wanted to rage at someone.

Just in case.

There was no *just in case* here. They would be ok. *They had to be.*

I move on autopilot toward the door. It was like cotton has been shoved in my ears. I didn't hear the noise of the room. I faintly heard someone call my name, but I had to go to them. I could feel the tears starting to come. The lump in my throat threatened to cut off my air supply. Everything felt slightly off kilter. I didn't notice at first when a I ran into a hard body that stepped in my path. I looked up into the eyes of my little brother, my brain slowing to process what he was doing.

Why was he stopping me? He didn't move, but instead blocked me from going around him. "Atticus, move. I have to get to them." I pushed against his chest, but nothing happened. The tears were falling hard, constantly now. I couldn't see anything clearly. I pushed again, shoving him with all my weight. Damn him for being bigger than me. His solid body mass made him immovable to me. "Move. *Now.*"

"No, Scout, please listen. You–"

No. No?

"If you don't get *the fuck* out of my way, Atticus, so help me God." Anger had taken over my panic. I had never been one for violence, but if my little brother thought he could stop me, he was sadly mistaken. I would fight dirty to get to my guys.

"Let me finish, dammit. You don't need to drive, let someone drive you, *please.*" His eyes were pleading with me. It was like looking into the face of the little boy he used to be. The one who would follow me around, wanting to play. The eyes of the sweet baby I got to hold the day he was born. He was protecting me. He wasn't trying to stop me. He just wanted me to be safe. My anger vanished as fast as it came. It left a hollow pit and a bone deep need to be with my men. Silent tears continued to slip down my cheeks. The trails they left were cool against my burning skin. I nodded in agreement, knowing that he was right. Atticus' arms came around me, holding me as my shoulders shook with silent sobs. "Come on, you. Oakland and Lettie can ride with me and Flint. They will be ok, sis. They will be."

"Wait, what about Mud? I can't just leave him here. He can tell something is wrong." When I had gotten up, he had followed and was now pressed close to my side. He let out a low whine, like he knew I was about to leave him. I looked down into his sweet eyes and ran my hand over his head. "I know, sweet boy. It's going to be ok."

"Why don't I stay here with Mud? That way he isn't alone, and you guys don't have to worry," Lettie offered. As much as I wanted her with me, I couldn't imagine leaving him here alone.

"Ok. Thank you." I sounded lifeless to my own ears, all the brightness in my voice gone. My ability to be polite and grateful warred with my anxiety. Manners and cheer were currently not winning. "Can we please go?"

Oakland was already a step ahead of me. She grabbed both our bags and was waiting at the door. We all headed out to the cars, leaving Mud and Lettie waving from the porch. As I climbed into the car, the same words kept repeating in my head like a mantra. If I said them enough, they have to be true. At least for now.

I love you.
I need you both.
Please be ok.

chapter 24

. . .

gatlin

I BLINKED A FEW TIMES, trying to clear my head. *What the fuck just happened?* I took a mental inventory of my body—nothing felt broken or out of place. When I moved, a blinding pain burst from the back of my head. I slowly reached one hand up to feel the spot. Pulling my hand back around showed it wasn't bleeding, thankfully. More than likely, I had a concussion. Shifting myself more to a sitting position, I realized that I hadn't fell as far as I thought. My backpack somehow snagged on something, causing me to stop before falling as far as Leland had.

Leland.

Shit where was he?

"LELAND!" I yell before grabbing my head. *Fucking hell.* My vision blurred for a moment. Squeezing my eyes tight against the blinding pain. I cracked one eye open, testing for pain. When I wasn't met with immediate unbearable pain I started to look around. My eyes caught on him toward the bottom of the slope. He was slumped forward, like he had fallen asleep. I squinted as I tried to look him over to see if he was seriously injured. I focused on his right arm. I could see from here it didn't look exactly right. I slipped the straps of my backpack off, tugging it free from the tree stump that had caught me. I picked my way slowly down, trying to disturb the least amount of the loose stones around me. I moved to his left side, my eyes scanning over him. I squatted down before trying to wake him up.

"Leland." I touched his uninjured arm. He didn't move. I knew he was breathing by the steady rise and fall of his chest. "Leland, baby, please wake up. Please." I touched his cheek before taking off his hat and running my fingers through his hair. He stirred at the contact, not quite coming around, but getting there. "Come on, teddy bear, I need you to open those gorgeous eyes and look at me." He opened his eyes, raising his head up to look at me. When he tried to reposition his body, he let out a low groan of pain. His teeth dug into his lip where he tried to stifle the sound. "Try not to move. Your arm is banged up. Are you hurting anywhere else?"

"No. *Fuck.* Just arm." His face was screwed up in pain. He looked at me again, his eyes growing wide. "Your head." He reached toward my forehead. "It's bleeding. You're hurt."

I reached up and gingerly touched the spot he pointed at. I let out a hiss of pain at the contact. It didn't feel deep, but head wounds are awful about bleeding. "It's ok, it's just a cut and it's not that deep. Just a little bleeding."

"What time is it?"

I looked at my watch, which was thankfully intact. "Close to 1:30. We should have been back to camp by now. They are going to start to worry, but they know what to do. If we don't come back, they will call the rangers." He shifted again, wincing in pain. "Don't move, bear. We don't know how serious your injuries are." I placed a hand on his chest.

"What are we supposed to do?"

"We wait. That is about all we can do."

I settled next to Leland and removed my backpack. While it wasn't fully stocked, it had a small first aid kit and emergency supplies. I set to getting stuff out that we needed. I knew the adrenaline would fade at some point, but right now, my focus was on keeping my mind busy. Once everything was out, I shifted to sit more in front of Leland. My plan was to clean my head and then work on him. Looking at where we fell from, it would be hard for anyone to see us. We would have to get something to draw their attention down here. We could have been killed. Leland quite possibly saved me by pushing me forward. I was so mad at him, but also so grateful I got the chance to be pissed at him. I would have never forgiven myself if something worse happened to him. I could have never looked Scout in the eye again.

Fuck.

Please, God, don't let her be alone.

"What day did Lettie and Oakland plan to go to the house?" I asked Leland, trying to keep him engaged. My head felt like someone was trying to drive a railroad spike through it.

"Tonight. Why?" It hit him the minute the question left his mouth. "Fuck. Who will they call first? Have you given the other leaders her info for emergencies?"

I started to nod my head and immediately regretted the movement. "Shit, shit, shit." My eyes were screwed shut with pain. I felt like my teeth were going to crack from the pressure of clenching them. A warm hand touched my cheek, and my body automatically leaned into the touch.

"Shh, you probably have a bad concussion. Turn around and let's check your head."

I cracked one eye open, my gaze locking on Leland's banged up arm, the cuts and scratches over his exposed skin. "I'm ok. As for the contact information, they already have it. They also know we are together so they will try to call her. She won't be alone though. Right now, we need to stabilize your arm."

"Gatlin. Turn around and let me check your head. Now." The command in his tone had my dick twitching.

Not the time, asshole.

I wordlessly moved for him to look. I knew that I just hit really hard, but my body refused to fight against his order. His finger traced down the back of my head, running across the knot that was already forming. I tried not to flinch at the contact, but epically failed.

"Sorry, bee. No blood back there, but there's a pretty serious knot. Do you want help with the cut?"

I turned back around to face him. "Could you hold the mirror?" I pulled out the little mirror with stuff to clean and cover the cut. Looking at my reflection, I could see the cut was a bit deeper than I thought. It would probably need a stitch or two, but that was a problem for later.

Cleaned and bandaged, I grabbed the other roll of bandage, bandana, and lastly the safety pins from a dry bag. Leland already had his arm in front of him, so we at least wouldn't have to move it too much. He tried to scoot his body so he was more upright, but cried out in pain when his arm started to slide off his lap.

"Stop trying to move on your own you stubborn ass, I'll help you. If your arm is broken, you could do internal damage by moving it so much. Hold it to your body with your good arm." I helped him get his arm up, supporting it while he got a hold of it. His face was pale from the pain, the muscles in his jaw bulging with tension. "I know it hurts. I'm so sorry, baby. We have to get you sitting up so I can wrap it. We also need to get the satellite phone from your pack. I promise the wrap will ease it a little. I will be as quick as possible. Here, use me to lean on. Good. Ok, now just shuffle your butt back. Perfect." I gave him a moment, taking his weight while he caught his breath. "When you're ready, I am going to grab the bandana and make a sling of sorts. Then we will wrap the bandage around your body. Basically, we need to keep it tucked tight to your torso so it doesn't move." He took a few seconds more before straightening.

"I'm ready." Because we have both done first aid, but also some advanced classes geared for the outdoors, he had an idea of where his arm needs to be.

I tied up the bandana then carefully wrapped the bandage, doing my best not to move him unless necessary. "Ok, how does that feel?" I sat back, looking at the makeshift sling. It should help with the pain by taking the need to hold the arm up away.

"It's good. Thank you." He sighed a little at the small relief.

I slid his pack around to face me before opening the flap. "It should be in a dry bag in the inner pocket." Everything in his bag had shifted and moved from the fall. I unzipped the pocket and pulled out the dry bag.

Fuck a duck.

I knew before opening the bag the phone was toast. When the top was unrolled and I looked into the bag my suspicions were confirmed. "Don't freak out." I pulled the phone out before setting the bag down. It was completely shattered but it definitely wasn't going to be useful.

"Dammit. Fuck, I am so sorry Gat." I heard Leland's head thunk back against the tree trunk. I set the phone on the bag before touching his leg to get his attention.

"Leland, look at me." I waited for his eyes to meet mine. "It's not your fault. The satellite phones are great but we have other measures in place to make sure we can be found. Plus this thing pings a location like every five or ten minutes. It might not get them an exact location but it will give them something." I reached out to squeeze his hand. When he silently nodded I straightened.

The temperature was starting to dip with the sun being hidden by the mountain. I grabbed an emergency blanket out and tucked it around Leland. Deciding to make some kind of signal, I grabbed another bandana from my bag, this one a bright yellow with some kind of reflective material woven in. When I stood up, I felt Leland's fingers wrap around my wrist to stop me.

"Where are you going?" Leland looked at me, his expression almost panicked.

"I'm going to go up closer to where we fell from and tie this up. It is hard to see us right now, so they could literally walk right past us and never know. I'm not going far, just enough that they can see the fabric."

He looked at me, then to where we fell. He knew I was right, but he didn't want to risk me getting hurt. "Just please be careful."

I leaned down, placing a kiss on his lips then his forehead. "I will. Promise."

leland

The sun continued to sink lower, taking the light with it. Gatlin grabbed what he needed to get a fire started then settled in next to me. As worried as I was about being out here and thinking of what could have happened, my brain kept going to Scout. They were going to call her first. She was going to panic. This was not something that crossed our minds when we gave the volunteers her number. Most of them had her number from past trips. Gatlin was right about the one silver lining was that she wouldn't be alone. If they called her first, Lettie would be there and Oakland. Our families would go to her and she also had Mud with her. The calmness that Mud provided her was amazing. She would need support. This was a terrifying situation, but it could have been so much worse. I knew that Gatlin was upset with me for basically sacrificing myself, but I would do it over and over if asked. I would literally stand in front of a speeding car if it meant he and Scout were safe. All I could think was at least they would have each other.

I laid my head back on the tree and let out a breath. Gatlin looked over at me, one eyebrow raised." You ok?"

"Just hurting." We both knew that was not what he was asking about. He thankfully let it slide for now. "Do you remember the first time me, you, and Scout went camping?" I let my head roll to the side to look at him. The soft glow of the fire flickered across his skin. He smiled, thinking back on the trip.

"That was a fun one. You were talking to that one guy. What was his name? Jeremy, or something? I remember hating that dude from day one. Then we said we were going on camping, and he lost his mind."

I chuckle at the memory. "Yes, it was Jeremy, and apparently, two-week anniversaries are a milestone to some. He wanted to go out and 'celebrate', even though I told him from the start about the trip with you and the Nature Nuggets." He started making remarks about how he didn't understand why I would want to spend the week with other people's kids. Then I turned to asking if I had to stay the whole week. The final straw was the comments about Gatlin and Scout not being good friends because they were taking me away on an important date. If they really cared about me, they would support my relationship with him. I realized then and there that his crazy train was not one I wanted to be attached to.

"I was so jealous of him."

"W-what? Why?"

"Well, I was struggling with all the feelings and realization in my head, and that asshat was just getting to have you. I knew deep down that it was something I craved. You had been talking to him. Scout had been on a few dates, and I was kicking myself in the ass for not growing a pair and doing something about what I was feeling toward y'all." His gaze connected with mine. A mixture of emotions played across his face. "Also, Nan was the reason yours and Scout's tents went 'missing'. The old woman stole them. I found them in the back of the bakery two weeks later. She bet Oakland that we would sleep together that weekend."

"We didn't have sex that weekend! We would never do something like that with the kids around."

"Um, teddy bear, you and I *did* do things with the kids around. Literally, this morning. But that is the thing with making a bet against Nan. The devil is in the details. She didn't say sex or intercourse. She said sleep together. Where did you and Scout sleep when we figured out you didn't have tents?"

"In your tent. Was she behind the sleeping bags, too?"

"What do you think?" *Yes, she was.*

I shook my head at my grandmother's antics. "So she what, stole Scout's sleeping bag and only left the two bags that could be zipped together?"

"That's exactly what that old bat did. She knew that you and I had shared the sleeping bags before. She also knew that Scout hated being cold with every fiber of her being. She is damn sneaky."

That woman. I believe in her past life, she was a matchmaker or a con artist. Both seem probable

"She might have also mentioned it to Jeremy, the jerk, that we had shared before, and that if it got too cold, we would probably all have to share."

"That was the reason I stopped talking to him. He started acting crazy jealous of you and Scout. He didn't want me eating with y'all or really being around you both. I shut that shit down real fast. When he questioned our friendship, I told him to kick rocks with open-toed shoes and never looked back." I huffed out a laugh. "I swear, Nan has been gunning for this relationship since we were in elementary school. Then Scout entered the picture, and she went feral. I can't be mad at her, though. That was a great trip. Does Scout know about all this?"

"It was. And yeah, on one of the girls' night Oakland got drunk and spilled the beans. She had just lost another bet to Nan and was mad."

We both laughed, knowing how mad Oakland and Nan both get pissed when they lose a bet. When we stopped laughing, we turned to look at each other for a moment before our gazes drifted back to the fire. Gatlin's fingers were now laced in between mine. My thumb rubbed small circles on his skin. Silence settled for a few minutes, both of us just soaking in the fire.

"Scout is going to be so pissed at you, you know that, right? Honestly, I am upset with you." I turned at his words, taking in his profile. His brows pulled together as he stared ahead, looking at the fire, but not actually seeing it. "I thought you were dead. I thought about having to go back and tell Scout that you were gone and it was my fault." I saw the tear start to slide down his cheek, the droplet disappearing in his beard. "You can't do that to us. We—" His words were cut off by voices and flashlight beams cutting across the trees. Gatlin grabbed the flashlight, turning it on to signal to get their attention.

"OVER THERE. GATLIN, LELAND, ARE YOU GUYS DOWN THERE?" a male voice called down to us.

"WE'RE HERE!" Gatlin yelled before winching in pain. He swayed like he was going to pass out. I automatically reached for him to stop him from falling. This caused me to cry out in pain, the world darkening again.

"Hang on, baby. They are going to get us out of here. Just hang on." Gatlin's rough palm was on my cheek. Where it would normally be warm, it was cool and felt like heaven. "We have to get back to our girl."

THE PROCESS of getting me up the steep edge was excruciating and painfully slow. By the time we got to the top, I was half-conscious and in need of some strong pain meds. I heard a radio somewhere around me, responding that an ambulance would meet us at the trailhead. I didn't know what time it was, but the sun had been down for a while at that point.

"Hey, what time is it?" I asked Gatlin who was sitting in the bed of the side-by-side I was laid in. The fact that the rescue crew carried my big ass out was still a bit of a shock. He glanced down at his watch before replying.

"Coming up on 10:45 now." He started to worry his bottom lip between his teeth. The side-by-side was moving now. I reached my good hand up and soothed it over his lip.

"The only people I want to see biting that lip is me or honeysuckle." He caught my hand, bringing it to his lap and tangling our fingers together. We rode the rest of the way in silence to the awaiting ambulance.

I'm loaded up in the rig, with Gatlin following behind me to sit on the bench. One of the EMTs moved to the back where we were now. She was looking down at first, but then looked up.

"Gatlin? Oh my gosh! You are not who I expected to see tonight." My hackles rose as she spoke. "So what happened, guys?" She started going through everything, directing almost every question to Gatlin. She *gasped* and *ah'ed* as he told her what happened. "That is awful. I'm so glad you're ok." *Wow, the professional bar has never been met by this one.*

"Thanks, Julie. It would have been worse. Just glad I knew what to do to help the person that saved my life." His eyes found mine, boring into my very soul. The conviction in his words had my eyes stinging. I tried to swallow around the lump in my throat. *This man.*

She addressed me for the first time, as if remembering I existed. "Oh my goodness, yes, Mr. Boone! Let's get you looked at. So, how is your pain right now?" She chewed the gum I just realized she had in her mouth. When I say *chewed*, it was like a cow chewing cud. She smacked and clicked it. *For fuck's sake.*

I hesitated to answer. I didn't want to be out of it with this woman giving heart eyes at my man. My gaze was cold as a tundra when I looked at her. "I'm fine." The words came out clipped. I knew I was being ridiculous and acting like a child throwing a tantrum, or a caveman. With hot pants, looking at Gatlin like she wanted to eat him, I was not inclined to like her nor trust her.

"Bear. You almost passed out from the pain. Take some fucking pain meds." He looked at me, daring me to tell him no. "It will make the ride faster and easier on you. Please, Leland."

The use of my name was like a bucket of cold water being dumped on me. He was right. I was being an ass. I let out a breath before I answered again, more honestly this time. "It's bad. I would say close to a nine on a scale of 1-10." There, I said it.

I didn't even notice, but she already had an IV in and was getting medication ready to give me. "No allergies to pain medications?"

Gatlin answered before I had the chance to. "No, he doesn't have any allergies."

Julie nodded. "Ok, we are going to give you something to get you comfortable. You will probably feel a little loopy and tired." She began to pop her gum almost mindlessly. *Fucking gum popping. Is she twelve?*

She put the medicine in, and within a few minutes, I felt its effects. My teeth unclenched, and my body relaxed as the pain eased. *This is the good stuff.*

"Well, what have you been up to, Gat?" Julie's voice brought me back around.

"Just working. You?" Gatlin asked, but his politeness was forced. Normally, he would be chatting up a storm. His easy friendliness with people always came out. Right now, he was giving the least to this conversation. He was currently digging in his bag and I was pretty sure only half listening.

"You know, just saving people." She sighs dramatically. I tried to roll my eyes, but I wasn't sure it worked with how fuzzy my brain was. I probably looked more like the dolls whose eyes opened and closed when you picked them up or laid them down. Unfortunately, not like a shiny new one. More like one that the eyes didn't want to work right. My whole body was loose and light, but also heavy. *Did she give me too much?* She was trying to kill me. Get me out of the way. *Too bad, bitch, we have a woman who would cut a hoe.* My head was so fuzzy and muddled. "I have actually been thinking about you. I was going to reach out about maybe doing a guided hike with you." She winked at Gatlin who was now staring at her with one brow raised. *She fucking winked.* My eye ping-ponged between them like I was at a tennis match.

Over my dead body, hot pants.

"Really?" I heard him reply. I cut my eyes to Gatlin. He was only half paying attention again, splitting it between his phone and this conversation. *What was he doing on his phone?* I tried to clear my throat at him to get him to pay attention. My throat and mouth like the rest of my body was heavy and not working. *EARTH TO GATLIN. THIS BITCH IS ABOUT TO GET MURDERED.*

Julie, the oblivious, continues, "Yes, I had been thinking about you and how we had so much fun and thought that maybe—"

I heard someone speaking, my brain was slow to catch and realize it was me talking. I would normally be mortified, but Pain Medication Leland was protecting his man's dignity. "For the love of all that is good and holy. Shut up and halt the gum popping so I can be sure you hear me. Stop hitting on my boyfriend. We are in a very committed relationship with a drop dead, gorgeous woman who would absolutely eat you for breakfast. I am a big, mean bear and Scout is a feral honey badger. Also, hot pants, I licked him. He is mine."

Julie sat, stunned, blinking like an owl. Gatlin was covering his mouth, trying to stifle a laugh. He cleared his throat, then he spoke. "Sorry, he is right. We are together with our other partner. I was distracted trying to get my phone to send a message to Scout."

"That's—wow, ok." Julie's attempt at conversing was cut off when we pulled to a stop. She jumped up when the doors were pulled opened. *The ride was definitely shorter than I thought.* Gatlin left the back first to be out of the way. I watched Julie *the professional* stare at his delectable ass as he left.

I cleared my throat again and her eyes snapped to mine. Her cheeks turned pink with embarrassment. I squint menacingly at her—or at least tried to. With my good arm, I give her the "I'm watching you" signal, before whisper-yelling, "Mine. I licked him. And Scout. I licked them both. Mine." As I was pulled out, I did the only mature thing I could think of and stuck my tongue out at her.

"Let it go, Papa bear. You know who has my heart." He winked at me as we headed into the hospital.

"Trying to steal my man. Can't believe–" My eyes started feeling heavy. The words I was trying to say come out more slurred than anything.

"Just rest, bear. Everything is ok now."

I relaxed and did just that. I had one part of my soul, now I just needed the other with me and I would be perfect.

chapter 25

leland

I WOKE up in a hospital room in the early morning hours. The room had a window and I could just see the sky lighted with the sunrise. The beep of the machines around me filtered into my brain. I moved and let out a low groan of pain. I felt like I had been hit by a truck. Scratch that —I felt like a whole fleet of trucks had driven over me a few times.

"I'll get the nurse." I heard a voice but couldn't place it.

Lips pressed to my forehead. Scout and Gatlin's scents surrounded me, soothing me. "You're ok, bear. Gatlin and I are here. Our families are in the waiting room. Oakland stayed back here with us." I felt Gatlin smooth a hand over my hair. I breathed, pulling more of their smell into my nose. My body relaxed knowing they were here. I knew that everything would be ok. I let out a sigh of contentment. Even with the pain, happiness was bubbling up inside me because I got to be with them.

Damn, I could write poetry. *The painkiller poet.* I snorted at myself. I had always been a hopeless romantic. I couldn't stop the mushy, sweet feeling and thoughts about Scout and Gatlin. I would never want to. They were my world.

"Hey there, Mr. Boone. Can you open your eyes for me?" Someone

I assumed was the nurse was now on one side of the bed. The overly floral scent of her perfume made my stomach turn flips. Thank all the good lord and all the angels she wasn't smacking gum. *Fucking hot pants Julie.* I would normally be embarrassed by how I acted but damn, that woman was trying to move in on my man. I stand by every word and action I took.

I cracked one eye open before peeling the other open. My eyes found two of the most important people to me. Scout stood in front of Gatlin. Her eyes were red and swollen from crying, with no makeup covering any of it. I hated to see her this way. She must have been terrified. She had her hair in a messy bun that looked close to falling. She was wearing leggings and one of my sweatshirts that was more like a dress than a shirt on her. She had never looked more beautiful. Gatlin had changed into sweats and one of my sweatshirts. His hair was down, my finger itched to comb through it. The cut on his head was freshly bandaged. He had his hands around Scout, a soft smile played across his lips. I knew they were both upset with me. Even with the soft smiles and loving gazes, they were not happy with me. I still didn't regret it. I couldn't pull me eyes from them. I want to memorize every inch of them. I must have not answered in a reasonable amount of time.

"Bear, the nurse is asking how you are feeling." He smirked at this, Scout stifled a giggle.

"Sorry." I looked to the nurse, my face burning hot with being caught ogling my partners. "I'm hurting pretty bad." I now looked at my arm. It was bandaged up and resting on pillows.

"You're ok, sweetie. I hear you are *very passionate* about your partners." She winked at me. In the few minutes I had spent looking at Scout and Gatlin, I had forgotten.

Julie, the gum-smacking EMT. She would forever be associated with fucking popping and smacking of gum.

I groan this time from embarrassment instead of pain. Maybe I was a little embarrassed by all the things I said. "Oh God."

"I mean, licking somebody is quite the claim," my evil twin added. I scowled at her, but she just cackled.

The nurses laughed under her breath before speaking. "Well, I admire a man who claims who he loves." She typed away on the computer, entering all my vitals in. "Ok, you are due for more pain medication and then the doctor will be in to talk to you. If you need anything, just press the button or someone can snag me. Ok?"

"Thank you so much," Scout said to the nurse. Once she was gone, Scout turned back to me. Her expression was filled with white-hot rage. Silent tears ran down her face. I knew what came next was going to hurt. I had hurt and scared her and Gatlin. I braced for the words.

Who am I fucking kidding? I'm done for.

scout

I knew my anger wasn't rational, but Leland could have been killed. Hell, they both could have. I literally almost lost both of them. I took a deep breath to calm my racing heart. I could hear the blood roaring in my ears. I didn't want to explode on either of the guys. Most if not all of the feelings that were currently churning in my stomach stemmed from fear. Since learning they were missing, my mind had run through every scenario that could have possibly happened. Most of the solutions included me sneaking out of the house like a teenager to go look for them. I had never snuck out, so I doubted I would have been successful. I would have tried, though. Would that have made it worse for everyone? Yes, but sitting and waiting to hear anything had been torture. Then, only to be told they were on the way to the hospital and given nothing else had almost killed me. Tears continued to run down my face. I wiped them away angrily before clenching my fist. The next breath came a bit easier. I was about to speak, but was interrupted by Oakland.

"I'm going to go find, well, somewhere else to be. Good luck, teddy. Don't let him off easy, Scout." Oakland shut the door with a soft click.

"You could have died." My voice was low, almost a whisper. "I know why you did it. The rescuers said that you potentially saved Gat's life. But you are damn lucky to be alive. They said that you would have more than likely busted your head open if you had not caught whatever with your arm. I'm sorry I am so mad. No, you know what? I am not sorry." *Fuck it.* "I love both of you too damn much to lose you." There, I said it. I had known it for a long time and had just not been ready to let it out. I had loved them as my best friends for a long time. The love I had for them now was soul-deep, Earth-shattering, all-consuming love. "I know this is super cliche to say it after a life-threatening event, but I own a bookstore and I am a book nerd, so it makes sense." I grabbed Leland's good hand, threading our fingers together. Gatlin tangled his fingers with my other hand. "I love you both. I have never felt anything close before to what I feel for you. You have shown me that I deserve to be loved and accepted for who I am." I gently squeezed their hands. "You are the two halves of my heart. You don't have to say anything back, but I wanted you both to know. Also, if you ever do anything like this again, I will go as feral as a honey badger on both of you. I will hunt you to the ends of the Earth and beyond. I licked you both, too." I smirked at Leland, who rolled his eyes. Gatlin's chest shook against my back. After a moment, I sobered. "I want to have a long life with you both filled with love, laughter, and adventures." Gatlin kissed the top of my head while Leland brought my hand to his lips.

Before either of them could respond, there was a knock at the door. "Knock, Knock. I'm Dr. Sutton, the on-duty doctor today. I hear you guys had quite the adventure." The man who entered the room was not who I had pictured. The guy was as big as Leland. He looked like he was one wrong move from hulking out of his coat. He was older than Leland and Gatlin. You could see little streaks of silver at his temples and in the neatly trimmed beard he had. "So, how is your pain right now? The nurse should be coming in with your medication in just a minute." As he finished the sentence, she appeared. Gatlin and I both moved back from the bed, giving them plenty of room to work.

"There we go." The nurse finished and left as fast as she came in. She winked at myself and Gatlin. The nurses had all got a kick out of Leland's passionate claims in the ambulance.

"Ok, well now that's handled, let's go over your injuries."

A phone started to vibrate somewhere. I looked around at the same time Gatlin did, both noticing that it was his. He swiped the phone off the arm of the chair he had been sitting in and looked at the screen.

"Sorry."

With the phone silenced and in his pocket, Dr. Sutton started again. "It's all good. So, as far as injuries, they could have been worse. I'm sure they have told you how lucky you are to be alive. Both of you, honestly." He looked to Gatlin before returning his gaze to Leland. "You came in with a dislocated shoulder and a fractured elbow. Your shoulder has been set, and luckily, the fractures in your elbow were not severe enough to warrant surgeries. You will stay in the cast for between six and eight weeks so the fractures can heal. You can still go about your normal day, including physical activities, just don't use that arm." He pointedly looked at the three of us each.

Physical activities?—Wait does he mean sex? Is this man telling us that sex is ok?

"Any questions for me?"

"I guess just one. When will I get to go home?"

The doctor moved to the computer, pulling up what I can only assume was Leland's chart. He scanned through it, clicking various things. "Looking at everything here, we should get you guys out of here today. You were dehydrated, but have no other serious injuries. I will go ahead and get the paperwork started so we can break you all out."

I think we all let out a collective sigh of relief that we got to leave sooner rather than later. "Thank you, Dr. Sutton."

"Of course." He gave us a genuine smile before turning for the door. He was almost to it when it swung in, nearly hitting him in the nose. Oakland came barreling through the door, paying no mind to the fact that the doctor was standing right there.

"Listen, I know you guys are probably in here wanting to get down an—" Her words were cut short when she ran into the broad chest of Dr. Sutton. The coffee she was holding in her hand was poured down the front of her shirt. "Holy Christ on a cracker, that is cold."

Small mercy it wasn't hot, I guess.

Dr. Sutton steadied Oakland with a firm grip on both her shoulders. "Are you ok?" He looked her up and down, assessing for potential injury.

"I'm ok," she spoke while wiping at her shirt. "Except for my coffee, I guess. Did I get you?" That's when she looked up from her shirt. Her eyes went wide. "Oh my God. It's—" She was cut off by Dr. Sutton.

"No, I believe it all went your way." Dr. Sutton still gripped Oakland's elbow. "You need to be careful coming into places like that. This time your coffee was cold, but next time, it could be scalding hot. What if you had poured that on you?" He paused, as if waiting for Oakland to answer.

"It would have burned me?"

"Yes, it would have." His attention had been laser focused on her. "Please, be more careful. I would hate to see you in here because you are hurt. Will you do that for me?" Where his tone was almost commanding, a softness had bled in. Affection was laced into his words.

"Yes. I will." Oakland was now looking down at her feet. She looked like a child who had just been scolded by her parents. I couldn't see her face, but her fair skin would show the slightest flush like Leland. I wouldn't be surprised if her face was as red as a tomato.

"Good girl."

We would definitely be talking about that later. Miss Oakland had some explaining to do.

"I hope you all have a great day. I will pop back in before you head out." To Oakland, he said, "Come with me, please." She moved, following him out the door. The only sound was the door snicking shut. *What the hell was that?*

"Well that was fucking weird." Gatlin broke the tension that had built in the room. I looked back to Leland and immediately started to giggle. His head was cocked to the side like a confused puppy.

"I don't think I have ever seen her take orders. Are y'all sure I'm not dead?"

Gatlin and I were both laughing now. Leland shook his head before letting out a low chuckle. As our laughs subsided, the seriousness of before returned. Leland shifted around on the bed. He moved closer to the rails on his injured side. The bed had to be made for bigger people, because it actually looked like a comfortable size for him. He patted the bed and looked to me. "Come here, honeysuckle." I moved onto the bed, taking care not to move him. I snuggled in under his arm, my head on his chest. The strong beating of his heart calmed me to my bones. "Ok, bee, now you." Gatlin looked from us to the bed.

"I don't think that is supposed to hold that many people. I can just—"

"Get in the damn bed." Leland cut off his words. I stifled a laugh, but sighed when I felt Gatlin's warm body pressed into mine.

Gatlin reached one arm across my torso, it rested on Leland's stomach below where the pillows were. He was the big spoon to my little spoon. Leland reached so his good arm wrapped around us as much as possible. We wouldn't be able to stay here long, but I think we all three needed the contact.

"I'm sorry. I am so sorry I scared you both. The thing I will not apologize for is what I did to try and save the man I love." Gatlin sucked in a breath at Leland's words. "I would walk through fire for both of you. I would make the same choice any day to protect you over myself. I have always been too tall, too fat, too quiet, and many more things. I felt so alone in school. Oakland made friends so easy and that wasn't the case for me. The day I walked into that classroom, I prayed that just this once, someone would want to be my friend." I felt his chest vibrate with a soft laugh. "I didn't know it then, but he would be the sweet to my sour." I looked up to his face, his eyes were misty with unshed tears. I heard Gatlin sniffle behind me. "I then got to spend my life with him by my side. I was ok with where we were in life, but the universe answered a pray I kept hidden in my soul. That he would give me someone to love and cherish. I will never understand how I am deserving enough for not one soulmate, but two." Tears now streaked down his face, his voice thick with emotion. "Bumblebee, I have love you most of my life. From the first time I saw you, I knew that you would be someone special to me. I love you, my sweet bumblebee." He paused for a second. His gazes moved to mine. A soft smile spread across his handsome face. "You, my sweet honeysuckle, were the most beautiful, amazing surprise. The piece of our puzzle we hadn't realized was missing until we saw you. I fell harder every minute I spent with you. I love you, my precious honey-suckle." He pressed a soft kiss to my forehead. "I love you both so very much."

Gatlin sat up on the bed, moving so he can see both of us. The bed groaned, but didn't protest more than that. Leland's hand slid down to meet Gatlin's at my waist. I felt their warm palms on my skin. I slid my hand up to where they are. My finger tangled with one of them, the other sandwiched the other side. I didn't know how they were doing it, but I loved it. Gatlin wiped his eyes, but gave up when more tears replace them. "You are imprinted on my soul. I couldn't tell you where I end and you begin. There is no me without you. I don't have all the beautiful words you both had, but I can tell you with absolute certainty I am hopeless, wildly, and unequivocally in love with you both." Gatlin's hand moved from my waist. He moved us to a sitting position on the bed before he kissed me softly. It was a slow, lazy kiss. We savored each other's taste. He pulled back to look at me. "I love you, honeysuckle." He moved off the bed and around to the side closer to Leland. With one hand wrapped around the back of his neck, he leaned in close without their lips meeting. "Please don't scare us again like that. You are too important, my love." His words ghosted across Leland's mouth before they shared their own kiss. I watched them, my desire growing. It wasn't the right time or place, but damn they were so beautiful together. They pulled apart, their foreheads touching for a moment before Leland reached his good arm to pull Gatlin's head down to kiss his forehead.

When the nurse came in with the discharge paperwork, I moved off the bed and started to get our stuff together. Gatlin's phone started pinging with messages. He pulled his phone out, looking at the screen. "Oh fucking hell." He looked at the nurse. "Sorry, ma'am." His face was tinted pink.

"Darling, you wouldn't believe the things I have heard people say." She laughed under her breath like she was remembering something. "Give us a few and we will let you out of here, ok?"

"Sounds good. Thank you, ma'am," Leland replied warmly to the older nurse. She gave us a smile before leaving.

"What's wrong?" I turned a concerned look to Gatlin, who was scrolling his phone.

"That was Orrin calling, reminding me that his parents are in town. They have made a point to mention they will be downtown. I haven't seen or spoken to them in years. Most of the time, I'm out with the Nature Nuggets or I book trips with clients the week they come. I bet you fucking money they will come into the bakery and then try my store." He started to rub a hand through his hair and brushed the bandage. He hissed at the contact.

"I mean, if they come in, nothing says either of you have to be there. You normally don't open full days after the Nature Nugget trip, so you can get things cleaned, aired out, and put away. So you shouldn't have to see them." I looked to Leland. "With you being hurt, you won't be at the bakery because you need to rest and they don't know me." I looked between them, my gaze stopping on Gatlin shaking his head. "What?"

"Last time they came was right after we met you. Leland tried to stay in the back and away from them. Finch was out front when they went to leave, moving something for Seb. My asshole of an uncle made a remark, 'That of course the abomination wouldn't show his face.' Finch almost beat the shit out of him. He got a couple hits in before we pulled him off. Orrin convinced my uncle not to waste his time pressing charges and that was it. I'm so–"

"Stop. Do not apologize for him. He is a grown man who makes his own choices." My words came out harsher than intended, but they were the truth.

"I refuse to hide again. It doesn't make a difference if I stay away from them. I will not feel shame over who I love. Let them come in. Hell, invite them to come. I will be there, after that, they will be banned from the bakery." Leland's low voice came from the bed, the anger simmering just under the surface.

"I know. I know. I don't want that, bear, I promise." Gatlin took a second to collect himself. "We will figure it out. We always do." He smiled before adding, "I'm going to go let the parents know that we are busting out and probably call Orrin really quick." Gatlin kissed us both. "I love you both."

This should be fun.

As fun as having your whole body waxed.

chapter 26

. . .

gatlin

SON OF A BITCH.

I did not want to have to deal with my uncle. I tried to call Orrin while we were still at the hospital, but the call went to voicemail. After heading back to the room, the nurse didn't take long to come get Leland. Our parents had stopped by before the nurse to let us know they were heading out. I pulled my parents aside to let them know what Orrin had said. They, like me, hated when they came to town. Over the years, they had tried and failed to get my parents to "*see reason*." They had tried to guilt them when one of my grandparents got sick. My mom flat out refused to entertain anything that had to do with them.

When we got home and got Leland comfortable, I loved on Mud. I had missed him on the campout, but was more thankful he was here with Scout when she found everything out. The big dog lumbered over, leaning into me where I squatted in front of him. "Hey, Mudders, how is my boy? Did you have fun with Aunt Lettie?" His tail swished where it rested on the floor. Lettie had stayed with Mud last night while we were getting patched up. She and Scout were chatting before she left.

I normally felt more social than this, but I was mentally drained after the last few days. I wanted to crawl into bed and cuddle up to my loves. I smiled at the thought of Scout and Leland. They loved me and I loved them. I could have never pictured this would be my life, but damn, was it a good one.

I sat down, letting Mud completely take over my lap. That is where Scout found me after Lettie left. "Hey, baby, you ok? You didn't get dizzy, did you?" She squatted down to eye level, running her fingers through my hair.

"No, I was just giving our boy some pets."

She reached down, petting our sweet boy's face. She looked at him with so much love. "We missed you, Mr. Muddington." He sighed, as if answering. "I know it was only one night, but you are our bestest boy." His tail wagged at that, lifting his head enough to give her hand a gentle lick. After a few more pets, she stood, holding her hand out to me. "Come on, let's go take a nap with our bear. He is probably so lonely in that big old bed." I let her help me stand before pulling her to me to slant my mouth over hers. I licked the seam of her lips, taking advantage when she moaned to possess her mouth. I felt eyes on me. I assume Scout felt the same because we pulled apart at the same moment.

"Please keep going." Leland stood in the doorway. He was shirtless with his sling on and grey sweatpants. *Fucking grey sweatpants.* He eyes were hooded and hungry. Scout grabbed my cheeks, turning me back to her. She dove back in, consuming me with her kiss. I let her lead before turning and backing her towards the doorway. She let out a puff of air when her back met the wall. I moved over, allowing Leland to move in, essentially boxing her in.

"What do you want to do, honeysuckle? Want to get down on your knees for us? Want to take turns, sucking our cocks while we watch?" I felt lust drunk in that moment.

"Or we can take you into the living room. You can wrap those pretty lips around my cock, while bee bends you over the couch and fucks that needy little pussy from behind."

Oh, that is a very good idea.

Scout licked her lips. She had started to squirm, searching for friction and relief. "Please. Need you. Need to be filled."

"Fuck, you are so greedy. Just can't wait to have your holes filled, can you?" I stroked her face, causing her to shiver. I stepped back to grab my wallet, pulling out the lube that was stashed there just in case. When we got started, there was no telling if we would need supplies or not. When I looked up, Leland had her pressed up against the wall. I could see his hips grinding into hers. I stepped up behind him, pressing my hardening dick into his backside.

"Mmm, fuck yes." His words came out a groan. He pulled back, leaving Scout chasing his lip. "I want you to go to the living room and get those clothes off. Can you do that?"

"Yes, sir." Scout moved from the wall and went straight to the living room. Leland turned, grabbing my t-shirt and pulling me close. He palmed my cock through the sweats I was still wearing. His finger slipped down the waistband. When his fist closed around me, I tried to thrust farther into his tight grip. His big hand continued to stroke me loosely, before giving me a gentle squeeze.

"Ngh, feels so good."

"Good. I want you to pound our girl until she is nothing but a pile of Jell-O. You'll do that for me, won't you?" His fist circled my tip, my hips twitched again. "So sensitive. It's going to feel so good in her hot tight cunt." He released me. I immediately missed the loss of contact. I didn't move at first, trying to bring my brain back online. "Get to it, I want you naked, too, baby." As I passed him, he swatted my ass.

"Yes, sir."

"That's my good boy."

Holy shit.

leland

I walked into the living room to find Scout bent forward over the arm of the couch. Her beautiful body on full display. Gatlin was down on his knees between her legs, eating her out like a starved man. They were both moaning as Gatlin worked her over. They were a fucking sight to behold. I fisted my dick, stroking it lazily as I moved around them. Scout's face was buried in a pillow as she tried to muffle the sinful sounds coming out of her. Gatlin ran a finger through her folds, coating it in her juices. A low mewl came from behind the pillow when his finger slid inside her. He slowly thrusted before adding another finger. He worked her through one orgasm before pulling his fingers from her. I caught his hand, taking them into my mouth. The mixture of Scout's sweet and salty release mixed with the woodsy, manly flavor of Gatlin exploded in my mouth. I popped his clean fingers from my mouth with a languid hum.

"You ready for us, gorgeous?"

"Yes, I'm so wet. Want you both to use me. I want to be full of you. Please."

Who are we to deny our girl?

"Raise up on your hands, love." With the sling and bum arm, I needed the couch to stabilize myself in front of her. Lifting one leg onto the couch, I used my good arm to hold on to the back until I felt stable enough. Gatlin moved to stand between Scout's legs. I looked at him, knowing we were on the same page. We waited for a few seconds until our sweet honeysuckle started to shift.

"Please, give me your dicks—"

If she planned to add anything else, it was cut off by Gatlin driving into the hilt. Once he was seated, he gave her a second to adjust and let me get into that delicious mouth. Scout looked up at me, her face flushed and blissed out. She opened her mouth, letting her tongue hang out. Gripping my shaft, I tapped my dick on her tongue, giving her a little taste of my precum. "Open wide." She did just that. "That's my good girl. God, you are both so good for me." I slowly slide into the tight heat of her mouth. I began to thrust, not pushing too deep, but getting just to the edge of her mouth. Gatlin was also moving at this point. Every movement he made was slow and measured. We continued at a leisurely pace before need began to win out for all of us.

Scout began to take more of me to the back of her throat. Spit and precum mixed, running down my shaft and balls. Our gazes connected, allowing me the privilege to take in her debauched appearance. Her eyes were watering as she forced herself to the limit to take my cock. I slid the finger of my good hand through her hair and tugged her off my dick. Gatlin stopped, his cock buried deep inside Scout.

"More?"

"Use me. Make me your dirty cum slut. I want my pussy and throat to be raw by how hard you both take me."

My restraint snapped. With my fingers still in her hair, I used that to guide her back to my dick. Carefully, I shifted forward so that when Gatlin drove forward, it would drive her onto me. Once in place, we thrusted into her together. I fucked into her throat as she was pounded from behind. Gatlin fucked her into to me and her need for a breath forced her back on to him.

She would probably have bruises from how Gatlin's fingers pressed into the skin of her hips. "Fuck yeah, baby. Take that dick. God, your pussy is gripping me so tight. Just sucking me deeper in."

Scout's moans vibrated up my shaft and went straight to my balls. "I'm close." At my words, Gatlin released her hips and bent over her back. He put one hand on the arm of the couch before reaching the other between Scout's legs. She cried out when he began to thrust while also playing with her clit. "Fuck, fuck. If you don't want a mouth full, pull off, baby." In response, the little minx sucked harder. In two more pumps, I was releasing down her throat. "Take it all, baby. Milk my cock with that tight throat." As I fell from her mouth, she reached her own shaking climax with Gatlin following behind her with a shout, shooting his load into her waiting pussy.

"I'm going to need to do that again," Scout murmured as she moved to sit beside me on the couch. "That was fucking amazing."

Gatlin fell onto the couch on my other side and let out a pleased hum. "My brain is goop. Scout took brain matter with how hard she was clenched around me."

"Best welcome home present ever."

chapter 27

. . .

scout

WE WERE able to convince Leland to stay home for all of two days. By Tuesday night, he had put his foot down that he was going to the bakery on Wednesday. We could either drive him and he would take his pain medicine, or he would skip it and drive himself. No medicine was obviously not happening, so we relented. We had been getting periodic updates on Gatlin's family. I felt like they were asshole boogiemen just waiting to pop out and spread their hate. The guys had shared more with me about them and why everyone would rather they just stay away. They seemed to enjoy coming to town to make people uncomfortable and angry. From all of the time I had spent around Gatlin's mom over the last few years, for her to turn her back on her own brother was a telling sign. The woman was a genuine saint, but had a fiery streak she let slip out.

While everyone else avoided Gatlin's aunt and uncle, Nan went looking for them. She was like a predator on the prowl. Oakland had told us that she cornered them on more than one occasion over the last few days and forced them to talk to her. Her reasoning is they would never be so disrespectful not to speak, so she wasted as much of their time as possible. One of her favorite things so far has been telling overly elaborate stories. However she doesn't change the story, she just adds to it. Every time she has "bumped" into them, she tells them the same story, never missing a word from the first time, but adds more at the end. They get the same story, but somehow it's longer every time. This is just another reason why I believe Nan could be president, a mob leader, or a dictator and people would be happy about it. She is a force and no one will stop her.

We pulled up behind the bookstore together in Gatlin's truck. I leaned between the seats when he didn't move to get out. Leland also paused. We both looked to our boyfriend. His expression was cloudy and masked. "Bumblebee?" I placed my hand on his arm. He turned to look at me, his eyes clearing slightly. While he shared a lot of what had gone on, there are things that his uncle said that he refused to repeat. He also never said if the things were about him to just to him about Leland. I'm not sure I would want to know.

"I'm ok. I just want to protect you both from them and anyone like them. It scares me that I won't be able to. I know you are both grown adults but I am ashamed that I share blood with people that think the way they do." He looked down where Leland has placed his open palm between the seats. He took Leland's outstretched hand, tangling their fingers together. I ran my fingers through the back of his hair, trying to soothe some of the tension away.

"Bee, you know there will always be people who don't understand what we have. But know this, my love, you are not fighting alone. Until my last breath, I will be right there with both of you. I have met people like them before. The only thing that holds me back from losing it completely on your uncle is respect for you and your parents." The conviction in Leland's voice drove home just how much he meant every word.

"We protect each other. We also have amazing people around us who love and accept us. If someone cares about who we love, that is their problem, and we don't need them." I rubbed down his arm as I finished placing my hand on theirs.

Gatlin let out a shaky breath before looking between us. "Let's get this day started so we can go home."

We get out, heading into our businesses for the morning.
Please let the boogiemen stay away.

I THOUGHT we would get lucky when they hadn't been seen by lunch. From what Oakland said, they never hang around long once they make their presence known. They like to disrupt and then disappear. I asked why they even visited at all because it confused the hell out of me. Apparently, they still have friends living here and Gatlin's cousin that they wanted to see. It is still just such an odd, uncomfortable situation. Orrin also did not make it seem like he enjoyed these visits.

After lunch, I was standing at the checkout, fighting with the computer when Leland came from the back. He had said he would probably come over here for a bit after lunch. I would never complain about spending time with either of my men. After the events of the last few weeks having them close was something I craved. Even though he shouldn't have been working per the doctor's order, he would try and work if he was at the bakery.

"Did Cleo or Seb kick you out? Or did Fin get tired of telling you to stop lifting things?" I asked before going to my tiptoes for a kiss, being careful not to bump his arm. One of my arms snaked around his middle as I looked up into his handsome face.

His cheeks pinkened slightly as he answered. "Seb said he would make Fin throw me out if I didn't leave. Fin agreed. Then I heard Cleo thank God, so I figured I should get out of their hair."

I laughed, not surprised they ganged up on him to get him to leave and rest. It was sweet how much they cared for each other. They immediately jumped into action when They found out about Leland and Gatlin. Finch and Seb went by and got my keys from Lettie to hang a sign at Gatlin's store. Cleo arrived before we got home and stocked the fridge and freezer with food. She was a kick-ass bakery and decorator, but she was also an amazing cook. Everyone circled around us I appreciated it all more than they would ever know. I pressed my cheek into

Leland's chest, resting my ear there to hear his heart. The steady beat calmed something in me. Leaning back after a moment and with one more quick kiss, he wandered around the store. I told him about some new romance books I ordered, so I knew that was where he was heading. The day I found out the big teddy bear baker next door liked to read granny, pearl-clutching romance books, it would be a lie to say I wasn't a little surprised. It also made me curious about him. Once I got to know Leland, I discovered it was because of Nan. They have read them together for years. Now, I buy them constantly, even finding some vintage ones that I save for the two of them.

I fiddled with the computer until he walked back over with a couple of the books. He pulled one of the barstools that sat behind the counter over to and cracked open one of the books. We sat there in companionable silence. I was reaching the point that if I didn't walk away from the computer, I would hurl it out the front door, which was neither good for the environment nor my business. When I went to move away, I squealed when he hooked his good arm around my waist. He turned the chair where I was standing between his legs. I could feel the warmth from his palm press against my lower back, forcing me closer to him. "What time was Gatlin planning on being done?" His voice was low and gravely with lust. I glanced at the book and then back to him.

"Get some ideas of things to try?" I glanced at where he laid the book down. It was a historical romance with two men and a woman. I may have purchased that before we became more. His fingers slipped up the back of the shirt I wore with my baggie overalls. His warm fingers trailed across my skin, sparking goosebumps to cover my body. "I'll take that as a yes." He pulled me in close, pressing his mouth to mine. We were caught up in kissing when I heard the bell over the door. I pulled away quickly.

"Welcome to Blue Mountain books, let me know if you need—Oh hey, Orrin." I felt Leland press close to my back, his body vibrating with tension. Shit. If Orrin was coming in, that meant—the bell chimed again. His parents. *Lovely.* The high noon showdown was happening now. In my store. The only thing missing was the scattering of town folk and Western music to set the scene.

Orrin flashed an apologetic grimace that I think was supposed to be a smile as they made their way across the store. "Hey, Scout, Leland." He nodded at us. "Scout, these are my folks. Mom has been wanting to come into the store for a while."

"I used to come here as a child." I looked at her and smiled. This being a family business, we got that a lot. Before she or I could speak, the man who looked like an older version of Orrin spoke.

"I guess that was all just a phase back when you were younger, eh, Leland?" While I tried to mask my *what the fuck* expression. You could have heard a pin drop. The audacity of this man was unending.

"Dad." Orrin tried to stop his dad from continuing.

"It's ok, son. I'm saying it is a good thing he grew out of all that whole liking men stuff." He looked so pleased with himself for coming to this realization, and all the past wrongs were righted because Leland supposedly didn't like men anymore. "I mean, you have a pretty young lady now. Man and woman together how it is supposed to be. He smiled. Actually, smiled at Leland and me. "Glad you were able to get past all of it." His words made my skin crawl. I wanted to punch him in the throat and puke at the same time. How could someone be so blind and stupid to the world around them? I looked to where Orrin stood. His pale expression shifted from disbelief to shame and fury over his father's words.

"What the fuck did you just say?" Leland spat the words at him. Each one a venomous dart aimed at the hateful man.

"Excuse me?" For the first time, the asshole read the room. His face was a mask of something close to shock. He genuinely believed that we would be happy with the hate he was spouting.

"I think you heard him just fine." Gatlin stepped from the back, coming to the counter and standing behind me.

"Gatlin, we were head—" his dad cut off Orrin's mom's words.

"You better apologize for using that kind of language in front of my wife, boy. I was merrily congratulating you on finding a good woman to settle down with. I'm sure your parents are happy they will have a daughter-in-law instead of a son-in-law. Even if it's not really a marriage if it's between two men. Right?" He laughed at his own joke. *Fucking laughed.*

I was going to murder this man.

"I think they will probably be happy to be getting both." Leland spoke calmly from behind me. Orrin's dad took a moment to register what he had said before his eyes locked on where Leland's hand was around Gatlin's waist. His face drained of color before the red returned. It was like watching a thermometer warm and rise. *Uh oh. Stand back, he's gonna blow.* He stumbled over his words, not being able to string a single word together. "Nothing to say now? What, cat got your tongue? You did say it was supposed to be man and woman. In our case, it's two men and one woman." Leland taunted him.

Not being one to back down, he opened his big mouth. "Well, it figures you would need another man present to be able to satisfy a woman. Pathetic. Gatlin, I am ashamed—"

"ENOUGH." Orrin's voice boomed from beside his dad. "That. Is. Enough. I have had to listen to your toxic fucking bullshit since I was a child."

"Orrin, language." His mother looked like he had slapped her.

"Mom, honestly, the fact that you care more about the words I am using rather than what is coming out of his mouth speaks volumes. I am done. You hear? Fucking. Done. You have been paid for the house. It is legally mine. I am tired of living a half-life because the two of you have your head so far up your own asses. You have never noticed your only child has been slowly fading away. I chipped pieces of myself away, hoping you would wake up one day." He paused, taking a steadying breath. "I have kept a part of myself buried so deep that I have hurt people I loved, hell, *still love* because I hoped that I could one day be open with you. That you would *love* me for me. That I would be enough. I realize what a complete and utter fucking mistake that was. There is no hope for us to have a relationship now, possibly ever. I am bisexual. I like men and women. I always have. Of course, you already knew that, didn't you, Dad?" Orrin looked at his father unblinking. The anger was there but also lounging. It broke my heart he was having to go through this. "Yeah, I know all about what you did. Does mom know? What about Grams and Pop?"

A flash of panic and realization closed his father's face. In the next second, it was gone, replaced with pure loathing. "No." His dad's voice was angry now. His eyes burned with raw hatred. His expression morphed into one of white-hot rage. "No son of mine would ever disrespect me this way. I don't know what you think you are doing, but you will not disgrace me like this. You hear me, boy? I won't have an abomination for a son."

Orrin looked at Gatlin. The cousins shared a moment of silent conversation. Gatlin gave a subtle nod. Orrin returned the gesture before his focus was back on his dad. "Well then, Arthur, in that case, I will need you out of my house before tonight. Leave your keys on the counter." He looked at his mom, his eyes softening slightly. "Mom, you can stay. You don't have to keep doing this. I know you don't agree with him on all this."

"I can't. I am married to your father. Where he goes, so do I." She looked beat down and like her heart was shattered.

"Ok. In that case, I expect you both to be gone before I return to the house this evening. I will warn you I have security cameras. I am also not above involving the police. You are not welcome back. Also, don't try to contact me once you are gone. As of today, we are not family. If someday you realize how flawed and toxic you are, maybe then we can have a relationship again." He looked between them before movement behind us caught his attention. "Goodbye." He stepped around them, moving to stand with us. A throat cleared, drawing our attention to Amos, who stood at the doors that led to the back of the store. Orrin moved toward him without giving his parents a second glance. Amos glanced at me as he held the door open. I gave him a nod that it was ok to take Orrin into the back. He shot me a grateful look and placed a hand on the small of Orrin's back as he passed.

I turned back to the now unwelcome customers. Orrin's dad looked like he was about to have a stroke while his mom appeared seconds from collapsing. Gatlin broke the silence when he clapped. "Well, as much fun as this has been, I no longer consider you family. You have insulted Orrin, myself, and the two people I love most in the world. So kindly fuck right off and don't come back." He held his hand like a game show host showing a prize. With a huff, Arthur grabbed his wife's hand and walked out.

When the door closed, Gatlin deflated. "Well, that went about as well as expected." He covered his face with one hand. Leland and I moved to surround him and hold him. I knew he wasn't grieving the connection for himself but for Orrin, who he considered his brother. He was quiet for a few minutes before he looked at us. He kissed my lips softly before his words of love ghosted across my mouth. Leland then took his turn. The softness of their kiss and words to each other made my heart melt. I felt their love for me and each other in every fiber of my soul. Some people will find it hard to understand how our relationship works. While we have not hidden it, our town is not massive, and people do know us. Thankfully, though, the only person who voiced a negative opinion had just been booted from our lives.

"I'm going to check on Orrin, then do y'all want to head out once Lettie gets here?"

"Yes, please."

As if Gatlin's words summoned her, Lettie comes through the door. "I would say I am happy to see everyone, but I feel like I have walked into a funeral. I just saw the contractor guy with Orrin and they both looked tense. They were heading toward *Bob the Builder's* truck." She stopped talking for a moment, then like watching a light turn on, it hit her. The humor left her tone, replaced with seriousness. "Oh shiitake mushrooms. His parents. Did they come here?" She looked between us, waiting for answers. While Lettie didn't know everything, Gatlin knew I had talked to her about them—his uncle, in particular.

"They did come in and my uncle, of course, had to run his mouth. I have been ready to throw him out of my life. Orrin was with them today, and his dad ramped up the bullshit. Unfortunately, Orrin reached his breaking point. He basically just disowned his parents." Gatlin finished with a small shrug.

She looked like she was on the verge of tears. Her big heart was one of the things that made her the most amazing human. She hated that she cried when others did and felt so deeply, but I honestly didn't know what I would do without her and her big heart.

"I truly hate that it came to that, but I can't say I am not happy that someone finally told him where he could shove his awful opinions. Are you ok?" She looked to Gatlin, understanding that his proximity to it all made this hard for him.

"Me?"

"Yes, Gatlin. Are you ok?"

"Oh, yeah, I mean, he isn't my dad or anything. Technically, he is family, but I am more hurting for Orrin." He looked toward that back where Amos took his cousin.

We are all quiet for a moment, lost in our thoughts. I couldn't imagine not having my parents, but I also couldn't imagine having a father that nasty. Every word his dad said was like a physical blow. The true pain showed when his mom chose his dad. The hurt in his eyes revealed this to be a reoccurring event.

Lettie reached over to give my arm a gentle squeeze. "Since I'm here, why don't you guys head out? We don't have anything to do that requires both of us, right?"

"No, just manning the store, really." I glanced around the store, mentally running through my list to make sure there was nothing that required me to be there. Having worked together for so long and the store being well established, the old girl ran herself. Of course, I couldn't give up that kind of control. I honestly probably spent too much time here, but I genuinely loved this place.

Lettie was just about to reply when her phone rings pulled her attention. "Shoot, sorry. Seriously you guys go and relax or *whatever*." She waggled her eyebrows and then started to walk toward the front of the store to answer the call. She didn't look happy about the call, but now was not the time to ask her about it. I turned to the guys, reaching out to them. They each took a hand.

"Ready to go home and relax or do *whatever*?" Mimicking Lettie's words, I also waggled my eyebrows at them. The hunger in their gazes was answer enough for me.

I HADN'T TOLD them yet, but like Gatlin, I planned my own little surprise. I had been intrigued by anal and having both of the guys in me, but my nerves had kept getting the best of me. I had decided to hash it out with Lettie before trying to plan my approach to the guys. After

Gatlin had been so brave in asking for what he wanted, I had made the choice to grow some lady balls and talk to them. She had suggested that I do a little pre prep before the talk and the deed. That was why I had been wearing a plug all day. I have played with them before, but this one was a touch bigger. It had taken some getting used to, but I wanted this to feel good for all of us. It did, however, make the ride home difficult. My need to squirm had been hard to fight. There had been a few times one of the guys had caught me, giving me a questioning look. They would know soon enough.

When we got home, Gatlin went to take care of Mud while Leland and I waited in the kitchen. No sense in wasting a good opportunity to get my men hot and bothered. I moved around the island to stand between Leland and the counter. I hopped up, sitting on the edge which put us closer to the same height. I carefully wrapped my arms around his neck and pulled him between my spread legs. I kissed him softly on the lips, just one peck. I methodically worked my way down his jaw and cheek, pressing kisses to the delicate skin. Knowing what would drive our teddy bear wild, I scrapped my teeth down, following that with my tongue.

"Fuck baby. Feels good."His words came out on a breath.

I heard Gatlin come in the back door as I made my way over to Leland's ears. I reached my hand out to Gatlin, knowing he would come to us. He did, pressing into Leland's side, mirroring my movements. I then felt him shift to my neck. My head fell back at the scratch of his beard on my sensitive skin. The focus shifted from Leland to me, with them nipping and biting my neck. My eyelids slid closed as I just leaned into the sensation of them moving around me. Their warm hands were on my side, snaking their way up my shirt. They worked together to rid me of it. With it out of the way, Gatlin trailed his finger lightly over my skin while Leland reached around to unclasp my bra with one hand. They again worked together to remove my bra before each taking one of my nipples. I was so sensitive. My nipples already pebbled. Their touches were so different, but they still drove my need higher.

Gatlin teased, lightly touching before focusing on my nipple. Leland was more demanding. He kneaded my whole breast in his strong hands while still rolling the sensitive bud between his thumb and forefinger. A low moan worked its way up my throat at their focus. "So good." They continued to push me closer to the edge of release. I had never came from nipple play alone, but today might be a first. When I felt Gatlin's hand making its way up my thigh, I knew I needed to speak up for what I wanted to happen. "Wait." They both froze, pulling away immediately.

"Are you ok? Do you need to stop, love?" Leland looked at me concerned, his brows pulled together with worry.

"It's completely fine, honeysuckle. If there is something you didn't like or want–"

"No, that is not what I was trying to say," I cut Gatlin off. I didn't want them to think I was not completely on board with what we were currently doing. For the first time, I trusted that my partners would take care of me. I wanted to be vulnerable with them. "I want to keep going. I just have something I want to do. Or I guess try. I have been working up the courage to ask because I am a little nervous." Leland's gaze was searching, trying to read my mind while Gatlin looked at me with concern. "You guys are the freaking cutest. Shit, I'm getting off track." I took a breath before counting to three and blurting it out. "I want you both to fuck me. Like at the same time. You know, one in one, and the other..." I trailed off, not quite finishing the sentence. My face was on fire as I tried to look away from them.

"Don't hide from us, beautiful." Leland caught my chin, turning me back to them.

"So you want one of us in your tight ass and the other in your pussy, baby? That's so fucking hot." Gatlin leaned in, initiating a kiss. His tongue licked the seam of my lip. Once I opened to him, he devoured my mouth. Our mouths moved together in a dance. He pulled back, his head resting against mine. "Whatever you want, my love."

Leland, ever the caretaker and protector, had to know this was something I not only wanted but was prepared for. "I know you said you had done anal, but this will be different. We will have to stretch you to be able to fit. The last thing we would ever want to do is hurt you."

I sheepishly looked away before scooting off the island. I took my pants off, dropping them to the ground. Next, I tugged my underwear down, being sure not to expose my surprise before I was ready. Once I was completely naked, I turned around to face the island. When I stepped on foot back, both of the guys moved back, giving me room to bend forward. I pressed my chest forward onto the counter and spread my legs to expose my ass. The cool stone sent a wave of goosebumps across my skin. My already hardened nipples grew more sensitive to the cold. I heard Gatlin suck in a breath. He ran one hand down my back. The warmth of his hand was a sharp contrast to the counter. Leland reached forward to grip my ass cheek with his good hand. "I was trying to be good and do some extra prep work. I wanted to be able to take both of your big cocks."

Leland ran his hand down over the plug and to my center. He applied pressure to the toy, causing my whole body to clench up. I was soaking wet. The cool air of the house met my dripping pussy. My center fluttered as my ass squeezed the plug. I was so turned on between the plug being in all day and the heavy petting session. His fingers slid through my folds easily. He pulled his fingers back, showing them to Gatlin. "Damn, bee, look at how wet she is. She is fucking dripping like a faucet." Gatlin's hands joined Leland's hand, pulling my cheeks apart. I could feel myself trying to clench around the plug as they spread me wide. I glanced over my shoulder, watching as they hungrily took all of me in.

"Look at that needy little hole. Trying to choke the plug. You want us to fuck your greedy holes? Our sweet honeysuckle isn't happy with one hole being stuffed, she needs more?" The way these men dirty talked should be illegal. Gatlin squeezed my ass before giving it a swat. "So needy and ready to be filled."

"Yes. Please. Fill me up. Want to be full of you, feel you till tomorrow."

"I think we can make that happen. But let's take this to the bedroom, shall we?"

Gatlin scooped me up before I had a chance to move, carrying me bridal style down the hall. When we got to Leland's bed, he tossed me to the middle before crawling up the bed. He kissed me first, hard and controlling, then worked his way down my body to lay between my legs. I arched up into his touch. His warm lips ghosted down my body. Leland appeared at the door, his gaze heated at the show he was receiving. He came to sit on the bed while Gatlin ate me out like it was his job. Leland palmed his cock through his sweats. The bulge grew with each stroke. Gatlin teased and licked my folds and clit. He never stayed in one place long, living up to his nickname while he buzzed around me. When he slipped his tongue in my channel, my back arched off the bed. I fisted the sheets in a white-knuckle grip. Leland leaned in, pulling one of my nipples into his mouth. He sucked it, then flicked it with his tongue. He alternated between my nipples giving them each attention as he balanced on his good arm. The nip and scrap of his teeth rode the line of pain and pleasure.

I felt my core start to tighten as Gatlin added in two fingers, working them in deep. As he stroked my inner walls, Leland kept up his assault on my breast until I thought I would lose my mind. Gatlin found that magical little spot and that was it for me. My release was just on the edge when Leland sat up, taking my nipple and pinching it. It should have hurt, but holy fuck. I squeezed around Gatlin's fingers.

I needed more.

"Oh God yes, fuck, you both feel so good." I was riding the edge of climax and wanted it more than my next breath. "Gonna come. *Fuuck.*" My body shook as one climax led to another. The tremor continued to move through my core as Gatlin sucked my sensitive clit. I laid boneless on the bed. I squeezed around the plug feeling full and empty at the same time. "Please. Fuck give me more." My pleads came out as a whimper of lust. When Gatlin moved, my hips twitched, wanting him to come back.

"Shh, baby, I'm not going anywhere. We just need to do some rearranging." He leaned over, pressing a kiss to my sweaty forehead.

"Are you ready for us, baby?" My eyelids had drifted closed, so when Leland spoke, I wasn't sure where he was standing.

"Yes, please." My word sounded like a prayer.

Gatlin sat back down on the bed, stroking my forehead, combing his fingers through my hair. "With bear being hurt, it will easier for him to stand so he doesn't put weight on his arm. Are you okay with him being in your ass?"

"Yes. Please, someone start fucking me now."

Leland chuckled at my words. I always appreciated them checking in with me, but right now I wanted to get a good dicking down by my two loves.

"You heard the lady, bee. Strangle bee's cock, let him fill that sweet pussy up."

I shifted over to give Gatlin room to lay on the bed. I moved over him, resting my slick folds over his hard cock that rested against his stomach. I ground my hips a few times. I wanted them both wild and just as needy as me. His tip caught on my entrance. Gatlin grabbed my hip, driving up, fully seating him inside me. With his grip tight enough to bruise, he thrust, using my body weight and gravity to bring me down hard on him.

I came with a scream of pleasure at having Gatlin seated fully inside me. "Oh fuck."

"Damn it, baby, you feel so good. You want me to pump you full of cum? Fill you up until it drips out of you?"

"God, yes." A low moan echoed in the room.

"We have to wait, love. I want to feel bear pounding that ass while I'm buried inside you."

Leland ran his hand up my spine, gently pushing between my shoulders. This put my ass on display. He smacked my ass so hard I knew there would be a red mark. "Please do it again, sir." I felt Gatlin's hands squeeze my thighs. Leland let out a low groan of approval.

"Fuck, she maybe our good girl, but she wants her ass to be red with my handprint?"

"Yes, sir."

I was rewarded with his hand landing on my other cheek. "Again. Please, sir." I tightened around Gatlin. My walls tried to pull him deeper.

"Son of a bitch. Bear. She is so tight around me."

I whimpered when I felt Leland run his fingertips over where we were joined. At the contact, Gatlin thrust into me. "You want me to pop her ass again, bee? Make her squeeze that big cock."

"Please."

Gatlin moaned low. I wasn't sure what Leland was doing, but Gatlin liked it. "Please, sir."

"That's fucking right." With two swift smacks, Leland was done and running a soothing palm over my heated flesh. He pushed on the plug, applying pressure. Gatlin and I both let out low moans.

When I felt Leland playing with the plug, I tensed slightly. *Breathe.* Leland gave the plug a gentle pull to remove it. I bared down, trying to help it come out. There was a slight burn until it slipped free. I could feel myself trying to squeeze and clench around nothing. I whimpered at the feeling of emptiness.

Not for long.

My body reacted with a shiver as Leland spread cool lube over my entrance. "Mmm, your ass is perfect," Leland commented as he slid one finger in. Working it back and forth, he added a second and then a third. Thankfully, the toy had done a great job at getting me started. I know without it, this would have been a longer process. Gatlin and I were both squirming by the time he finished. "Ready?" I nodded my head. "Words, my love. We need words."

"Please fill me up with your cocks and cum," I turned my head to look at him before adding the last part, *"sir."* I loved the way he reacted when we called him sir. It made him almost feral. He always reacted to it in the best ways. What started as a joke was effective on him. His pupils were blown out. Gatlin reached to grip my cheeks, spreading them to expose my hole.

"She is so ready for you. Want to feel you inside with me, sir."

Leland notched his tip at my entrance. "Say it again. Tell me what you need me to do."

"Please fuck my ass, sir." I let all of my lust and hunger bleed into my tone. Gatlin had been slowly pumping into my pussy, keeping me right on the edge. When Leland's tip slipped in, I clenched, pulling a low groan from Gatlin. It took a few minutes of slow movements before I felt Leland's hips resting against my ass.

"Holy shit. I'm so full. Fuck," I moaned as an orgasm rolled over me.

"God, this is fucking heaven. Could fuck you both all day every day." Leland sounded like he was barely holding it together. I wanted him to let go. *Needed* him to.

chapter 28

· · ·

leland

BEING BURIED in Scout's ass was one of the best feelings in the world. I felt the same about being in Gatlin. The *sir* thing had thrown me. It was something I had not realized was such a turn-on. When it was coming from their lips, it drove me to the limit of my control. Like right now. I had not started to thrust because my control was wavering. Scout had other plans. Our lover was going to take her pleasure, and damn if we weren't both ready to let her take anything she wanted. She pulled forward and then slammed her hips back.

"Holy fucking shit." I gripped one hip tight enough to leave bruises.

"Fuck. Me. Now."

That was it. Gatlin and I began to move as one. I could feel his cock through the thin layer of skin. We were both thrusting, giving our girl the fucking she needed. I pounded her ass while he did the same to her cunt.

"So good. Yeah, fill me up with your hot seed. Oh God, I'm going to cum again." She tightened down on me, milking my dick for what she wanted. "Fuck. Fuck. Fuck. Right there." We continued until she was shattering around us. We fucked her through the orgasm and into another one. Her body shook with every climax.

"Gonna come. Get ready, baby."

"Me, too. I can't hold it back," I forced the words out while still driving my hip forward.

We both became erratic with our movements before thrusting in and filling her with cum. She clenched again, screaming our name as she vibrated with pleasure.

"Don't pull out, want you in me a little longer," Scout whispered from where her head was in the crook of Gatlin's neck.

"Of course, honeysuckle."

By the time we were pulling out, Scout was half asleep. We worked together to get her and the bed cleaned up before climbing in with her. I heard a whispered *I love you* from Scout. I smiled to myself at how cute she was.

"I love you both. So much."

"I love you." Gatlin leaned over to kiss me. We had sandwiched Scout between us. Everything we had done had been a little more intense. We wanted her to feel our love and comfort. "And I love you." He kissed Scout's forehead gently.

I wanted to live in this moment forever. I felt in my heart that I would have the chance to do just that.

EVERYTHING HAD CALMED after the trip and the visit from Gatlin's family. Without the cloud of his family potentially causing trouble, he had seemed lighter. He did worry about Orrin. They had talked a few times over the last few weeks and hung out. No one wanted to push him to talk, but Gatlin wanted him to know that he had us. Gatlin may be his blood family, but we were also his family.

"I'm ready to not have this fucking thing on my arm anymore," I snarled as I looked to where a tray of scones lay scattered across the floor. I was going to the doctor that afternoon and would hopefully be released to start actually doing things with my arm again. Everything was healing perfectly, so I was excited, to say the least. I felt arms wrap around my waist. My lids fell closed at the contact, a sigh coming as my body relaxed.

"It's almost time, bear. After today, you can start getting back to normal. Are you ready to go?"

With you and Gatlin? To the ends of the Earth and beyond.

"Very ready."

Scout sat on one of the stools while I finished with the very limited list of things I could manage. I glanced at the cover of the book she pulled from her bag and laughed at the title. "Nan got to you, didn't she? *Devotion of the Dukes.*" I leaned a hip against the table next to her. "Care to share what the book is about, my love?" She looked up at me, trying to squint and look menacing. All it did was make her look like an adorable pissed of kitten.

"I will have you know this is a beautiful love story. It has action, and angst, and—" She took a second and looked down at the book. "A great plot?" I waited, watching her squirm. I knew what the book was about —I had read it already. Scout, of course, read romance novels, most of them stayed in contemporary or fantasy genres. She would also read just about anything. The older style pearl clutch novels were a horse of a different color.

"It's smut. Spicy, hot and bothered, they take her up against a stone wall, smut." I leaned closer to her. Our faces were inches apart. "Wait until they are in the hunting cabin away from prying eyes." I winked at her and pulled back.

"Leland Alder Boone, you have read this book. I literally just got it in. When did you read it?"

"Well, Scout Eleanor Frazier, I read it a few years ago. Nan went through a phase where all the books she traded with me had something to do with a duke, lord, prince, or some other title. I spent a year not being able to convince her to read any other bodice rippers." Exchanging our granny smut novels had been mine and Nan's thing for years. The year of stuck-up dukes about ended that. "A year. The day she handed me a *Fiery Passion of a Texas Rose,* I almost cried."

Scout broke, laughing so hard she was crying and I couldn't help but join her. She tried to speak through her laughter, but only managed to wheeze incoherent words. My laugh calmed as I took a look at her. She was mesmerizing. These moments were the ones I kept close to my heart. There have been so many with the three of us, but also ones that were just of Scout and myself or Gatlin and I. They were just as important to me as any.

"Dang it, I am a little disappointed! I thought I had this on you and could recommend it to you. Nan, of course, beat me to it." Her smile gave away that she was teasing. I leaned to press a soft kiss to her lips. "Mmm, silencing my pouting with a kiss."

"How about I promise to make it up to you?" She turned on the stool, her legs now bracketed mine. "We can join forces and edge our bumblebee. He seems to like that."

"Don't tempt me with a good time. I will hold out as long as possible, sir." I glanced up to where Gatlin had just pushed through the door. His little smirk had me itching to bend him over. He was so damn bratty sometimes. I had seen the way he lit up at being praised, but he also lit up when he pushed my buttons. He moved farther into the kitchen. The noises of the various equipment and Fin's music drowned out anything we said.

"Careful, bee. You are going to make Papa bear mad." I looked at Scout with an eyebrow raised. She had pulled her bottom lip between her teeth to help fight the smile trying to form.

"Jesus, do the three of you only think about banging each other? You like to have carnal relations. We all get it. Give it a break." Cleo came from the front of the bakery. Gatlin jumped a good three inches off the ground. I broke first, unable to stop myself from laughing.

"What the hell, Cleo? Do you train as a ninja in your free time?" Gatlin clutched his chest, looking at my head baker like she was an oddity.

"No, you three are just very obvious." This time, everyone but Cleo jumped. Orrin came through the door behind Cleo. She looked at him and rolled her eyes.

"I'm going to put fucking bells on y'all. You are too quiet for my good. I 'm going to die of fright at this rate." Gatlin moved to stand behind Scout. She leaned into his body, resting her head against his abdomen.

"Employees only," Cleo snipped at Orrin. *Woah, what's that tone about?*

"Obviously." Orrin waved his hand toward Scout and Gatlin. "I can't help that I want to be near you, sweet Clementine." He batted his lashes at her and I thought she was going to deck him. She stared him down, not reacting to his words. The tension was palpable between them.

"Sooo we should get going. Right? Right." Gatlin would stir the pot all day but let a situation get awkward, and he wanted no part of it. We didn't answer at first. Then Scout slid off the stool. She and Gatlin went ahead and went out the back while I grabbed my bag from the office. I returned to hear the swinging door bang as Orrin pushed through it. Cleo was making her way over to go upstairs.

"Cleo?"

"Sorry, boss, won't happen again. I need to go grab some stuff from upstairs." In the blink of an eye, she was up the stairs.

What just happened?

chapter 29

. . .

IN THE WEEKS since we had taken Scout at the same time, I had learned a lot about myself. I liked to be praised in the bedroom. Maybe I also enjoyed in day to day life. I also liked to push Leland's buttons. He was always so controlled, and seeing him let go with us was amazing. Calling him sir had been me trying to get a rise out of him. I would have never guessed that he would like it. Scout had also taken to calling him that, but used it on me sometimes. We all traded off on control and it was the most amazing thing I had ever been a part of. I thought we had been close before, but our bond had grown even stronger since being together intimately and then after the accident. I looked over to where they slept. I had woken up before them and had taken the chance to make coffee and arrange a little breakfast in bed. They were both still sleeping when I returned with breakfast. Leland was curled protectively around Scout's back, her head resting just below his chin. She had curled up after I left the bed and looked like a little kitten. As if he felt me watching, Leland cracked open one eye to find mine. A soft smile pulled the corners of his lips.

"Good morning. Come back to bed, love." His gruff, sleep-filled voice called to me like a siren song.

"I thought we could do breakfast in bed. I think someone will wake up when they smell the coffee." Moving closer to the bed, Leland pressed a kiss to Scout's temple. She pulled in a deep breath before sighing, her bright green eyes peeking open.

"Mmm what's this? I get to wake up to my two favorite people and coffee?" Her hair was adorably tousled from sleep. She sat up her nightshirt, not hiding her perky nipples. From the end of the bed, Mud let out a huff of announce at not being acknowledged. "Sorry, Muddington, two of my favorite people *and* my most favorite puppy." He let out a pleased huff before he started to snort softly. Scout giggled at his antics, then reached out and pat the bed. "Come here, bee."

Leland sat up, shifting so there would be room for all of us and the tray. Once everyone had their coffee, we picked over the breakfast pastries and biscuits I had warmed up. We talked throughout breakfast, Leland and I sharing stories from school and growing up together. The amount of trouble he had kept me out of was astounding. If our parents knew half of it, they would still probably try to ground us.

"I wish I would have known you both then." Even with living in the same town, we had not gone to school together. "Going to a private school was great, but it was a bit isolating." Scout's grandparents had paid for her and Atticus to go to private school from start to finish. This meant we didn't get to meet our sweet honeysuckle until that fateful, rainy day.

"I wish we knew you, but I have to say I am just glad we get to know you now." She leaned in, meeting me halfway for a soft kiss. When we parted, I caught Leland watching us with a soft expression on his face. "Come here, teddy bear." The kiss was slow and sweet. I pulled back, smiling at him. He returned the smile before kissing our girl.

We returned to eating and talking. Scout gave us updates on the renovation. As she talked, a sinking feeling tried to settle in my stomach. It made every bit taste like cardboard. She would be moving out and back to her apartment soon. When I looked at Leland, he looked like he was in physical pain. Good to know we were on the same page. Looking to Scout, she was talking with almost forced happiness. The excitement was not there, she was also picking at her fingers. *What are we doing here?*

"Amos said that it should only be like another week. It's going to be weird being there now. But I mean, I did renovate it to live in." She ended the sentence with a half-hearted smile.

"No." I heard the word come out of my mouth before I could stop it.

"No?" Scout looked at me questioningly. Confused, but also was that hope?

Leland had leaned slightly forward like he was on the edge of his seat. I took a second, wanting to be sure that I said everything that I wanted. Hopefully, at the end, the answer will be yes.

"No, don't move back. Stay here. With us." I reached my hand across to take Leland's, lacing our fingers together. "I cannot imagine going to sleep with you not here or waking up without you in our bed."

"I can't just move in. That would—"

"Amazing? If I had of thought of it first, I would have suggested it. Please stay. This is it for me. Everything I am is yours." He took Scout's hand, placing it where our hands were already together. "I want this to be our home. To build a life here together. Please say you'll stay."

Scout looked between us, a small smile growing lighting up her beautiful face. "Ok."

"Ok? You'll move in?" I asked, moving and jostling the tray. Leland set the tray off on the floor, sensing the potential mess. *Smart man.*

"Yes, I will move in." Her words came as happy tears welled in her eyes. I lunged forward, causing her to fall back. The kiss was a hard clash of teeth and searching tongues. I reached one hand out, searching for Leland. He came willing. I turned my head and broke the kiss with Scout to take his mouth. He didn't allow me to keep control before he pushed his tongue in and dominated me. I moved us closer to Scout until we were all together locked in a messy, sexy as hell, three way kiss.

"Fuck. That was so hot. I don't think I'm going to let you to leave this room today—maybe ever." My dick twitched at Leland's words. Scout reached down to grab the hem of her shirt, pulling it over her head, laying back on the bed like a goddess. She slid one hand down into her patties, the other moving to one of her nipples.

"I think we need to celebrate." She began to work herself up. Leland and I sat watching her. Both of us stared at her mesmerized by how fucking sexy she was. "Ngh, please come fuck my needy hole."

I looked to Leland, asking for what, I didn't know. I didn't need his permission necessarily, but it felt right to ask. "Do you want me to fuck your tight hole?" he asked me. I nodded my head, looking like a bobble head. "Words."

"Yes."

"Fuck our girl's pretty pussy while I get you ready."

"Yes." I moved when I felt the swat to my ass cheek. The sting pulled a moan from my lips. "Fuck."

"Yes what?" *Oh, we were doing this today.*

Scout whimpered in front of me, her finger moving faster in her underwear. "Yes, sir." Her eyes blazed at the words.

"That's my good boy."

Leland opened me up with his mouth and fingers. My dick was buried in Scout, which made it seem like only seconds before I felt Leland move behind me. "This is going to be fast and hard. I won't last. I want you both too much." His words sounded like he was barely in control.

"Please fuck him into me, sir," Scout spoke before I could.

"Oh *fuuck.*" I felt his tip start to press into the tight ring of muscles. I tried to breathe and relax my body. Inch by inch, he pushed into me, driving me forward each time into Scout's tight pussy. Her inner walls massaged my sensitive cock. Leland paused when his hips met my ass, giving me a moment to adjust. When I started to try and move, he took over.

He set a brutal pace, pounding me down into Scout. We were both whimpering and moaning. All of our sounds mixed with Leland's grunts and groans of pleasure. I felt my balls start to draw up. "Fuck, gonna come."

"Give it to me. Fucking breed me. Come inside me," Scout begged. She had already climaxed twice. I think we can say with certainty that we had a bit of a breeding kink. Not that I'm complaining. There was nothing like it in the world. I had never gone bareback with a man or woman until Scout and Leland. It was heaven.

Leland kept driving into me. With three more thrusts, Scout was clenching around me, her whole body locking up with her third orgasm. I followed her over the edge with a shout.

"Where do you want me to come?" Leland panted.

"In my ass, please. Fuck me full of your cum." *Holy shit, I liked to talk dirty.*

With a final slam of his hips, Leland did exactly what I asked. He filled me with so much of his hot release I could feel some trying to leak out from around where he was still lodged in my ass. We collapsed into a pile on the bed. "I love you." I looked between them. My chest rose and fell as I tried to steady my breathing.

"And I love you both," Scout spoke, her voice still blissed out.

"I love you, my soulmates."

We laid in bed and cuddled the day away, getting out to eat before coming back and lazily making love. This was just a glimpse at what our lives would be like. Sandwiched between us, Scout let out a content sigh. From now until my last day, I would live for moments like this with them.

epilogue

scout

"MUDDINGTON BEAN ESPRESSO FORD the First, get in this house. We do have things to do today, mister." Gatlin stood at the back door of the house, yelling out to Mud. "I swear, you two spoil him and now he never listens to me." He shot a glare at Leland and I, where we stood at the kitchen island. While he wasn't wrong that we spoiled him, Mud never liked to come in after he had a taste of freedom. Just as Gatlin was about to give up, the stubborn pup came bounding up the back steps. "Thank you for taking your time, sir. I raised you better than this." Mud, not caring about anything his dad had to say, walked past him and went to lay down. Leland moved around the island to where Gatlin was standing. He moved so that he was in front of Gatlin before putting his hands on his shoulders.

"Bee, I love you, but that dog has never listened when it's time to come in. He is a great dog in all the other areas, but he likes his morning runs in the yard." Leland gave a soft smile before kissing Gatlin's forehead. "Also, we aren't the only ones who spoil him." Moving away from Gatlin and back to me, he gave me a quick kiss. I tried to deepen the kiss,

"

when Leland pulled back. "Honeysuckle, we will have time for that all weekend."

I felt another body move in behind me as Gatlin pressed close. "Just think, we will be out in the middle of nowhere. No one will be around." His lips ghosted over my neck, causing me to shiver. "You can be a loud as you'd like." He nipped my earlobe before pressing a kiss below my ear. "So while we run to the store and get the supplies and maybe some other things, you just relax and think about all the things we can do while we're away." With a final kiss on my neck, he moved away.

"Dammit, you better get a move on or I will start the part without you right here in the kitchen," I grumbled. My pouting was met by two chuckles. *Jerks.* "I love you, be careful."

"We love you and we will." Leland responded for both of them before they headed out the door.

"Mud, come on. You're coming with us. We need to have a talk." Gatlin tried to project a serious tone, but seeing as he was talking to the dog, it fell short. "Also, I got some dog stuff I want to test to see if you will wear any of it." Mud stood, walking over to bump my leg with his head before following Gatlin from the kitchen.

The guys had planned a camping trip for the three of us to have some time to ourselves. Between the businesses, family, and side projects, it seemed like we were always on the go. Everything had pieced together, though. The Boones and Fords just pulled my parents into the fold and now they took vacations together. Our dads had poker nights, and our mothers were now plotting for grandchildren. Nan, of course, was the ringleader of meddling. Thankfully, she currently had her sights set on other people, so we don't get the full weight. Oakland was her main target currently, which she hated but we all loved.

I moved around the kitchen, putting the last of the food supplies into totes for the trip before heading to our room. I finished packing up my clothes and tidying up. My transition from temporary roommate to permanent was an easy one. We now had one very large bed in what used to be Leland's room. We turned one bedroom into an office and library, and we had two bedrooms to spare. After I moved into the house, the apartment above the store sat empty until Atticus graduated college. When I offered it for free, he refused and started paying rent.

The guys thought it was so he could have a true "adult" bachelor pad. Gatlin's exact words were, "He is a young, single guy. If he pays rent, then there is only so much big sis can say," then he winked and walked off. The images those words conjured now haunt me. I gave a shake of my head, trying to stop that train of thought and tried to refocus on the book I had been reading. The guys should be close to being back. Relaxing back into to bed, I was caught off guard when my phone rang. It sat charging on the nightstand, but I could see that it was Oakland calling. I reached over, grabbing it before answering.

"Hello *Oakleaf*, since when do we call?" I waited, but got no answer. "Uh, Oakland? You ok?" Nothing. but then I hear a noise in the background. *Is that?* I strained to make out what I believed was—

"On your knees pretty girl."

Oh dear Lord in heaven. Wait. Where had I heard that voice?

A very deep male voice spoke. "Look at her so ready—"

There was what sounded like fabric rustling before a female voice moaned low.

Oakland moaned.

Oh, fucking fuck. That was Oakland moaning.

What was I listening to? Who was I listening to? Wait. Shit. *Why was I still listening?* I smashed the end button and sat, staring at my phone. I was still sitting there when I heard the front door. Mud came clicking down the hall before walking into the bedroom. I felt his head plop down on my leg before he huffed. I looked over at him and realized why he was huffing.

He was currently wearing a new harness, which from his tone, he was not pleased about. "Oh Mudders, what is this? A new harness? You look so handsome!" I rubbed his head, but he turned and walked back out before I could say anything else. *Well, I guess he doesn't agree.* I stood up, following him down the hall. I didn't see or hear the guys when I left the bedroom.

"Hey, bee, I don't think Mud–" I froze when I came into the living room. Mud was sitting in front of Leland and Gatlin. "Is everything ok?"

They were both looking at me with soft smiles. "Go ahead, Mud." Gatlin coaxed him back to me. I walked closer, squatting down to be eye level with the big dog. He walked over, sitting down in front of me, leaning forward to boop me with his nose.

"What is going on?"

"Collar," was Leland's only reply.

I reached for Mud's collar. I had not noticed before, but there was a new tag on it. I looked at the tag, my brain not processing what it said. I read the words out loud like that was going to make them more real. "Will you be my mom?" I was still looking at the pup when I heard movement. Glancing up, Leland and Gatlin each held a small box. I was stunned, looking between them. Mud moved to lay at my side as I was still squatting down.

"From the first day I saw you, I knew that I wanted my life to be intertwined with yours. I didn't realize that on a rainy day I would find the other half of my heart. The other half had belonged to the same person who became my best friend as a child." Leland looked to Gatlin before turning back to me. "We know that we can't get married in the legal sense, but I want to be tied to you both in every way I can. That starts now." Opening the box, there were two beautiful rings. There were two bands, each with an almost floral pattern, intertwining with the stones around the surface of the ring. They were absolutely stunning. "Scout Eleanor Fraizer, will you marry me?" I nodded, tears starting to form. Leland waited to slide the rings on my finger, turning to Gatlin. Gatlin started to speak before I could ask any questions.

"I can't imagine my life without you both. My sweet teddy bear and precious honeysuckle. I never knew that I could love two people as much as I love you both. You both own every part of my soul. I will work every day to show you just how much I love you. Scout, my love, will you marry me? But also marry us?" They each held a band now, waiting for my answer.

I nodded, not able to form words.

"Before we give you the bands we have, there is another ring in Gat's box." I looked, realizing Gatlin hadn't opened his box. "Our parents knew this was coming and wanted to give something to symbolize the love they have for us and the family we are creating." Leland reached where Gatlin held the box and opened it. The ring was made up of three stones. The center stone was a beautiful oval diamond. On each side were two round stones. I realized the bands fit perfectly around the center ring, like they were made for each other. "The center stone belonged to Nan's grandmother. The stone on the left was from my mom."

"The stone on the right was from my mom." The stone caught the light as Gatlin pulled it out. "The gold is from your parents."

"Scout, would will you allow us to give you these rings as a sign to show the world that you are ours and we are yours?"

"Yes. Oh my gosh, yes. Of course I will." I looked down once the rings were on my finger, the bands surrounding the middle ring. "They are beautiful. I can't believe this. I love you both so much." I moved forward, reaching for them, pulling one into a kiss and then the other.

I shifted away from them. "Well, I guess there's no reason to wait." I got up and went to my purse. I returned with two bands. One that Leland and I picked for Gatlin. The other Gatlin and I chose for Leland. I had secretly went with both of them to pick rings for the other. "I have been keeping a secret. Well, two, I guess." I held the rings in my hand, looking at them. "I never knew this was the life I was destined to have. To not only have one great love, but two. I cannot wait to do life with you both. I know I already agreed to marry you, both but will you marry me?" They both looked at each other before turning to me.

"You sneaky little thing," Leland said, smirking at me.

"You both were pretty sneaky, too. Now, I believe you both have something to ask each other. Now that I have asked, I will patiently await my answer." I looked at them pointedly and waited.

"Leland, I loved you long before I realized it. I am so sorry that it took so long. I was too scared to admit it when I figured it out." Gatlin pressed his lips to Leland's in a soft kiss. "I have a yes from one of my loves. What about the other? Will you marry me?"

"Only if you will marry me?" He winked at him. His expression turned serious. "You have nothing to apologize for, bee. It happened when it was supposed to. I would be honored to spend the rest of my life with both of you."

"So, bumblebee, what's it gonna be?" I waggled my eyebrows like I didn't know the answer.

"Fuck yes, I will. We are going to figure out some way to actually do this. Name changes or something." We met again, kissing and touching. When I placed their rings on their fingers, everything felt right in my world. I never realized that taking over my family bookstore would lead me to find these two beautiful men. Sandwiched between them on out living room floor, I laughed, repeating the same words Gatlin had said to me that first day we met.

"You are definitely better than bookends."

THE END

Dried Apricot Jam

1 lb Apricots
4 lbs Sugar
3½ pts boiling water
Wash & quarter apricots
Pour boiling water over &
stand 24 hours.
Put in pan, boil ¾ hr,
add sugar & boil 20-30 mins

Apricot & Pineapple Jam

1 lb Aps cut up & steep overnight
breakfast cups water (5 teacups)
tin pineapple, cut up
3 lbs sugar
...steep overnight, bring to the boil,
add sugar & boil 20 mins.

9